NOBLE LORD

NOBLE LORD

Peter Lauder

STEIN AND DAY/*Publishers*/New York

First published in the United States of America in 1986
Copyright © 1986 by Peter Lauder
All rights reserved, Stein and Day, Incorporated
Printed in the United States of America
STEIN AND DAY/*Publishers*
Scarborough House
Briarcliff Manor, N.Y. 10510

Library of Congress Cataloging-in-Publication Data

Lauder, Peter
  Noble Lord.

  I. Title.
PR6058.I343N6   1986   823'.914   86-42696
ISBN 0-8128-3116-0

For Carol

For now I see the true old times are dead,

When every morning brought a noble chance

And every chance brought out a noble knight.

Tennyson

NOBLE LORD

PROLOGUE

THE SMALL BOAT'S oars made no noise as they dipped in the water. They steered it carefully through the dark harbor, avoiding the anchor lines of the yachts and cruisers swaying at their moorings. The oarsman could hear the clinking of glasses and the occasional sound of laughter wafting across the bay on the light breeze. A million stars sparkled in the tropical sky. Some yachts were illuminated bow to stern like props in a fairy tale, their lights reflected in the water, while others sat somber and brooding, for the moment forgotten.

The boatman threaded his way expertly through them all. His clothes were dark and his skin was as black as the night. It was his harbor and had been for twenty years. Here he had worked and played until he had gone away. Now he was back again.

He recognized without difficulty the different craft as he passed them silently by. Unseen and unheard, that had to be his way. His heartbeat quickened a little, and he licked his lips, which had become dry with apprehension. He concentrated on his passage to the beach, now a huge shadow one hundred yards away. To his left was a Frenchman from Guadeloupe, this his favorite weekend spot with a girlfriend. Behind him a charter, Americans by the sound of them he thought. He recognized a forty-footer from Saint Vincent to the right and a trimaran from Tortuga with its washing still hanging out.

He was behind a darkened motor launch now, a flat thirty-five-footer, when he saw the shadow of movement to his right. He shipped oars instantly and grabbing the larger boat's anchor line waited, hidden in its lee. An unmarked yacht had slipped silently in from sea, a single jib giving her momentum.

The oarsman breathed a sigh of relief. He had seen her before, this night visitor who stayed never more than thirty minutes; yet tonight was the conclusion of a voyage that she had begun at least two weeks before in the Colombian port of Barranquilla. In a few moments she would offload her precious white cargo, which had made its way from the very far side of the Cordillera Oriental and was now in transit to Main Street, U.S.A.

The boatman slipped his oars into the warm Caribbean and continued his journey. He had picked his night well. The lady from Barranquilla never made an error. The nights she put in were notable for the absence of any harbor police. The boatman knew the system although he was not part of it. He continued on for the shore.

There was a soft crunch of sand, and he vaulted lightly into the tide, pulling his small craft behind him up onto the beach, out of the water's influence. Then he ran to the bushes at the beachhead and made his way through them, without sound and invisible.

He came to the edge of the shrubbery and parted the leaves of a dense sea grape. The lights of the bedrooms were now only ten feet away. He put on a pair of tight, black, cotton gloves. Then he ran across a shadowy open area and stopped, panting slightly, outside the sliding French windows of the first room. It took him half a minute to be sure that no one was in. They were all at dinner, just as he knew they would be, just as they had been last year and the year before. He went to work on the simple door lock with a penknife. A moment later the aluminum panel slid back and he was in.

A black nylon bag had appeared in his hand, and into it he put the Leica in its leather case that was by the bedside. A small ring on the bathroom basin followed and an electric razor. His heart thumped audibly now as the extreme tension of robbery began to tell. Abruptly his nerve snapped, and he left the room at speed, sliding the door home. Back in the protective shadows of the shrubs he sat down, his back to a tree, beads of perspiration on his face. He had been in the hotel room for ninety-five seconds. He had a great urge to escape with his haul—but what was a camera worth? And a small ring?

He almost missed the jewelry box in the next room. It was wedged under a suitcase in the wardrobe. He shook it and when it rattled promisingly, bagged it. Later on he would marvel at his good fortune—most guests kept such valuables in the hotel safe. He went through a man's suit pockets and found a roll of East Caribbean dollars. He smiled. Things were looking up.

He had begun to regain his sure touch now, and as he did so his confidence returned. In the third room he allowed himself a more systematic search, in control for the moment of the ever present undercurrent of fear that is the bane of a thief. No longer was the blood pounding in his ears—he could use them to listen for danger now, quite detached in their function to his eyes, which dissected the room with clinical precision. He found a gold pen lying in a drawer. He shrugged and put it in the bag. A wallet of credit cards and another camera, this time a cheap Japanese instamatic, followed. He moved on.

The fourth bedroom had a classy feel about it. The suitcases were made of real leather, the clothes in the wardrobe felt expensive to his agile fingers, there was the smell of hundred-dollar perfume. The wardrobe yielded nothing of value. He pulled out all the drawers from the dressing table and tipped their contents onto the middle of the large double bed. He sifted them urgently. Nothing but clothes. He opened the drawers of the tables at either side of the bed. Whoever it was did not believe in keeping much in the way of value around. He shut the drawers, cursing silently. He was spending too long here. He tossed the pillows onto the bed, seeking for hidden objects. By now the room was thoroughly ransacked. He decided to check the bathroom before he left.

A large range of cosmetic bottles cluttered a small table. A pair of matching hairbrushes with silver backs glinted at him for an instant before disappearing into the bag. He turned to leave, but something in the corner of his eye made him stop. He stared at the heated towel rail and shelf behind the bath, so nearly obscured by the plastic shower curtain. Plump towels, neatly folded, were stacked there. But their shape was wrong.

He flung the towels into the bath. A brightly polished, black briefcase, its brass combination locks winking in the bathroom light, fell with an earsplitting crash onto the hard, white enamel. He froze, not daring even to breathe. His heart was thumping away again, threatening to deafen him. Then the instinct for survival coupled with near panic took over as he grabbed the black leather handle in one hand and his nylon bag in the other and ran full tilt from the room, back to the beach and the sanctuary of the bushes. Five minutes later he was retracing his noiseless way back across the bay, back to a spot that the tourists never saw.

He was calm again now and was looking forward to opening the rewards of his labor. There was no sound on the receding beach, no signs of pursuit. Voices still drifted from yachts, people were still enjoying the warm night. He breathed deeply savoring the clear night air. He had done it again, although each time made him feel he had died a little.

He looked about him as he rowed. The stars were still brilliant in the sky, but the lady from Barranquilla was gone.

14

PART ONE

April 2-May 21

CHAPTER
ONE

THE TWO MEN who lay huddled on the north-facing hillside had achieved almost total camouflage. A very persistent bird-watcher might have spotted them—the Army Air Corps Lynx that had just clattered overhead did not.

The men's foxhole, a slight, natural hollow in the hillside, had not been casually chosen. Branches of heavy, green gorse, cut from the bushes around them, had been placed over where they lay. Their position was three hundred feet up the slope, overlooking a small valley of patchwork farms and a few whitewashed cottages. A bubbling stream ran across the floor of the valley and under a winding country road that crossed the landscape at right angles to their hill. It was 7:00 A.M. A slow misty rain drifted over everything. It was a typical early April day in picturesque South Armagh.

The two men watched the valley intently. They were dressed in full, mottled-colored battledress. Dark brown balaclavas encased their heads so that only eyes and mouths were visible. Their hands had been stained black. They lay side by side, peering out through the gorse into the curtain of drizzle.

One of the men, the taller of the two, raised a pair of British Army binoculars to his eyes. It was useless. Visibility was no more than two hundred yards. The other man was much smaller, stocky and compact; he lay propped up by his elbows. His eyes were fixed unwaveringly on the scene below. Cradled between his hands was a small, rectangular radio transmitter complete with joystick, which he had purchased a week before from a hobby shop in Londonderry.

The transmitter was the beginning of a disruptive train that ended in four large aluminum milk churns wedged in an old drainage pipe, which ran under the road below. Six hours before, the waiting men had been driven over the border to this spot. They had gingerly positioned the twenty-gallon containers in the culvert. The churns were packed with a home-brew of cooked fertilizer crystals, metal filings, and diesel. A small amount of picric acid—the last of their stock—had been added. They were extremely careful. Two months previously three of the boys had blown themselves to bits on such a job.

From the mouth of one churn protruded the small, silver aerial of the amplifier, which had come in the same box as the radio transmitter. It was wired in turn to a solenoid, which when activated would complete the circuit of a six-volt battery and send intense heat to a tiny lump of lead azide no bigger than a pea. This whole arrangement sat at the top of the churn in two pounds of commercial explosives. When the distant transmitter was switched on, a violent, exothermic reaction would follow, which would cause an instantaneous rearrangement of the atoms in the milk churns, the drainage pipe, and anything else above or below within a ten-yard radius.

The taller of the men, his feet numb with cold, suddenly picked out the twin sidelights of a car at the very edge of his vision.

"Here they are!" he whispered.

He chanced a look at the man next to him. The stocky figure was rocking gently on the ground. It was the taller man's first such mission, but he had heard the stories and seen the fear that the very name of his companion kindled in even the most ruthless of their kind. In awe he stared. The radio transmitter rocked with the movement of the stocky body.

"Come on you bastards," came the strange broken voice. "You fucking bastards."

The car carrying the two officers of the Royal Ulster Constabulary was not doing more than twenty. It was a heavy, armor-plated Cortina. Dressed in light, bottle-green uniforms, their hats on the back seat, the policemen tried to discern the potholed roads ahead of them, sharp ridges and dips marking where the boggy earth had moved underneath.

The driver was familiar with these roads, which like a spider's web crisscross this part of the land border with the Republic. He knew the smugglers who crossed here at the dead of night with their cargoes of wheat and barley, vans filled with whiskey and videos, and trailer loads of squealing pigs. He knew the routes to the south and to safety taken by the men from Belfast and Londonderry when the going got too hot. And he knew the Fenian mind, intent on displacing the rightful plantations of three centuries before, the influx of civilizing souls who had tried to give a better way of life.

At fifty-six, his family reared, comfortable and respected, he could allow himself to feel a little proud of his part in the long effort, the vigil that maintained things as they were, as they would always be.

However, he did not envy his companion, a young man of twenty-two, soon to be married, today his first tour of duty on the border. If he only knew what lay ahead, the older man thought. The long hours, the constant threat to your life, the feeling of working in a jungle where a thousand pairs of wild eyes were always looking at you from the thicket, waiting, forever waiting for their chance to see your back turned. And there seemed to be no end to it in sight.

"What a godforsaken place," said the young officer.

The older man smiled. He opened his mouth to reply, but the words he intended to speak would never be heard. At that moment the Cortina's front wheels reached a point on the road immediately over the drainage culvert, and the terrorist on the hill above pressed the switch on the small transmitter. The thirty-pound amplifier picked up the familiar frequency. An immediate, chemical chain reaction followed. The tightly packed explosives decomposed into a gas with a huge and simultaneous liberation of heat. Kinetic force expanded at a rate of 9,000 meters a second.

The result was spectacular.

The heavy car was punched twenty feet into the air, nose first. There was a noise like thunder. The car's steel floor buckled upward to its roof. Its sides, front and rear were pushed powerfully outward by the accelerating shock of the detonation. The occupants were impelled indiscriminately through the jagged apertures that were now becoming part of the airborne one-and-a-half-ton vehicle.

A six-by-twenty crater had appeared in the road and was rapidly filling with water from the abruptly diverted stream. It was back into this that the mass of flaming, disfigured steel fell. A large cloud of smoke and dust hung over the morning.

There was no sign whatsoever of what had ten seconds previously been two members of the Royal Ulster Constabulary.

On the hillside the taller man was on his feet. For a moment he stared with awe at the level of damage that they had caused, but now it was time to get out. He spoke urgently.

"Come on! For Christ's sake come on!"

The stocky man did not appear to hear him. He had removed his balaclava and was lying on his back, head to one side, his eyes glazed. He was exhausted and panting. His pink tongue darted out and licked his thin lips. A mass of dark curls framed his milk-white face, which was now a death mask. He was not yet twenty-three.

"The fucking bastards," he gasped.

"Come on Kelly, for the love of God!" said the man who was standing. He was sure that he had spotted an infrared surveillance camera, slung under the belly of the Lynx as it had gone over. It would not take the Brits long to develop the film, and when they did the two men's presence on the hillside would show up as bright as a bonfire.

He looked down at the man he had addressed as Kelly, and then he knew that what they whispered was true. He turned away and pressed on up the hill, looking back a few times at the smoldering devastation in the valley but avoiding the mad eyes behind him.

Nor could he bring himself to look and confirm what he had unquestionably seen a few moments before: a spreading damp stain on the front of the other's battledress trousers. Holy Mother of God, he thought and crossed himself quickly as they reached the summit. Then the two men ran down the south side of the hill and into the Irish Republic.

THE ELECTRONIC, BLACK gates of the Embassy opened smoothly on their well-oiled hinges. The Fiat Mirafiori swung out onto the road of the quiet Dublin suburb. Through the gates could be seen a large, square house set well back from the road in a wooded garden. A watchful surveillance camera on a tubular pole inside the gate made its clicking sound as it recorded the exit.

Commercial Counselor Gregori Bulnovsky looked in his rear-view mirror. The *Garda* sedan opposite had not moved. Bulnovsky knew that he needed special permission to go outside Dublin city limits, but the chances of being caught were remote. The Irish police force could spare only one patrol to survey the Embassy. If they followed every car that left, their surveillance would be at an end.

Bulnovsky drove toward Dublin. He passed a nursing home, went down a hill, up another, and then turned sharp right into a tree-lined avenue. It was quiet; most people were just beginning breakfast. He reached the end of the avenue, turned left, and then made two rights in quick succession.

He was now in a very quiet and secluded lane in which there were only two other vehicles. To his left he saw the high, green railings of a park, to his right a wall. A girl on a bicycle

21

passed him as he pulled in. In the center of the park a man in a track suit was throwing a ball to a dog; a couple of early-morning joggers went past. He let them get out of sight.

"*Von*," he said softly.

Assistant Counselor Dimitri Kornilov got up from the back floor where he had been lying. He opened the door of the Fiat and walked straight to the Mini-Metro in front of them.

Bulnovsky watched as Kornilov got in and drove off. He looked at his watch. He would allow ten minutes before driving back to the Embassy. He reclined the seat and closed his eyes.

THE METRO SPED out past Dublin Airport on the Belfast road. Traffic was light, but Kornilov kept at a steady fifty. The last thing he wanted was to be caught in a speed trap.

He passed through Swords and then the seaside village of Balbriggan before winding through the undulating Irish countryside into the busy town of Drogheda. He crossed over the bridge that gave the town its name and the famous River Boyne where, to the west, almost three centuries before, King William of Orange had finally stopped King James of England. He continued north toward Dundalk. The countryside is so lovely, thought Kornilov, as the richly green Mountains of Mourne appeared to his right. He thought of the stark beauty of the fertile, grassy plains in northern Kazakhstan where he had been born but had not returned to for many years. Their beauty was different, he decided.

The Metro had arrived in the outskirts of the town of Dundalk. It pulled into the parking lot of a modern hotel.

Kornilov checked his rear-view mirror yet again. However remote the chances were of being followed, one could never relax one's vigilance. He opened the window slightly and looked at his watch. After three or four minutes a black Ford Cortina, which had been parked twenty yards away, suddenly spluttered into life. It moved away from its position and came to a stop beside the Metro.

Unhurriedly, Kornilov got out and walked into the hotel.

The driver of the Cortina, who had left the engine running, opened his door. He walked behind the Metro, lifted its hatchback and removed a suitcase. He closed the hatchback again and walked swiftly to the Cortina. Within ten seconds he had pulled out and was headed in the direction of Belfast.

Dimitri Kornilov emerged from the hotel. He started up the Metro and, turning around, proceeded back down the road to Dublin at a leisurely pace.

If he was concerned about the fact that his suitcase containing two hundred thousand U.S. dollars had vanished, he did not show it.

Back at the hotel, behind the large moving van in an unmarked car, the detective sergeant from the Irish *Gardai* wrote the number of the Metro into his notebook.

OVER ONE HUNDRED miles from Dundalk, to the extreme northwest, three men sat in the darkened bedroom of a farmhouse.

They had been there right through the night, endless cups of coffee the only distraction from their intense discussion. The single table in the small room was covered with maps, papers, and diagrams. A stale smell hung in the air.

One of the men stood up and stretched. He was broad-shouldered with unruly, dark hair and a bushy mustache. He walked to the window and pulled the curtains apart, allowing daylight to flood the room. Of his two companions, who like himself looked tired and unshaven, one was a thickset young six-footer, the other a man in his mid-fifties with blond hair going gray.

"Have you finished?"

The question was asked by the older of the men. He had an English accent.

The man by the window nodded.

"In that case . . ." said the blond man, standing up stiffly. He ran his hands worriedly through his hair and then, adjusting his tie, begain to make his way to the door.

"It will all be in order," he said weakly.

"Good," said the man by the window, nodding again, a thin smile of arrogant triumph on his lips.

The older man hastily opened the door and without looking back, went down the steep, narrow stairs and out to the front of the house where a small car was parked from the night before. He squinted as the bright sunlight hit his red-rimmed eyes. There was no one about.

A feeling of utter depression and hopelessness, which had established itself in the pit of his belly hours before, now swam over him, making even the starting of the car a great effort. He drove past a steaming dungheap where hens scratched for tidbits. He peered ahead willing himself away.

The roads were at first potholed and winding—primitive country roads that made speed impossible. He pressed on, oblivious to the beauty of the countryside or the fresh delight of the morning. His hands clenched the steering wheel as if by the sheer application of strength he could cauterize from his mind the image now squatting there.

As the roads improved he pushed the rented car harder, his all-engulfing desire to put distance between himself and the men in the farmhouse uncontainable. In this fashion he drove for nearly four hours, forcing himself to the limit.

Not until that evening when he had settled back in the first-class seat of the Trident, a stiff drink in his hand, did the feeling begin to subside. Time was an unfailing friend on whose therapeutic power he had relied over and over again.

An hour later, when the plane reached London, he had begun to breathe more easily. He took a taxi in from Heathrow, each click of the meter bolstering his recovery. By the time he had eaten a solitary supper in his club, accompanied by a bottle of decent claret, the dreadful gnawing was only a distant memory.

That night in his West End home, as he lay in bed beside the sleeping figure of his wife, he had completely forgotten.

CHAPTER
TWO

THE NARROW LOBBY of the Algonquin on West Forty-fourth Street was crowded. Bright-eyed, would-be starlets stood in line, waiting to be beckoned by the maitre d' to a free table in the oak-paneled lounge where they would sit endlessly over their first and last drink; agents brooded, chewing cigars; theatrical-looking men and women assembled themselves around small tables. It was five o'clock on Monday, May 2.

A man strode in from the street. He walked with an aura of command, his wide shoulders thrown back. He was very tall, fortyish with dark, thinning hair swept straight back on a long, rectangular head that ended in a lanternlike jaw; the shape of his head should have made him appear stupid but somehow transmitted an air of natural authority. His large and powerful hands hung straight down by his sides. Great, bulging veins stood out on them, running from the wrists through the knuckles and down to spatulate fingers and thumbs. He wore expensive clothes, shoes with gold buckles, an Italian silk tie.

He moved through the lobby, declining the offer of a porter

to take his coat, into the bar. He ignored the maitre d'. His eyes surveyed the room until they found whom they sought. He would never let it show that the meeting he was about to have filled him with a feeling that a lesser man would call dread.

Walking purposefully across the bar he sat down beside a thickset man with dark skin that had not much faded since he had first left his native island in the Mediterranean. He had a thick, drooping mustache and very white teeth.

"A scotch," said the tall man to a hovering waiter.

The dark-skinned man raised his glass to his lips.

"An unusual pleasure, Quorn," he said.

The man he addressed did not respond directly. He took some peanuts from a bowl and munched them. He had planned his approach with care.

"I have positive news about the transfer," he said evenly. The dark man smiled slightly and nodded.

"*Bene*," he said softly, "you deliver as always."

"The agreed amount should be in Zurich tomorrow—U.S. dollars."

The other man shrugged.

"Everything as planned," he said.

"I will take delivery from you in two weeks," said the man called Quorn. "That is, if you are agreeable."

"With so much merchandise it will be important that the loading has the benefit of the privacy you promised."

"That is not a problem. It's a private wharf with only one access. I saw it two days ago. It's perfect."

The whisky arrived and fresh bowls of nuts were placed on the table. The two men drank in silence. The swarthy man with the mustache looked at his guest speculatively. He could imagine necks being snapped by those powerful hands. He wondered how they would deal with a stiletto.

It was two and a half hours since he had got the call to his home in Newark.

He had recognized the voice immediately.

"What number do you want?" he asked, slipping into their prearranged code.

26

The man now opposite him had recited a number

"I'm sorry, this is not it," he said and hung up.

He had driven to the Holland Tunnel and, on emerging in Manhattan, turned right on Canal Street, making his way downtown until he reached the very tip of the island at Battery Park.

Having found a parking space he walked north again for five minutes and into the shimmering vastness of the World Trade Center where he descended into its teeming bowels, his eyes tirelessly scanning the hurrying crowds for a repeated face. Ten minutes of browsing in a bookstore and he began to relax. He left the subterranean store and joined the crowds milling toward the subway. His fingers touched the brass token in his pocket. He waited until the last moment before boarding the E train, but even then changed cars twice on the journey uptown. He stayed with it until Fifty-third and Fifth; there he alighted and took a cab back down to Forty-fourth Street. It was with confidence that he had entered the Algonquin.

Now he beckoned the waiter for more drinks. The meeting had not been requested for small talk. He sat back and waited. He had known Quorn for almost six years. At the beginning it had been just small stuff, some handguns, probably for private clients in Europe. But as an arms dealer Quorn had come a long way. Now he was into rocket launchers, mortars, the works. The deal they had recently concluded was a biggie, mainly Armalites, and a lot of them.

The man with the long jaw shifted slightly in his seat. His second whisky was almost gone.

"There has been an accident, Emilio," he said.

The coal-black Sicilian eyes became suddenly hard.

"An accident?"

The tall man had withdrawn a piece of paper from his pocket and handed it across.

"This came in at midday. I called you right away."

The dark man took the fiche and scanned it very rapidly and then again line by line. He shook his head slowly.

"Curnutu!" He spat the word out in a guttural voice. *"Stronzo inglese!"*

The other man did not move. His companion's face had become suffused with color through his rage. Emilio was just a messenger and had to repeat everything back to his brother and their father. Quorn knew this. They made all the decisions leaving Emilio as the link. He would not get any prizes when he repeated back what he was reading. He folded the message and thrust it into his pocket.

"Jesus Christ, this is serious," he said, taking a gulp from his drink.

"I know," said Quorn.

"That end of it was your production. That has always been agreed."

Quorn spread his large hands wide.

"No dispute," he said coolly.

"You trusted that stupid bastard too much, Quorn," he hissed. "Christ!" He took out his handkerchief and wiped his face. "What was in it, what exactly?'

"Lists of the merchandise involved, serial numbers, costings."

"Names? Sources? Destination?"

"He says not."

"He says not! What can we now believe? This message says he's shitting himself."

Quorn lighted a Camel and sucked the first smoke deep into his lungs. "Look, I really don't think there's any problem we can't get over. Take location into account. Assuming that someone bothered to read it—which is most unlikely—do you think they would understand? I doubt it "

The deep, black eyes blazed.

"A written account of my family's business is floating around. Only two or three people in the world could provide such hardware."

He shook his head again.

"Jesus, Papa will go fucking mad," he said.

Quorn signaled for more drinks. Whatever else, there would be no further business with the sender of the telex.

The swarthy man opposite him was fuming in Italian. He took a long drink.

"Such stupidity I have never heard," he said.

"It should not affect the deal," said Quorn, sipping his whisky. "It's just an unfortunate accident which will probably come to nothing."

"Let us hope, let us hope."

"He has always delivered, including this time. At least he let us know right away."

"Papa was sweet on this deal," said the dark man.

Quorn ate some more peanuts. His companion seemed to be calming down.

"I've been thinking about the best approach to take," Quorn said. "I've made some inquiries, and it appears that a number of people on either side of him were hit as well."

The dark man raised his eyebrows.

"So?"

"Well, in one case jewelry was taken, in another a wallet of credit cards. It seems they may make their way up here." He handed across a sheet of paper. "Here is a list of the cards with the names on them, and this is a description of the jewelry."

He sat back in his chair. The man opposite him was really quite slow. Quorn spoke softly.

"You can do it better than anyone," he said. "Find the plastic, my friend, find the rocks, and you have found your man."

Emilio grabbed the list and knocked back his drink.

"I hope nothing comes of this, Quorn," he said, "for all our sakes."

He then stood up and, without looking back, walked out.

Ten minutes later Quorn signaled for the bill and having paid it left the hotel. He had a dull pain in his stomach.

He hoped that the business was not giving him an ulcer.

CHAPTER
THREE

AT 11:30 A.M. on Monday May 9, Patrolman John Tilson and Patrolman Vincent Puzzotti were cruising down the East River Drive in the mid-seventies.

The two front windows of their patrol car were rolled down allowing the morning air to circulate. Nothing unusual had occurred on their tour of duty. Patrolman Tilson yawned and looked at his watch as Patrolman Puzzotti exited from the Drive and made his regular turn toward the Heliport on the river at East Sixtieth Street.

Abruptly, the morning was shattered by the high-pitched scream of a woman, coming from the direction of the Heliport. Tilson sat upright and instinctively unclipped the safety catch of his revolver with his right hand. Puzzotti stood on the accelerator, at the same time flicking the switch that activated the flashing siren on the car's roof. They screeched at speed to where a number of cars were parked. A middle-aged woman with blond hair was running toward them from the Heliport. Her two arms were outstretched and, when she saw the police car, she began to scream again.

Tilson was first out, his eyes scanning the road for an

assailant. The woman began to sob. She pointed toward the water. She was shaking violently.

"Oh my God," she wailed, "oh my God."

The two policemen ran into the Heliport. A few people were by the wharf rail looking down. A man quietly ushered his wife away. They were shaking their heads.

The policemen reached the wharf and looked down Beneath them a naked black body bobbed face downward in the water. In their combined twenty years of police experience neither Tilson nor Puzzotti had been quite prepared for what they now saw.

As Tilson hurried back to the car radio, Puzzotti vomited generously into New York's East River.

CHAPTER
FOUR

AT THE SOUTHERN end of the Leeward Islands in the east
Caribbean lies the tiny, independent state of Antigua. Once a
prolific producer of sugar cane for the Empire, this small
island of the Lesser Antilles boasts the best natural harbor in
the Caribbean. It was in English Harbour that the young
Nelson sited his winter dockyard for the earlier campaigns.
Today, the most diverse display of floating hardware in the
tropics lies at anchor in the shelter of the coastal indentation
that has been called God's Marina.

Nelson's Dockyard, the small town behind the harbor, is a
mixture of restored stone and shingle houses, gable to gable
with clapboard structures, many in need of paint.

On Friday May 13 at 5:00 P.M. the telephone rang in a
wooden building beside the fruit market. It was answered by
an attractive black girl in her early twenties. Sitting behind a
typewriter in a small office, she wore a stiffly starched shirt,
open at the neck, with an epaulette on each shoulder.

"Nelson's Dockyard Police Station," she said.

She listened to the caller and then said: "One moment, sir."
She cranked a handle on the old switchboard, and another

telephone could be heard to ring in the office behind her. This office had two large windows. It had once been the drawing room of a senior naval officer who had sailed with Nelson. The room was warm although the sun was now hidden behind the giant frond that grew outside. One wall of the office was covered by a large-scale map of Antigua. The wall facing the desk had at its center a single, large, colored photograph in an old gilt frame; it was of the Queen, taken at the coronation.

A man sat at the desk, writing. He was thirty-five, tall, athletic and fit. The muscles of his broad shoulders rippled through the thin fabric of his casual, batik shirt. He could still run a mile in four and a half minutes. He had a small mustache. On his desk were mounds of papers, their locations indicating their importance. To the left, summonses to be served for driving offenses, breach of the peace, failure to pay rent. In the middle, lists of cases to be heard at the next sittings, statements from plaintiffs, statements from witnesses. On the right, correspondence from police headquarters in St. John's, a circular from the Police Club and a copy of *Time*.

He put down his pen and stretched back, yawning, every muscle in his body luxuriously taut, his mouth wide open.

He picked up the ringing telephone.

"O.K., put him through," he said. "Good evening, sir."

He listened very attentively, saying "yes, sir" with regularity. Every word the man on the other end spoke caused his scalp to tingle a little. At last he said: "I'll be there straightaway, sir, yes, sir," and replaced the telephone. He looked out the window.

A blond girl of about seventeen had passed by five minutes ago and was now walking back toward the yachts, a pineapple in each hand. She was barefoot and very tanned. He adjusted his head slightly to follow her progress, past the sawmill and lumber store, on toward the jetties.

A forest of sailing masts rocked gently back and forth over the tops of the buildings in front of his office. Immediately below where he sat, beside the dirt road, a group of locals were gathered on a bench around a game of *warri*. Women from the market were beginning their walk home, baskets bundled high on their heads. A transistor crackled out the commentary on a distant cricket match.

He stood up, a feeling of foreboding replacing what had five minutes ago been the pleasurable anticipation of his night off. He picked up a brown file from a stack lying on a table.

In the outer office, at a desk beside the policewoman, a very large young constable was typing a report with one finger.

"Anything special, Sergeant?" said the constable, looking up.

"I've got to go to St. John's. That was the commissioner."

The young constable raised his eyebrows. It was not every day that there was a summons to visit the mountaintop. Must be something big, he thought. The look on his boss's face discouraged further questions.

"Good night," he said to them and went down the wooden steps to the road outside.

The young woman officer looked after him wistfully.

"Good night, Sergeant Hope," she said with a smile.

POLICE COMMISSIONER RICHARDSON reached for his pipe and thoughtfully began to pack tobacco into its bowl. A large fan revolved in the ceiling, battling with little success against the eighty degrees of May evening heat that still poured into his office.

Commissioner Richardson was fifty-eight years old, stood six foot four in his socks, and weighed two hundred and forty-five pounds. With an awesome reputation on the beat, his methods of dealing with petty criminals had guaranteed years of peace in large areas of St. John's. His reputation as a law keeper was only surpassed by his fame as a wicket keeper, for Constable Richardson had held that position for fifteen years, traveling on no fewer than five West Indies Test teams. Many an English and Australian batsman had learned to their cost what it meant to have this mountainous black man towering behind their wicket.

He had slowly but surely shown his worth. His unflappable nature, the instinctive respect that he commanded, marked him out as a functioning policeman of the highest order. He rose steadily through the ranks. He avoided the more complex cases, leaving them to officers who had shown promise in that field. He got on well with his white superiors at police headquarters and received the distinction of being made the first black assistant commissioner in Antiguan history.

When Antigua went independent in 1981, there was only one man for the top police job. Commissioner Richardson assumed the role easily and concentrated on keeping the streets safe for the increasing number of tourists to walk in.

But there were developments over the past three years that had caused the commissioner to look forward more and more to his retirement. Greater pressure was being brought to bear on the government of Antigua to do something about the dealers who were using Antigua as a safe drop for the millions of dollars worth of South American drugs on their way to the United States.

Washington was beginning to turn the screw: the foreign aid program was being reviewed. One of the inputs, prior to renewing Antigua's line of credit, was an update on how successful the Antiguan drug squad had been over the past six months. The prime minister personally had phoned Richardson the week before. What progress, he demanded, could they show to Washington? When Richardson had demurred, the phone at the other end had been slammed down. The truth was that, apart from busting a few young Americans for possession, the ambivalence of the local population toward drugs created an environment in which vigilant policing was very difficult. Many people were Rastafarian, and smoking ganja was their way of life.

The increasing pressure, the result of shortage of funds in the government, was ultimately born by Commissioner

Richardson. Despite his outwardly calm assurance that everything possible was being done, he knew that he had neither the men nor the equipment to stop what was happening. He needed sophisticated oceangoing launches constantly patrolling the coastline, capable of chase and interception at high speed. That would mean harassment of the yachting fraternity who would go over to Martinique or Guadeloupe if they became fed up with Antigua. Tourist revenue would be lost. Anyway the money just did not exist to buy the hardware: to fund such a program would mean diverting precious funds from schools and hospitals—and there were few votes in that.

The telex that now lay on his desk had created a feeling of exceptional unease beneath his calm exterior when he received it earlier that morning. It was from Interpol, New York, reporting the discovery of a body there nearly a week ago— that of an Ernest Wilson, a petty criminal and a native of Antigua. The marks on the body, found in the East River, were reported as being "consistent with execution methods used before by organized crime."

The telex simply confirmed to the commissioner what everyone already knew: South American drugs were being run through Antigua. Locals were obviously involved, and now one of them had come to a sticky end in New York. Probably tried to double-cross somebody.

Then the commissioner had got the spark of an idea. At first it was just a spark, but the more he thought about it the more it became a promising glow. He had paced his office for a full hour, grinding on his pipe, before finally reaching for the phone and asking for a number in New York.

The discussion had gone well; the man on the other end had eventually agreed. Commissioner Richardson had gone to lunch with the feeling that he had a plan that would show Antigua's utmost good faith in tackling the drugs problem. The PM would be pleased and there was even a chance it might work.

Now his telephone rang; Sergeant Hope had arrived in the

outer office. Commissioner Richardson looked out of the window at the quiet scene below him in American Road. Pretty schoolgirls in bright uniforms were going home. He thought of all the years it had taken him to get to where he now sat. He thought of his wife and the holiday he had promised her when he finally stepped down, a great career at a dignified end.

"Show him in," he said.

Winston Hope had to be the man for the job. After all, he had been married to Ernest Wilson's sister.

THE TWO WEST Indians, the one vast and imposing, the other young and tall, faced each other across the expanse of teak desk. Sergeant Hope put down his file and took the telex that Commissioner Richardson handed him wordlessly.

"What do you think, Sergeant?" he asked eventually. "I am, of course, personally speaking, sorry for your trouble."

"Thank you, sir."

To Hope the news of Wilson's death was essentially a relief. It was the same relief he felt when three years ago Wilson had gone to live with his brother in Miami.

Although Hope's wife had died over two years ago miscarrying their first child, there was still a strong connection with her family. But it had done Hope no good at all to have an in-law around who was widely acknowledged to be a thief with a number of juvenile convictions to his name. Wilson had come home roughly once a year for periods of about three weeks; each time there had been burglaries in the larger hotels.

This annual visitation with its usual consequences had last taken place just over twenty-one days ago. Hope took the file from the desk to his knee.

"Well, Sergeant?" The voice came from within enormous clouds of pipe smoke, illuminated from behind by the rays of the sinking sun. Hope quickly consulted his file.

"Wilson arrived in Antigua on April twentieth, sir, and

returned to New York on May first. In that period there were three cases of robbery reported which still remain unsolved. It is my intention," he cleared his throat, "it was my intention to detain Wilson when he next came home to Antigua and to question him about the incidents."

There was a long silence.

"Is that all, Sergeant?"

"What more could I do, sir? Now we shall never know."

"That, Sergeant, is where I believe you are wrong," Richardson said. "That is where I believe you are very wrong. Look at this organized crime connection," he stabbed his pipe at the telex. "We all know what that means. It's drugs, Sergeant, drugs. Why does Wilson come here just once a year? What does he do in New York? And why is he 'executed' by organized crime? Because he is a petty thief? Never. This is the Mafia, Sergeant. They are in this. They are behind the drugs being run through Antigua. They have made a mistake. This is the break we want."

Hope shook his head slowly.

"I am sorry, sir, but I do not believe so. It just does not fit Ernest Wilson."

"Look, Sergeant, people go to New York, to the United States, and they change. Burglary, prostitution, dealing in drugs, smuggling drugs, what's the difference?"

"Perhaps, sir, but not Wilson."

"Nonsense!" The commissioner crashed his great fist onto the desk. "What day did you say Wilson left? May first wasn't it? Well take a look at this, Sergeant."

He shoved two sheets of paper across the desk. The first had no heading but detailed the dates, names, and tonnages of boats entering and leaving English Harbour in the last three weeks. The second was a copy of the official Antiguan coast-guard's report for the same period. The official list was shorter.

"This unheaded list, Sergeant," said the commissioner, "comes to us from the American CIA, who follow all shipping movements in and out of Antigua by satellite. It proves that our own service is less than completely efficient when it comes to policing our visitors. Now look at this." He pointed to an entry on April 30, underlined in red. "Not in our records, you will notice."

Hope read the words "*Maria Isabella*, registered Barranquilla, Colombia." She had spent approximately thirty minutes in English Harbour on the night of April 30.

It still did not fit Ernest Wilson. The commissioner had stood up and was pacing up and down the room.

"Obviously Wilson was running drugs. Coming from Antigua and living in New York he had the perfect cover to visit here. He was spotted by someone in organized crime who set up the drop on April thirtieth. Why else would a Colombian-registered yacht slip into Antigua for half an hour at the dead of night? The next day Wilson leaves for New York. No, Sergeant, it's drugs all right and this is the opportunity we need."

"Sir?"

Richardson sat down again and leaned forward, this time speaking persuasively.

"I have been speaking to Interpol, Sergeant, and they have come up with an idea." He looked at the police sergeant intently. "The New York police have come to a dead end. They cannot connect Wilson directly to any drug dealers although they are certain he was in it up to his neck." He lowered his voice. "Wilson was living with his sister and her husband in New York, your in-laws, Sergeant. New York, that's where the answer is." He paused. "I want you to go there, Sergeant, on Monday."

Hope blinked, but Richardson plowed on.

"It's only natural, Sergeant, that as family you should go. No one knows you up there. It's a visit of condolence. You'll fit in perfectly. No one will ask any questions. Mix with his friends, probe the background. Find the connection, Sergeant. Find who was running Wilson. And get me the information we need to cut out this cancer that is killing our island."

Hope thought to protest, but the commissioner was speaking again.

"Find the connection, Sergeant, find the link in Antigua. You are in a position to discover things up there that the New York police never will. Put a feather in our cap, Sergeant Hope. Things like this are not forgotten."

Hope thought he detected a note of pleading in the old man's voice.

"Constable Tomkinson will take charge in Nelson's, sir," he said quietly.

"Excellent, Sergeant. I can see you are well organized. You are booked on a flight, Monday morning. Your ticket and money will be ready for you here, together with a visa which I have arranged. We have told Interpol you are going, but in a strictly private capacity. They'll want to see you, of course."

He stood up and walked around the desk, putting a fatherly arm about Hope's broad shoulders as they made their way to the door.

"I have every confidence in you, Sergeant. And remember, this is a strictly private affair. You have no jurisdiction up there. Just get names. And Sergeant, you report to me directly, understand? To me directly."

"Yes, sir," Hope said and quietly made his way out.

Back at his desk Richardson thought about what he had just done. It might work and at least it showed enthusiastic cooperation from Antigua at a time when results were extremely thin. The commissioner sighed. Sometimes things had to be expended for the greater plan. Hope was an excellent station sergeant, and he would be hard to replace should anything go wrong.

SERGEANT HOPE DROVE slowly back to Falmouth where he lived. He went to the front room of his house taking the Wilson file with him and began to read through his last report; the incidents of three weeks before began to come into focus again.

It had been a typically sunny morning. With Tomkinson he had gone first thing to The Pirates, which had reported thefts the night before. The hotel was on two levels: reception, bar, and dining room at the top of a hill; bedrooms on the harbor below. From reception he had seen figures jogging on the beach. A rubber dinghy, powered by an outboard motor, pulled away from a yacht and headed toward Nelson's Dockyard.

Simms, the owner, had fussed about. He had been eager to pacify his guests but not for any publicity.

"Some of them went completely berserk when it happened," he had said. "Think I've calmed them down now though."

After a cup of coffee he had brought them to the bedrooms, down a very steep, almost vertical road pitted with large potholes. The two-story bedroom blocks were right on the beach, surrounded by abundant shrubs and capped with bright bougainvillaea. Small blue hummingbirds moved from bush to flower; black birds with yellow breasts darted about in search of crumbs.

Three thefts had been reported by Simms. Hope listened while Constable Tomkinson took the three signed statements that now sat on the file.

It all began to come back. There was the Englishman, extremely disgruntled by the loss of his wife's jewelry, worth over twenty thousand pounds, and all his cash, five thousand dollars.

"Bloody disgraceful," he had said.

Then the middle-aged American couple; their expensive camera and his credit cards were gone. They had been much more relaxed, seasoned campaigners who took the view that after New York nothing could surprise them.

Next door to them, the honeymooners from Detroit, about four days into their holiday by the color of them, putting a brave face on the loss of her wedding ring.

To them all, Hope had murmured words of reassurance: everything possible would be done, but realistically one had to expect the worst—and were they insured?

Hope narrowed his eyes as he tried to recall what had happened next. He had left Tomkinson at the car and strolled down the beach. He had walked past a large, rusted anchor upright in the sand, the relic of a great ship, its chain still intact. Some of the locals who worked this beach might never come up to the Dockyard. A group of them had sat on a little jetty waiting for someone to ski. Several had long Rasta locks; the heavy, sweet smell of ganja hung in the air. There was a chorus of amicable greeting as Hope sat down.

For fifteen minutes they chatted easily with him. They knew this was their own man who had treated them fairly down the years. They had nothing to hide.

He asked about several people: who was coming and going in the hinterland of the harbor. The larcenies of the night before were common knowledge to them all, transmitted through the flawless island information network. Many of their wives were hotel chambermaids—always the first on whom suspicion fell; thus a theft of this kind was bitterly resented. Ripples were felt in different ways: the tourists were unhappy and might not come back, the hotels began freshly to scrutinize their staff. Now it would be all the harder for her to come home at night with a well-earned pound of prime fillet strapped to her thigh.

Hope had bid them good-by, slapping their upraised palms in the local way. He had a good idea of what had happened the night before. It had to be Wilson.

He had made his way back down to the car where Tomkinson waited. The hotel barbecue was cooking hamburgers for lunch. As the image returned he could almost smell the meat on the griddle.

There had been something.

He felt his neck tingle as the memory flooded back. He had been walking to his car, which was parked under a giant, cooling palm. A taxi driver was loading suitcases into the back of an old Buick, and he greeted Hope cheerfully.

As he did so, a couple had emerged from the nearby bedroom and walked toward the taxi. They carried overcoats, out of place in the tropical heat, indicating the beginning of a journey that would end in a colder place. The man was smoking a long cigar. He had blond hair going gray and now he ran a hand through it. Hope had got into his car and looked again at them as Tomkinson pulled away. Their face color was that of people arriving for a holiday, not leaving. As they drew level, to a distance of not more than four feet, it was the man's eyes, seen just for an instant, that Hope remembered.

They were the eyes of a man in fear of his very life, at the moment when he has just been told that it is in danger.

THE RED DATSUN Sunny pulled up at the hotel door, and the tall West Indian got out. He was dressed in a dark suit, a white shirt and sunglasses. A suitcase lay on the back seat; Sergeant Hope was on his way to New York.

The lobby of the hotel was quiet and cool. Maids in bright pink uniforms carried breakfast trays on their heads. An old dog lay asleep on the stone-flagged floor. Hope hit the small bell at reception, and a thin man in his late twenties with glasses and straggling, dark hair came out.

"Is Mr. Simms in please?" asked Hope.

"I'm sorry, but Mr. and Mrs. Simms are in England."

"Who is in charge please?"

"I am the assistant manager," said the man. "Can I help you?"

Hope had never seen the man before. He introduced himself with his police ID. The assistant manager appeared unimpressed.

"We haven't met before. I am from Nelson's Dockyard," said Hope.

"I am Mr. Croake," said the assistant manager.

Sergeant Hope looked at him.

"On the night of April thirtieth last," he said, "there were a number of rooms broken into and guests' valuables taken. On May first I came here and took statements. On the way out I

44

noticed two guests who were leaving in Mr. Cotter's taxi. Could you please let me have their names?"

Croake made a face. "Lots of people come and go each day," he said. "You want to know them all?"

"Just May first," replied Hope pleasantly, "and to make it easy for you, I'm looking for a couple who had probably arrived only two or three days before."

"Well that's impossible," said Croake. "All our guests stay for minimum one week—our basic charge covers seven nights."

"Please look it up," said Hope.

"If you insist."

In about a minute Croake had found the information.

"The only people to fit your description are an English couple, Sir Tristram and Lady Hoare," he said. "Arrived April twenty-eighth, checked out at noon, May first. I checked them out myself as it so happens."

Hope wrote down the names.

"Why did they leave so soon?" he asked.

Croake tilted back his head and looked at Hope with an air of fraying patience.

"It so happens that Sir Tristram Hoare has a heart condition," he said. "He had taken a turn the night before, and his wife insisted they return at once to London to see his doctor. Now if you will excuse me, Sergeant . . ."

Hope turned to go, but then turned back.

"One last question, was this their first stay in this hotel?"

"No," said Croake bitingly, "but I expect it will be their last. They weren't very keen on being robbed blind on their third night here. I think they expected a little more law and order in Antigua."

Hope stood there.

"Does that strike you as odd, Sergeant?"

"Yes," said Hope slowly. "I was never asked to take a statement from these people—their theft was never reported to me."

Croake had busied himself behind a typewriter and was making out a dinner menu.

"I shouldn't worry, Sergeant. All they wanted to do was to go home."

Hope walked slowly to his car.

It was with few expectations of success that he drove through St. John's out to Coolidge airport to catch his flight to Kennedy.

CHAPTER FIVE

THE NEWMARKET TRAFFIC was heavy as usual for the Guineas. The early May Saturday was bright and sunny, and there was a light breeze.

Jeremy Carvill bit a fingernail as he sat at the wheel of the white Mercedes 500SL that had cost him fifty thousand pounds. He wiped a lock of black hair from his eyes and swore viciously. He was strikingly good-looking, in his late twenties, very dark and tall, with an open, innocent face. Penny, his wife, sat beside him. Her pretty face was framed by straw-blond hair falling to her shoulders. Two pairs of binoculars lay in her lap. It was twenty minutes to three o'clock.

"Oh fuck this," said Jeremy again.

He swung the wheel of the two-seater hard right and at the same time stood on the gas. Leaping out of line the gleaming car streaked up the outside lane, its five-liter V8 engine reaching sixty with a high-pitched whine in just over seven seconds. They made about three hundred yards passing car after car. The road they were on now met a junction leading directly to Newmarket racecourse. They could see the stands and the bright silks of jockeys flashing in the distance as they went down for the start of the second race. Helicopters landed and took off in an area of Newmarket Heath in front of the enclosures.

Jeremy stabbed the button that electrically controlled his window. He leaned out to the police officer who was directing traffic at the intersection.

"Jeremy Carvill, Officer," he shouted. "I've got less than five minutes to declare a horse for the Guineas."

The policeman nodded. He held up his hand and brought all the main road traffic to a halt. Then he waved Carvill through.

"Thank God for that," murmured Penny as they shot over the road and up by the racecourse to the main entrance. She dreaded to think what would happen if they failed to declare the favorite for the Two Thousand Guineas. It was most unlike her husband to put such an important task at risk. He had been in Newmarket all morning and had only got back to their farm outside Ritchbridgeton at noon. Barely enough time to change, get to the racecourse, and declare the colt. It was going to be touch and go. Even one minute late was too late for a clerk of the scales.

They screeched to a halt at the entrance to Newmarket racecourse. The clock on the dashboard said there was a minute left. Jeremy jammed the lever into neutral and jumped out leaving the engine running.

"See you inside," he shouted running in, quickly passing through a door marked "Owners and Trainers." The weighing room was fifty yards away. He sprinted for it, down a line of white marquees where companies were treating their customers for the day. There was the clatter of glassware and cutlery. Jeremy cursed himself furiously for leaving it so close with so much at stake. Still, there had not been much of a choice.

He had spent two hours that morning in a bedroom of the

White Hart in Newmarket giving a forty-year-old billionaire the greatest blow job of his life.

PENNY CARVILL PARKED the Mercedes. She put on a wide-brimmed straw hat tied around with a bright, red ribbon. Taking the Zeiss binoculars, she made her way into the racecourse and walked to the weighing room. Jeremy emerged. He was carrying a small racing saddle, a lead cloth, and a number fourteen on his arm.

"Thank goodness," said Penny when she saw the saddle.

"Jesus Christ," he replied, still breathless. "I only had seconds in hand at the end."

Race goers milled past them heading for the enclosure where the winner of the second race was being unsaddled.

"Why on earth did you leave things so late?" asked Penny. "It's so unlike you."

"All I need now is a lecture," he said turning away. "I'm going over to the stables."

They walked through the crowds toward the stables, which were located at the far side of Newmarket Heath, Jeremy's long stride carrying him along in front of Penny who hurried behind. Earlier that morning the horse had been brought there by the senior stable lads.

As they crossed the enclosure a number of people greeted him.

"Buy you a bottle later," said a small man with a ruddy face. Drinking champagne at race meetings went hand-in-hand with the need to entertain one's owners constantly. Penny had learned to smile gamely hours after the last race as yet another bottle was opened in the Owners and Trainers bar. The owners were out for their fun; a horse in training was a toy. Jeremy's early patrons had come to him not because of his outstanding record as a trainer—any analysis would show it to have been hopeless—but because they had allowed him to talk them into it. When darkness fell and the owners decided to go home, it was always Penny who made the drive back home, her husband stretched out beside her.

But that was all years behind them now. Today was different. Jeremy Carvill's training yard was in Ritchbridgeton, and Newmarket was the local meeting. Today he would have his first ever runner in the most important race of Newmarket's year. Newmarket: the cradle of English racing with its great open plains, where for three centuries men have matched their horses against each other; the little town to which the second Charles brought his tempestuous Nell for the sport that was the great pleasure of the King. From here the supreme authority of English racing—the Jockey Club—has for over two centuries dispensed the judgments and made the rules that control all horse racing and breeding. To this club the English aristocracy have for generations given their unstinting service in the stewardship of a sport that, by virtue of the massive gambling involved, has a turnover of nearly three billion pounds sterling and employs sixty thousand people all over England.

For Newmarket, this was the highlight of the year. Jeremy and Penny Carvill arrived at the gate leading to the stable yard. The security man signed them through. They walked down a block of stables buzzing with action. Lads scurried about with buckets of water and baskets full of brushes and tack. Horses that had run in the second were being walked in cooling circles by their lads, great clouds of steam rising from their still heaving flanks, their nostrils red and dilated from the recent contest. Others were being led to the parade ring for the big race, stable rugs of colored felt on their gleaming backs.

The Carvills turned left down another block. They stopped before the second box and looked over the door. A magnificent, almost black, three-year-old colt with a white blaze on his forehead stood there. A boy held a lead attached to the animal's leather head collar while an older man stroked the horse's quarters with a soft body brush. As he groomed, the man spoke to the horse all the time in a soft, soothing voice.

50

"Everything all right?" asked Jeremy, opening the stable door and stepping inside with the saddle.

The man who was grooming stopped and looked up.

"He's ready to run for his life," he said, a broad beam on his wizened face. Bob Charlesworth had been with Jeremy from the start. He was known to everyone as "Chalkie," reflecting an earlier career as a jockey when infrequent rides caused his name to be written up in temporary fashion on the riders' board.

"He'd bloody talk to you," he said to Jeremy. "You should have seen the way he looked at those other horses on his way here, as much as to say, 'Who the hell are you?' He just knows he's the best."

Jeremy felt a surge of pride run through him. He felt, not for the first time, an affection bordering on love for this colt whose name was now on everyone's lips: Noble Lord. The colt's sire had won the Derby and been second in the Two Thousand Guineas while his dam had won the Epsom Oaks. His grandfather also had won the Derby and the St. Leger and his great-grandfather had won the Derby in Kentucky. Noble Lord was a prince among aristocrats. He had been purchased at auction in Kentucky for an amazing fifteen million dollars as a yearling, before he ever had a saddle on his back. His royal breeding and outstanding physical confirmation had guaranteed something special. When the contest was finally over and the auctioneer's hammer fell, the name that was on everyone's lips was a newcomer to racing: Prince Abdullah bin Yasir al-Fahd. The record price was a sensation, and so was the new owner's decision to give the colt to a second-league English trainer named Jeremy Carvill.

THE ARABS WERE now a major force on the international racing scene. Up to the first oil crisis there had not been an Arab owner of any note in England. The Japanese had provided the hard cash necessary to keep breeding prices on the up. The British aristocracy were never going to let themselves be outbid by a Jap! But the odd little men from Tokyo kept waving their catalogues, and a procession of the best blood in English racing set out for the Far East. It did not matter to them that they were sometimes stuffed with a barren mare or a stallion just over the effects of equine VD. They were building up their own thoroughbred horse-racing industry, and they knew a lot more about horses than was generally assumed. They became the backbone of English breeding for nearly six years.

Then suddenly they vanished, almost overnight. The thoroughbred sales were left with only domestic bidders; there was a slump. People said the good times were over. Those who bought foals at high prices in the hope of selling them on for even more as yearlings went to the wall. Projections were produced showing how a plateau had been reached and how there would at best be a slow, orderly decline.

Watching the nine o'clock news, which showed the Israeli tanks pouring into the Sinai, it was hard to realize the far-reaching consequences that the war would have. As the price of oil doubled and then doubled again, purchasing power moved from the West to the Middle East. Suddenly there was a new persona at large in the world of the megarich: the monied Arab. Many of them came from lands that historically had looked to England for their protection. The social pecking order of the English was something to which the Arabs had always aspired without ever achieving success. Now that they had money by the bushel, there was a way to buy themselves acceptance in the society that they had been brought up to admire and envy from a distance: they bought horses.

Ten years ago no self-respecting member of the Jockey Club would have been seen dead talking to an Arab, whose habits and personal hygiene were the subject of endless fascination. Now things were different. Arabs were the most sought-after clients in the racing world; there were even Arab members of the Jockey Club. They came in droves to Newmarket, Epsom, and Royal Ascot, their flowing robes suddenly as much part of the English racing scene as top hats and striped morning suits. It was Arab money that caused thoroughbred breeding stock to quadruple in price the world over. And whether it was Chantilly, Newmarket, or Kentucky, Arab money snapped up stud farms that had been in families for generations. The men at the Jockey Club put their best foot forward, flung their doors open and forgot, for the moment, about the unusual habits and the hygiene.

Wherever the Arabs came they brought their wealth with them. They arrived from their desert kingdoms in private, commercial-size jets, complete with fitted bathrooms and bedrooms. They commuted in private helicopters to newly acquired country estates where retinues of servants were kept on standby throughout the year. Being at heart simple men of the desert, many maintained their old ways, even when in residence in Berkshire. They converted their new houses into fairyland *majlis*, importing exotic silks and fabrics to create the tented interiors they were used to. They brought along their cronies to chat to, and their favorites to provide periodic variety from the wearying British climate. Their wealth was fabulous, and with it the thoroughbred horse-breeding industry in Europe and the United States flourished.

NOW JEREMY CARVILL looked again at Noble Lord. He had never before known what it was to have nearly half a ton of such synchronized muscle and blood under his control. This horse, when requested, accelerated in such a devastating burst of speed that his rivals were left wallowing behind—running, as it were, in a different race.

Jeremy knew acutely what it was to have been in the second division of racehorse trainers. At eighteen, against everyone's advice, he had taken out a training license. He soon realized that his ability lay more in the training of the owners than the horses. His background, a public school education and the fact that his grandfather had been a minor peer, gave him social entrées that he used to the hilt. But the money that his owners were prepared to put up was strictly petty cash. Training horses was expensive; his take-home pay at the end of the day was often less than that of a middle-grade clerk in the insurance business.

Jeremy got into the business of puffing. He would see a horse he liked before a sale and persuade one of his patrons to buy it. If it was a yearling colt, for example, there was the prospect—tantalizing if remote—of making a fortune, should the animal turn out to be a star and win a Classic. Jeremy would approach the animal's vendor. He would disclose that he had an interested client but that he would only bid for the horse if it was agreed to slip him a private commission afterward—say five percent of the sale price. He would then go and arrange with an accomplice to bid against him so that the price was bid up or puffed until the limit of his patron's instructions had been reached. This practice, which put money in Jeremy's pocket, had the inevitable result of filling his stables with very expensive animals of dubious ability. Eventually the owners got fed up with paying for the keep of these pricey duds and pulled out.

When the crisis came Jeremy was down to four owners and sixteen horses, many of which he had had to take a share in himself. He had not had a winner for five months, and his stable yard was beginning to acquire the appearance of an abandoned, outback cattle station. His bank manager had promised to return any of his checks that were not covered. He and Penny were fighting regularly.

It was against this background in July three years ago that he had bought himself a round-trip, economy-class ticket to Lexington, Kentucky, for the bloodstock sales. Jeremy had been lucky, for it was at the Keenland Sales that he had met Prince Abdullah bin Yasir al-Fahd.

Many other English horse trainers had been trying for years to achieve what Jeremy wrapped up in five minutes flat. It had been in the bloodstock sales complex on the evening of the first select yearling offering. Jeremy had flown in that morning via New York and had booked into the cheapest motel he could find in Lexington. Now he was following each transaction, catalogue in hand, from the edge of the ring.

A nuclear device dropped at that moment on the arena would have caused the redistribution of a significant percentage of the world's wealth. They were all there. Syndicates of money from Miami looking for an easily transferable asset, aging shipowners from Greece, art dealers from Paris and Rome with ravishing young women at their sides; and the real pros, the Irish, a great group of them at the back of the auditorium entering the bidding at chosen moments, when each nod of the head was worth a hundred thousand dollars.

Jeremy felt very much alone. The prices were impossibly high, and he looked about vainly in the crowd to see if he knew someone who might provide an introduction to a person with the one thing he so desperately needed: money. The English trainers he knew were jealously shepherding their owners, many of them Arabs, through the proceedings. Jeremy saw Major Langdon who trained five miles from Ritchbridgeton—a virtual neighbor—and Maxwell Rae, another Newmarket trainer whom he knew well. His attempts to get them to meet his eye were either ignored or met with a short, frozen smile. He was unaware of the intense interest with which he was being regarded by the dark-skinned man in the Western suit on his left.

Jeremy left the sales ring and walked through the crowded lobby area until he reached a sign that read "Rest Rooms." He walked to a toilet cubicle. It was empty. He opened the door and entered. Suddenly he felt a sharp push in his back and stumbled forward. He put out his hands to save himself. He could hear the door being closed. He turned around ready to lash out with his fist. But the small area in the cubicle simply meant that he was wedged chest to chest against a dark man of about forty, his own height.

"What the fuck . . ." shouted Jeremy.

A strong, coffee-colored hand clasped over his mouth. In

panic he felt another hand unzipping his fly and searching for his penis. He looked down and saw that his assailant was also unbuttoned, for his throbbing phallus now stood hugely erect as it pressed into him. To his amazement he felt himself go rock hard. The dark-skinned man slowly released his grip on Jeremy's mouth and sank to his knees, his lips searching for the pink-skinned erection. There was no protest now from Jeremy, only a feeling of intense sexual need and an awareness of the serene smile of contentment on the other man's face.

Later that night in the Radisson in Lexington, Jeremy sipped a champagne framboise in the sumptuous suite of his new stable patron, Prince Abdullah bin Yasir al-Fahd. On the table between them lay the sales catalogue for the following day's proceedings. Jeremy was trying to keep his head. He knew that Arabs spent money like water, but he had not been prepared for the real thing when it came along.

"My friend Jeremy," said the prince, "you will buy for me tomorrow whatever five horses—colts—that you desire."

"Yes, Yaw, thank you," said Jeremy. "But I think you should have a look at some of the pedigrees."

Yaw, as he had asked Jeremy to call him, smiled.

"My friend," he said, "my pedigree is money. I have told you, you may spend one million U.S. dollars in total. That is all."

That is all! thought Jeremy. That sort of money or anything like it had always been a dream before. He feverishly scanned the sales book, marking pages that interested him, making notes. Yaw had made two more drinks and was bringing them over.

Jeremy wondered how he could be sure that his new patron was genuine. He had heard these fellows did not drink alcohol. This one was certainly different. If he had to bid for these horses himself and Yaw suddenly disappeared, then Jeremy would never be allowed into a horse sale again. His fears were quickly put to rest. The Arab sat down quietly beside him on the multicolored, padded settee. He placed their two glasses on the table. Under Jeremy's, there was a rectangular piece of paper. He picked it up and looked at it. His ears buzzed with excitement. It was a demand draft on Morgan Guaranty, New York, for one million dollars, made out to the Keenland Association, Lexington, Kentucky.

Jeremy did not go back to the motel that night.

The next day he carried out his new patron's instructions. Five thoroughbred colts were purchased. Moreover, Yaw had fifty thousand dollars change. He gave Jeremy a check for twenty-five thousand and left for the Middle East in a private plane. A jubilant Jeremy upgraded to first class and flew back to London. He was not slow to notice the changed attitudes of the other trainers to his new fortune. It was they who now tried to catch Jeremy's eye.

The yearlings arrived home and were broken under Chalkie Charlesworth's expert supervision. They thrived, and as they did, so did everything around them. Carpenters arrived to repair stables and fit new doors. The stable yard was given its first coat of paint in ten years. A team of gardeners toiled to restore the lawns and shrubberies to their former glory. The Carvills' life was transformed. No longer was there the daily threat of impending financial doom. Instead a healthy stream of cash flowed into the operation from their new client's substantial monthly training fees. Even their bank manager was friendly and came out once to dinner.

Jeremy's contact with the prince was minimal as a firm of London solicitors paid all his bills. Jeremy tried to make some inquiries but without much success. It appeared that his new owner was the son of an aging, fabulously wealthy ruler in the Gulf. Occasionally Yaw would call Jeremy, usually in the late evening. He could never be sure from where the call was coming, but several times the prince had been put through from New York, and once Jeremy had to phone a number in Tripoli for a decision on the color of his racing silks. (White, emerald green star back and front.)

In the year following their meeting in Kentucky, Yaw had come once to Newmarket. He had declined an invitation to come out to Ritchbridgeton for dinner and to see his horses. Instead he had requested that Jeremy come to the White Hart in Newmarket to see him—alone. In the months that had passed, Jeremy had allowed himself to believe that the sordid side of their relationship might have been just a bad dream. In Lexington it had been necessary for him to play along with a bit of harmless romping in order to get a client. Home in Newmarket, on his own doorstep things would be very different. He would make damn sure of it.

After ten minutes in Yaw's bedroom he realized how wrong one could be. As the sweat poured down his naked back Jeremy contemplated the outlandish situation. This was his new owner. But who owned whom?

The first season's racing with the new horses was a quiet success. One of them was promising, three were average, and one was useless. They won five between them, and everyone said that Jeremy Carvill was on his way. His confidence in his own ability to train racehorses also grew. Without the daily need to hustle for new business he was able to cut down on the socializing and concentrate his waking hours on training the horses in his yard. A couple of his old patrons left when Jeremy no longer went out of his way to entertain them. He made no attempt to stop their going. In fact, his new success attracted the attention of totally new patrons.

Then two years ago, on the anniversary of his first meeting with the prince, Jeremy went back to Kentucky. Yaw had asked him to suggest more yearling purchases, which made Jeremy doubly elated as he then knew he was safe for at least another year. The original colts were entering their three-year-old careers where they would face their most important races; even though none of them was going to win a Classic, they would do well enough in a number of other valuable and prestigious contests.

At their second meeting in Lexington, Yaw was particularly demanding. He insisted that Jeremy move into his suite with him. His sexual appetite was insatiable and also variable. After a vigorous first afternoon together—an afternoon that should have been spent reviewing prospective yearlings in their stalls—Yaw opened the door to the adjoining suite.

Two girls sat on the bed. They were completely naked and very tanned, one brushing the other's waist-length, platinum-blond hair. They looked up as the two men came in. He blinked and looked again. They were identical twins, not a day over sixteen, tall with firm, young bodies and full, round breasts. Their faces had the open, attractive healthiness that Jeremy associated with California and Coca-Cola ads. Without a word the two girls moved to the center of the large bed and began to make slow, erotic love, their long limbs entwined, their tongues seeking each other's mouths. Instantly Jeremy felt himself aroused. He and the prince sat down.

"Yaw," Jeremy said.

Yaw inclined his head toward Jeremy without taking his eyes from the scene on the bed.

"Yaw," said Jeremy again, "I've got a lot of horses to see. I've missed a whole day already." Yaw did not move, but spoke softly.

"Jeremy, my friend, when you see this with me, what can you miss?"

"I know, Yaw," said Jeremy, "but I've got to look at some horses if I am going to buy you anything worthwhile."

The two girls had altered their positions. One was now kneeling between the other's knees. Her hands were massaging the smooth insides of her firm thighs, her tongue caressing her navel and working down to her golden mound. Yaw's eyes bulged.

"Yaw," said Jeremy, "you don't mind if I go?"

Yaw slowly turned to his racehorse trainer. The look on his face was one of total authority, that of a master addressing a servant who has disturbed him. It was a look that Jeremy had not seen before.

"This year, Jeremy, we buy one horse. A colt. Premier Yearling Sale, tomorrow evening." Yaw turned his attention back to the bed.

"But which colt, Yaw?" persisted Jeremy in exasperation.

Yaw shrugged his shoulders.

"The best," he said simply. Then he pointed toward the girls on the bed. The girl lying on her back, her legs splayed wide, was now rocking violently toward her climax.

"You finish her," commanded the prince.

As Jeremy made his way to the bed his ears were buzzing again. Did this fellow know how much the top-priced colt was going to make tomorrow? Did even Yaw have that much spending money? He entered the beautiful girl slowly, and as he did she climaxed almost immediately, locking her legs around his. He thrust more urgently. A low moaning came from his right. Yaw was working himself in steady rhythm to Jeremy's penetrations. They both came simultaneously.

THAT YEAR IN Lexington, the best meant only one horse: the colt by South Pacific. Even as a yearling his majestic presence, the promise in his deportment and his pedigree—the off-spring of a mating of eagles as the press put it—underwrote the fact that this horse would sell for big money.

Jeremy had a lot to drink that evening in the horse sales complex. Yaw had asked to be left alone with some cronies for the night, and so it was nearly 2:00 A.M. when Jeremy found himself in a nightclub in downtown Lexington looking across a bottle of Dom Perignon at J. J. Reilly, the legendary Irish trainer. Reilly had amassed substantial wealth; he was the trainer whom everyone wanted. He had trained so many Classic winners, he had forgotten the exact number. He had the eyes of a ferret and the nose of a fox. He was barely touching his champagne. Music blared out the latest hits, and people knocked against each other on a tiny dance floor.

60

"You Irish are dishonest whores," said Jeremy heavily. "I have never met an honest Irishman."

Reilly laughed.

"We had to turn dishonest to stop the English stealing from us," he replied with spirit.

Jeremy slurped his drink. "You're fucking thieves," he repeated, "thieves, thieves."

"This business makes villains of us all," said Reilly.

"How did you get all your money, Reilly?" asked Jeremy. "How many poor fuckers did you screw to get where you are?"

If Jeremy had been able to focus properly he would have seen a shadow of anger cross the Irishman's face. "There's one thing you won't steal from me I can tell you," he said truculently. "By Jesus you won't."

"What's that?" asked Reilly.

Jeremy leaned over conspiratorially. "I'm going to buy the South Pacific colt tomorrow," he said, slurring. "What d'you think of that?"

Reilly raised his eyebrows. Jeremy had finished the bottle and was signaling for another.

"That will cost you a few shillings," Reilly said. "He's the best looker I think I have ever seen. We're interested in him too, of course."

"Then you'd better have a deep pocket, Reilly, my old son," Jeremy said. "I've my instructions."

The Irishman's eyes narrowed. "Any horse is only worth so much," he said shrewdly.

"A horse is worth what you pay for him," said Jeremy and knocked his glass to the ground.

"How much is that?" asked Reilly.

Jeremy looked at him belligerently.

"Whatever a hundred thousand on top of your highest bid is, that's how much," said Jeremy. "I've my riding instructions." He laughed. "You're fucked, Reilly, fucked. He's as good as mine already."

The next day's bidding was now part of racing folklore. Jeremy was in at the very start. The colt opened at two million and went rapidly to six. There was that hushed tension in the auditorium that is created by a very special event. A couple of bloodstock agencies and Langdon, the English trainer, had been shaken off. Now it was Jeremy and old Nicos Yannopoulis, the tanker king, who were bid for bid. Yaw sat impassively beside Jeremy. He had been quite specific: buy him. At eight two the Greek shook his head; the auctioneer tried to coax another bid from him, but the old man was emphatic. Suddenly there was a cry from a spotter: a new bidder! A great hum rippled through the crowd. Jeremy's heart began to do overtime.

"Eight three can I say four, can I say four?" sang the auctioneer.

"Four," bid Jeremy.

"Four I'm bid. Four I'm bid. Five I'm bid. Can I say six?"

Jeremy continued to nod, once allowing the other bidder to come within an ace of succeeding. He caught a frozen stare from Yaw. The price had gone to eleven million dollars. No one in history had ever gone this high for a yearling horse.

Jeremy bid on. He could now see the opposition, high behind him in the auditorium. It was J. J. Reilly, the little shit. Surely he hadn't this sort of money? Jeremy looked at Yaw. It was not taking a feather out of him.

"Fourteen nine, fourteen nine, fourteen nine give me fifteen!" yelled the auctioneer in his singsong voice.

"Fifteen I'm bid!" he cried with a great shout on the fifteen. "I'm bid fifteen million dollars for this son of South Pacific. Who'll say fifteen one? Who'll say one, who'll say one?"

This is complete madness, thought Jeremy, as he discreetly raised his hand.

"Fifteen million, one hundred thousand dollars!" sang the auctioneer.

Forty seconds later the hammer came down, a new world record had been created, and the prince had a new horse. He was delighted by all the fuss and the thought of owning such a unique commodity; Jeremy was delighted by the prospect of training this fantastic animal; and the colt's breeders were delighted by the amazing price that the Arab had paid. Over fifteen million dollars! The very top they had expected was five. That was why, over breakfast that morning, they had sold a half-share in the colt for three million cash to the legendary little Irish wizard, J. J. Reilly.

AND NOW THE same top-priced colt was just half an hour away from his most important race to date: the Two Thousand Guineas.

As a two year old he had fast become the horse people came racing to see. The animal's appearance even at this early age was that of a great athlete in the making. His flawless limbs, which would guarantee him unhindered acceleration at the right time, the carriage of his head, his perfect temperament, the great depth of girth and chest—the powerhouse within which his big heart beat—all combined to make this the most exciting horse of his generation. The faultless manner in which he won two races in England and one in France meant that today the bookmakers were taking no chances. Noble Lord was their favorite—by a mile.

"Is Prince al-Fahd here yet?" asked Penny.

She had met their principal patron only once, and that had also been at Newmarket last autumn when the colt had won his last two-year-old race.

"I haven't seen him," replied Jeremy.

There was something about their patron that Penny did not like, but she could not put her finger on it. She kept her doubts to herself.

"What are they betting?" asked Chalkie.

"He's two to one on," said Jeremy. "Southern Cross is threes, and Pentle Bay is four to one. It's any price you like the rest."

"Southern Cross is bloody fast," said Chalkie. "Remember

the way he finished at Doncaster last back-end after getting a bad run? God, he came like a little train."

"This fellow should have the measure of him," said Jeremy, patting Noble Lord's neck. Despite his outward confidence there was always a nagging doubt that something would go wrong, that he had misjudged the timing of the horse's preparation, that he might at that very moment be incubating some virus that would show itself only when the pressure of the race came on. And then there were all the other horses, all doing their damnedest to see that his colt did not win.

What a world of difference there was between a horse at two and three years. Surprises were legendary; last year's duds suddenly turned the tables on horses who previously had beaten them out of sight. Although Noble Lord had won his warm-up race two weeks ago, who knew what might come out of the pack to trounce him today? And if that happened, Noble Lord's name would be instantly forgotten, eclipsed forever by the new hero of the hour.

Some trainers went through life without ever winning a race like this, and here he was, his first runner the out-and-out favorite. It was too good to be true.

The saddling process was complete.

"See you in the ring, Chalkie," said Jeremy as he and Penny left the stable and began their walk back to the enclosures. The final build-up for the big event of the day had begun.

Interest in the Two Thousand Guineas was intense. Run over the Rowley Mile at Newmarket and reserved for three-year-old colts, the best of their generation, entries were made the year before by trainers all over Europe. Bookmakers had been quoting odds about the participants since they were two year olds and the racing public had the long winter to calculate their preference.

The winning colt of the Two Thousand Guineas would receive a prize of just under a hundred thousand pounds and would automatically be quoted short odds for the biggest race of them all—the Epsom Derby, to be held on June 3. More important, the Guineas' winner would be a stallion in his own right when his racing career was finished, with a price on his head of not less than ten million dollars. If a horse achieved this kind of distinction, not only his owner, but equally his trainer and jockey, shared in the dividends that would flow. It was a game of very high stakes.

THE CROWD WAS twelve deep as Noble Lord was led around the track on the perimeter of the parade ring. Jeremy and Penny pushed their way through to the railing and then ducked between two horses into the grassy center. Noble Lord looked superb, his coat glistened like living silk, dancing on his toes, Chalkie at his head, talking to him as they walked. Little groups of owners with their trainers stood looking at the horses being led around. J. J. Reilly, the trainer of Southern Cross, raised his hat courteously to Penny. Maxwell Rae stood talking to his owners. He trained a colt called Pavarotti who was expected to find the mile too short. Major Langdon who trained Pentle Bay smiled at them as they went by. The Carvills stood alone, near the center of the ring. The jockeys would be in at any moment.

"Do you think he's going to turn up?" asked Penny.

Jeremy was about to answer her when suddenly there was a murmur from the crowd. Jeremy turned to see what people were looking at. Then he saw a bright flash at the corner of the parade ring. An imposing figure in long, flowing Arab robes of the most immaculate white had entered and was making his way toward them, his dark face composed and regal, not noticing the excitement and hubbub he was causing. Two large men walked on either side of him. Yaw had arrived.

They shook hands, the prince showing meticulous attention to Penny, complimenting her on how she looked. Then he turned to Jeremy.

"The big day, my friend," he said, smiling.

"He'll run very well," Jeremy said to Yaw. "He'll have to finish in the first three."

In his heart and soul he knew that the colt had a major chance of winning the race by a distance. He had been over the contest in his mind a thousand times. But still there was the doubt. And there was no point in getting one's owners unduly excited.

"He's looking well, isn't he?" Jeremy said.

They turned and admired the magnificent animal being led around by Chalkie. Even to the uninitiated the horse as a physical specimen was in a class of his own.

The jockeys were entering the parade ring in their bright colored silks. One, in pure white with a green star front and back, was making his way over to the Carvills and the prince.

Bill "Stroker" Roche was forty years old. He had been riding races since he was fifteen. Twenty-five years of dieting and holding his man's body prisoner in a teenager's frame had given him a ravaged, wasted look. His head looked disproportionately large to the rest of him. Folds of unwanted flesh fell beneath his chin. His eyes were dark and darting. He could have been a monkey out for the day. But he was the best. With fourteen Classics to his credit and nine championship jockey titles, Stroker was among the legends in racing. His name came from his ability to coax the last ounce of effort from a horse, particularly a young horse, without being too hard on the animal in the process. Jeremy had come to a special agreement with Stroker that he ride Noble Lord in all his races. The partnership had been a devastating success.

Stroker tipped his cap deferentially to the prince and then to the Carvills.

"Afternoon all," he said chirpily.

There were three minutes to go before he would have to mount. Jeremy drew him slightly to one side.

"He's in top form as you see," he said.

He had spent hours working out the strategy.

"Settle him early and keep him covered up for the first half mile," Jeremy said. "Make your way toward the front after that and with two to go, kick for home. For Christ's sake don't get boxed in on the rails. There will be a lot of tired horses going backward when you're making your move. And keep your eye on Southern Cross. He'll be going fastest of the others at the end."

Stroker nodded slightly. He knew his horse. He was going to piss in. "All right," he said briefly.

"Jockeys get mounted," a man said into a hand-held megaphone, and the horses were led by their handlers toward the middle of the ring. Chalkie led Noble Lord over and Jeremy slid off the colt's bright felt rug. Noble Lord danced around as the fresh, spring breeze caught his warm coat. Jeremy checked the saddle girths for tightness, and then he came around to the horse's left side and gave Stroker a quick leg up.

"Good luck," he said.

Yaw bowed slightly to Stroker who tipped his cap again. Then they were on their way, Noble Lord sidestepping to the parade ring gate, still being led by Chalkie, out onto the racetrack where a formal parade would take place in front of the thousands of people in the stands.

Jeremy led Penny and Yaw up to the position in the grandstand reserved for owners and trainers. There was a huge crowd, and by the time they climbed to the top of the stand the horses were exactly one mile away down the great Newmarket plain, barely visible in the hazy English afternoon.

Jeremy's stomach was a knot of fear. All he wanted was just one Classic. With just one Classic he could start telling this Arab fairy where to get off. He glanced over at Penny. She was looking very pretty today. She saw his worried look and smiled, giving him a big wink. He peered through his binoculars down the track. The horses were being led behind the aluminum starting gates that would soon spring open on electronic hinges.

One by one the horses were loaded in. Noble Lord was one of the last to enter.

"They're under starter's orders."

Jeremy felt the heart hammering in his chest. A lifetime's ambition was being put to the test.

"They're off!"

Ten thousand pairs of binoculars swung up simultaneously to peer down the straight mile track at the eighteen thoroughbred colts that had just leaped from the starting gates to run in the most important race of their lives. An estimated twenty-six million people in the British Isles and as far away as Australia had turned on their TV sets within the past ten minutes to watch.

All that could be seen from the stands, even with binoculars, was a small, slowly growing bunch of color that clung to the right-hand rail of the racetrack about a mile away. The commentator's voice rattled out the names of the leading six horses and then skimmed through the remaining ones. A TV monitor in the stand enabled Jeremy to follow the early action. Noble Lord was a clear last.

Two furlongs had been eaten up by the horses, the leaders going flat out, testing the stamina of their opponents to the full. Gradually they became more visible. The jockeys on the more fancied horses, who had been lying in wait, could now be seen to make their moves, their heads with goggles bobbing at their horses' necks, their supple bodies not yet asking for the ultimate effort that would in seconds be demanded. Now they were nearly half-way home and Jeremy could see that the pace was a cracking good one. Pentle Bay was well placed behind the leaders as was Southern Cross. Noble Lord was still not mentioned.

"They're at the halfway mark."

The commentator's voice rattled on. Jeremy looked briefly at Yaw. The Arab was looking intently through a pair of expensive binoculars. His right hand also clasped a string of worry beads. Jeremy turned back to the race. This was where he had told Stroker to start to make his move and on the outside. A terrible shock ran through his body. With panic he realized that Noble Lord was not there.

"They have just over three furlongs to run."

Wildly, Jeremy scanned the group of horses, now in much clearer view. Some jockeys smacked their mounts a reminder down the neck and were going for their race. The Irish horse had come easily through on the rails and was fractionally the leader. Pentle Bay was being asked for his effort. Val-d'Isère, an unfancied French colt, was running smoothly on the outside. The rest were dead.

"Jesus Christ," Jeremy whimpered.

Then he saw him.

Jeremy's only concern had been that Noble Lord should run his race on the outside. That way he would eliminate the risk of being boxed in behind slower horses that could impede his run and cost him the race. Jeremy now saw the situation with sickening clarity. Noble Lord was about four places from the end, squeezed tight in against the rails with a wall of horses in front of him. There was just no possibility of his getting through. And to drop back and come on the outside around all the horses might have been an option up to the half-way mark. But now it was too late. Jeremy swore viciously and felt the tears welling up in his eyes.

"They have now got two furlongs to go," said the commentator, "and Southern Cross has taken it up. The favorite, Noble Lord, looks as if he has far too much to do at this stage."

Jeremy saw that Stroker was standing almost upright in his stirrups.

"It's Southern Cross and Pentle Bay with Val-d'Isère going easily on the outer. These three are drawing away from the rest of the field."

Jeremy saw the little horse that he reckoned they would trounce, streak up the track for home pursued by the game Pentle Bay and the French challenger. He focused again to Noble Lord. The colt was straining hugely at his bit, desperately wanting to run but with nowhere to go. Stroker had eased the horse even more, so that now they were almost last. Something must be wrong, thought Jeremy. Then in a flash he suddenly saw the strategy.

The idiot was trying to come on the outside after all. The

jockey yanked the horse's head hard right and in four strides had placed themselves on the outside of all the other horses. They were now on the extreme left of the field, as the people in the stand saw it. However, the maneuver had cost Noble Lord a further few lengths. Although his way was now clear he was definitely last.

"They're at the furlong pole."

Jeremy saw Stroker balance his mount. Then the little man crouched low over the colt, and with his heels kicking like pistons and his arms pumping with a life of their own, he set sail. People there who saw the next eleven seconds would remember it for the rest of their lives.

It was as if a rocket booster had been ignited. At first nothing much seemed to happen as the powerful colt began to lengthen his awesome stride. Gradually he built up his speed, his long legs eating up the green turf, until suddenly he reached the point of maximum momentum, which meant that he was being propelled forward at a velocity far greater than all the other horses. In a blinding flash of black muscle and white silk, Noble Lord shot up the track on the outside. The crowd was cheering deliriously. The horse was traveling so fast that he had drawn level with the three leaders. Jeremy began to jump up and down. Penny was shouting at the top of her voice. Noble Lord crossed the finishing line below them, the winner by a head from Southern Cross.

Penny threw her arms around Jeremy's neck and shouted for joy. Jeremy turned to Yaw, his face beaming. The Arab was smiling hugely. People around them were offering congratulations. They made their way down to the enclosure where the winner is led in. Crowds milled around trying to get a close-up glimpse of this rare champion. Reporters with their notebooks out were peppering Jeremy with questions.

"The Derby next, Mr. Carvill?"

"Crawfords are quoting him six to four for the Derby, what do you think, Mr. Carvill?"

It was all a blur to Jeremy. He was quite dizzy. He had gone from abject despair to the peak of victory in under a minute. He shepherded Penny and Yaw into the Winners enclosure, bedecked with beds of brightly colored flowers. Stroker rode a steaming Noble Lord in. There was a great cheer from the crowd gathered there.

"Jesus, you gave me a heart attack," Jeremy said to Stroker, as the jockey took off the horse's saddle.

The little man shrugged his shoulders. "He's the best there is," he said.

"Well done, jockey," said Yaw.

"Thanks, Your Highness," said Stroker and went into the weighing room.

Jeremy turned to Yaw as Noble Lord was being led back to his stable. "The Epsom Derby, now," he said gleefully, "and I think we'll walk it."

They strolled out of the Winners enclosure. Jeremy knew that celebratory drinks were not on. Yaw never drank alcohol in public.

"The trophy will be presented in about fifteen minutes," said Penny to the Prince, whose two bodyguards had reappeared at his side.

"Thank you," said the Arab, turning toward Penny, "but a flight plan is filed for my journey to the Gulf. We must leave for London."

They had seen his private helicopter waiting in the middle of Newmarket plain.

"I would be so happy," he continued, "if Mrs. Carvill would accept the trophy on my behalf."

"Of course, Your Highness," said Penny with a bright smile.

They reached the front of the racetrack, leading toward the parking lot. Yaw stopped and motioned Jeremy to one side. Jeremy turned to his wife.

"See you in the bar in a moment," he said to her. Yaw turned toward Penny and bowed once more. She left for the bar with a light step. Yaw then turned his attention to Jeremy.

"Well done, my friend," he said.

"Well," shrugged Jeremy, "we did it, didn't we?"

"*You* did it, my friend," said the Arab. Jeremy felt light-headed. All the years of work had paid off. Sure there had been a price to pay, but what did you ever get for nothing? And now for the Derby he thought. Just four weeks away, the third of June. The prospect made him almost giddy. He laughed out loud.

"Do you know, I think we'll win the Derby," he said. "We're going to win the bloody Derby!"

The prince was lightly fingering his worry beads. He felt extremely satisifed. What had started off as bait to hook this marvelous looking young man had paid off in a quite unexpected direction. If the horse won the Derby he would be worth tens of millions of dollars. Not bad by any standards. Certainly it should stem any criticism of his excesses back home. Yaw began to feel that his choice of trainer was quite an inspired piece of work. Of course, with the success came financial independence for Jeremy, and that might mean the end of their encounters that the Prince relished so much. Even now as he looked at the slightly flushed face in front of him, a lock of dark hair falling on the forehead, Yaw felt a tinge of desire. The trainer had the body of a youth, but the strength of a man.

Nevertheless, it was time to deliver the message. He touched the slim, paper object in the folds of his robe. Promises had to be honored.

IT HAD BEEN hot that morning in the desert, his favorite place. The extra-wide balloon tires of the Range Rover carried him effortlessly across the sand dunes to the spot where the camels waited. That day, his party was exceptionally small—just he and his chief hawker, a gnarled chestnut of a man who bowed deeply as the prince arrived. A magnificent, predatory bird—a male saker falcon—flapped on the hawker's arm.

They set off to the east, the nodding *Qatariyat* carrying

them with the long, pacing stride with which they have served mankind since the dawn of history. The Gulf sun shone fiercely on the sand, whose undulating contours gave the desert its horizons, making him feel he was moving along the floor of a bowl.

A bustard strutted from the cover of green vegetation to the left and the hawker released the falcon. The bird rose in the air for a moment and then, its powerful eyes fixed on the target, it swooped unhesitatingly, talons readied. The force of the blow killed the bustard immediately, and the hawker dismounted to put the game in his bag and return the bird to his arm.

They rode in this fashion, always east, for over two hours. The prince had loved to hawk since he was a small boy; it gave the old man pleasure to be alone with his master.

All at once two figures—Bedouin, it seemed—appeared over a sand dune nearby. The prince observed their dark robes, which identified them as the migratory folk of the great desert of Al-Khali. They were on time.

One Bedouin spurred his camel toward them, and the prince, motioning his hawker to remain, rode out. They exchanged the customary greetings and then walking their mounts side by side, the Bedouin spoke to the aristocrat's inclined head.

"Fardan bids me bring your esteemed Highness his humble greetings."

"It is I," said the prince, "who am honored with such greetings from my old friend Fardan."

He had been surprised the night before when the message arrived. Now he thought of the slim, dark boy in the baths at Cairo nearly twenty-five years ago. The image bore little resemblance to the present, obese reality, a 250-pound monster who, it was said, had to be helped on to his camel's back.

The emissary continued: "Fardan wishes your Highness all success and victory with your Highness's great horse."

The prince raised his eyebrows. Very little escaped the

notice of the ubiquitous Fardan. He inclined his head gracefully. What in Allah's name the great fixer of the Middle East
wanted of him, he had no idea.

"Fardan asks a favor," the emissary was saying, "a favor for
Fardan himself."

He spoke rapidly, explaining his request, gesticulating with
his hands. The prince was surprised. It was a simple matter,
arranged with the flick of a fly swatter. At any rate one could
hardly refuse. One never knew nowadays when one might
need Fardan.

"That is all?" asked the prince finally. "Then you may tell
my old friend Fardan, that as surely as the sands of the desert
outnumber the stars in the sky, it is done."

The Bedouin smiled and handed the prince a brown envelope. Then bidding him the farewell proper to a man of his
exalted rank, he wheeled away. In a moment he and his
companion had been swallowed up by the sands.

The prince and his ancient retainer turned to retrace their
steps westward. The saker falcon, with three kills to its name
that morning, perched contentedly on the arm of the keeper.
The edge to its appetite, and with it the urge to kill, had
momentarily gone as the small party made their way home.

THE NOISE ROSE as photographers gathered around. Their
cameras flashed at racing's most successful current partnership. A television sports reporter was hovering, waiting for a
chance to interview one of them. Jeremy was talking excit-
edly to Yaw about the horse's program between now and the
Epsom Derby.

"It's just over four weeks away," he was saying. "I doubt
very much if I'll give him another race."

The prince held up his hand to stem any further discussion.
"My friend, I must go," said Yaw.

They walked to the gate. The Arab continued: "I am sure
you will send me a full report in the normal way. We shall
meet in London in early June the day before the Derby."

74

Jeremy was too happy to protest or to object to Yaw's suggestion.

"But I have a small favor to ask," said the Arab.

Jeremy raised his eyebrows. Yaw had produced a small, brown envelope from within his brilliantly white habit. He went on: "A friend of a friend, his son loves the horses. He is presently working in the Middle East, but he wants to come to England. He wants to work with a trainer."

He handed Jeremy the envelope. Jeremy took it, somewhat reluctantly. His yard was full at the moment, and all his lads had been hand picked. They were walking toward the entrance gates.

"That is his photograph," Yaw said. "I would appreciate it so much if you could take him in."

"Well, I'll certainly give him a hearing," Jeremy said.

"He will start next week," Yaw said. It was no longer a request. Fardan had been specific.

What the hell, Jeremy thought. If it keeps this bugger happy, what do I care?

The prince turned. "To the Derby, my friend," he smiled.

Then in a flourish of robes he was gone.

Jeremy stuffed the envelope into his pocket and headed for the bar. Without Yaw he felt on top of the world, an ecstatic happiness that made him want to jump up into the air and shout for sheer joy. He had made it. He had won the Two Thousand Guineas. He was now training the favorite for the Derby. Jeesus! Would there be a party in Newmarket tonight!

He skipped up the steps into the bar and made his way to a large group, that included Penny, in the corner. There was a cheer as he arrived, the man of the moment. A glass of champagne was shoved into his hand.

"Noble Lord!" someone shouted and another great cheer reverberated throughout the racetrack.

Jeremy put his arm around Penny's waist and, pulling her close, hugged her warmly. He felt that his whole life had been designed for this moment. The happiness and excitement flooded through him so hugely that he thought he would drown.

CHAPTER
SIX

A GROUP OF Haitians stood inside the subway at 125th Street and Broadway. They leered at the West Indian with the suitcase who was making his unfamiliar way from the trains toward a portly man with a red face selling newspapers behind a stand. It was 7:00 P.M. The black man put the suitcase down and asked the news vendor directions. There was no discernible response and so, thinking he had not been heard, he asked again. The red-faced man looked at him for a moment and then bawled: "So who am I? Your fuckin' motha?"

This was the part of Broadway where the subway changes from the underground into daylight, running north to the Bronx on its massive girdered railway. The side streets were more neighborly here on the edge of Harlem than in midtown. Shops were still open selling large, firm tomatoes and fresh fruit; a dry cleaner's dispatched customers home with clothes in plastic bags.

After ten minutes and two inquiries he came to the door of a tall apartment building. In the lobby he found the name he wanted among the mailboxes. He took the elevator to the sixth floor. He had called from the arrivals terminal to say he was coming in.

Constanza was much older than her late sister. She opened the door, and they shook hands formally. Hope had met her only once—at his wedding. The apartment was a two-bedroom affair with a small bathroom and kitchen off a larger area for eating and sitting and watching the black-and-white TV, which was on in the corner. Mats as thin as rice paper covered the wooden floor. She showed Hope to a bedroom that contained a single bed.

"It was Ernest's," she said, "when he was home."

There was no emotion in her voice. Her face was cold and tired; she was at least fifty.

"Where is . . . ?" Hope searched for her husband's name.

"He's on nights at the moment," she said.

Hope remembered that the husband—Francisco—worked in one of the big midtown hotels as a porter. They had no children. Hope went out, and they sat in two chairs, facing each other, the TV still going strong beside them.

"A rough time," Hope said.

Constanza shrugged. "It happens sooner or later," she said. She still had her West Indian lilt.

"Why do you say that?" he asked.

"Ernest thought he could be a big boy. He didn't realize that he was just a sprat swimming in an ocean full of sharks." She made a snap-snapping motion with her fingers and thumb. "They eat him up, man, just like that."

"I'm sorry," said Hope.

Constanza shrugged again. "Maybe he's better off. When he was here he give me nothing but trouble. Man, there'd be guys comin' to that door all night after he'd done a joint. The amount of stuff that came up and down in that elevator . . ."

Hope nodded.

"You knew he came back home end of last month? Well I believe he pulled off some business on the island. Some time-

78

sharing apartments, a few bedrooms in Pirates, his usual routine. He probably had the stuff on him when he got back home."

She appeared uninterested in trying to defend her deceased brother's reputation. "I believe so, yes," she said. "He traded some high-class rocks a couple of days before he disappeared."

"That would be it," said Hope. Constanza it seemed had little to hide. "Did he talk much about his trip home?"

"Quite a bit," said Constanza, "about the old places, who had died, who has left, you know, the usual."

"Did he talk about drugs?" asked Hope gently. The woman looked at him sharply.

"Dope? No way—never, man," she said emphatically. "That's what those white trash keep askin' me last week. Every day they come and ask questions. Francisco, he's on nights, man, they nearly drove him mad. He didn't even *like* Ernest." She lit a cigarette. "I only had him here 'cos he was family."

She went to the little kitchen and began to busy herself.

"You like chilli?" she asked.

"Sure," said Hope. He wondered how much she knew of the circumstances of her brother's death.

"Did anyone identify the body?" he asked.

"Francisco," she replied. "I think he kind of enjoyed it. He said they'd roughed him up real good, whoever killed him."

The strong smell of spices wafted into the room. She still cooked like an Antiguan although most of her adult life had been spent here in Upper Manhattan. Hope thought of the little man she had married, and her life, six floors up in this tiny apartment. Already he yearned for home.

"How'd he mean by that?"

"I don't know, understand? I don't want to know," she said. "He's been dead nearly two weeks. I'd nearly forgotten the whole thing until you called, man. Maybe you shouldn't have come." She stuck her head out. "They asked if I wanted to claim the body. What do I want with his body, I asked them. I just want to forget, man. Bad news, real bad news."

"I told your mother about it," said Hope.

"She's an old lady. What she say?"

"She cried a little."

Constanza shrugged.

"Did Ernest have any Mafia connections?" asked Hope. "You said he was eaten up by the big sharks—who are they?"

There was a pause, and Constanza came out of the kitchen.

"You're just like those trash, Winston, aren't you?" she said. "You're not here 'cos Ernest was family. You're here 'cos you're a cop. Well, Winston, you just listen good. You stay here as family, long as you want. But don't you try and play shit with me. I had it up to here with shit. I don't hold with them drugs they're pushin' down on the street, and neither did my brother. I don't know why he got himself killed, but now he's dead and all your damn fool questions aren't going to change that. So you stay, man, but no more shit, you hear?"

Hope sighed. His mission had started with no more promise than he had expected.

He ate his meal and then excused himself. There had been few words between them, her attention being absorbed by a romantic movie that was still on as Hope went to bed.

The walls of the apartment were wafer-thin, and despite his tiredness he soon abandoned any idea of sleep. Still lying on the bed, he began to examine the small room with his eyes. The room gave no clues as to the identity of its recent occupier. There were no pictures on the walls, no personal memorabilia, nothing to suggest who had gone before.

A narrow wardrobe stood at the foot of the bed beside a chair. Hope got quietly out of bed and opened its door. It creaked slightly—he paused; the blare from the TV continued. The inside of the wardrobe was bare, but on its floor, was the dim outline of a suitcase tied around with a leather strap. He removed it silently to the bed and, undoing the strap, began to go through the contents that made up the paltry estate of Ernest Wilson.

There were bright, patterned shirts, all laundered now, some underwear and socks and a pair of canvas-soled shoes, a dark suit that Hope thought he remembered, a tie, a pair of blue jeans, a black nylon bag with a cord at the neck, a belt, two magazines with pictures of naked women, a penknife, that was it. Hope went through the pockets of the suit. His fingers made familiar contact with something; he withdrew a single East Caribbean dollar. The other pockets yielded nothing. In the jeans he found a handkerchief and a book of matches. If Wilson was part of a sophisticated international drug ring he had left little trace of it behind him.

Hope returned the belongings to the suitcase.

It was with difficulty that he settled down to sleep.

THE NEXT MORNING Hope quietly made himself some coffee. Constanza and her loudly-snoring husband—back from his night shift—were in bed. Hope took the subway downtown and made his way to a Howard Johnson's off the Avenue of the Americas. He was sitting at a window table for no more than a minute when a man wearing an expensive raincoat full of straps and flaps approached him.

"Sergeant Hope?" he asked.

"Yes. Mr. Carrington?"

They shook hands, and the Interpol man sat down.

"I thought it was better we meet somewhere like this since you're here, ah, unofficially," he said. "Did you have a good flight? You got in last night, I believe."

Hope nodded.

"If it's O.K. with you, we'll take a ride downtown and speak with the police who are in charge of this investigation. My function is strictly liaison." He smiled slightly and they stood up. Hope was ushered out onto the street and into the back of a Cadillac at the curb that had its engine running. He settled into the comfort of the big car, and Carrington got in the other side.

"Do you smoke?" asked Carrington.

"No, thank you," replied Hope.

Carrington produced a gold cigarette case, took out a tipped cigarette, flicked a gold lighter, puffed the cigarette, snapped shut case and lighter, returned them to his pockets, sat up and turned to Hope.

"This your first time in New York?" he asked, smiling.

"First time in United States," said Hope.

Carrington pursed his lips and nodded his head as if some deep truth had just been spoken. Then he took another puff and assumed a businesslike air.

"Your commissioner feels quite strongly that this will lead us to a major break in the Antiguan drug ring," he said. "He thinks that with the family connection you should get us a major break. Me, I'm not so sure."

Hope raised his eyebrows.

"We're going down to the precinct station to speak with the detective in charge of the case," Carrington explained slowly in the manner of a tour guide. "When the police found the body they performed an autopsy. They took some prints and put them through the FBI computer in the normal way."

Buildings flashed by and neon signs winked on and off, advertising burgers, spectacles, bars. Carrington went on: "The FBI report back to the precinct identified the victim as Ernest Wilson, a twenty-four-year-old Antiguan with a previous record of petty larceny, chiefly in Miami. The police had nothing to go on, no motive, nothing. They had the option to let the matter drop. Due to the other—uh—facets of the case, they initially decided to call us in and see what we could contribute. We contacted Antigua in the normal way."

"What are these other facets, Mr. Carrington?"

They had pulled up in front of a large brownstone building. Several blue-and-white police cars were parked outside. Carrington had opened his door.

"Well," he replied, "why don't we just go in and meet with Detective Irving. Then we can get into a little more detail. Just one point. The police weren't exactly jumping for joy when I told them that you were being sent to New York. They're a bit sensitive, O.K.?"

Hope got out, and they walked into the precinct station. Carrington led the way through a duty room where a couple of policemen sat at desks, typing or on telephones. A cagelike affair at the back of the room contained the outstretched form of a man asleep. They went to a glass-fronted office, and Carrington knocked briefly at the dirty door and entered.

"Morning, Detective," he said. "Carrington, Interpol. I have Sergeant Hope of the Antiguan Police Department."

A small man with birdlike features sat behind a desk. His movements were quick and nervous. He remained seated.

"Sit down, sit down," he said, waving his hands briefly at two chairs in front of his desk.

Detective Irving looked at the Interpol man, the Ivy League appearance, the gold cigarette case that had suddenly appeared, the raincoat with the dozens of flaps. He saw the West Indian with the fine features in the dark suit. He removed his gold-rimmed glasses and pinched his eyes with thumb and forefinger, his face screwed up as if in pain. After ten seconds he suddenly put his glasses back on and, as if decided upon a course of action, turned to Sergeant Hope.

"Ernest Wilson," the name had come to him a millisecond before. "Could you please tell me what you know of Ernest Wilson, Sergeant uh," he looked at his desk, "uh, Sergeant Hope."

"You mean his record, sir?" asked Hope.

"Anything you know," said Irving, "anything which you think might assist the investigation—now that you are here."

"Well, Ernest Wilson was born twenty-four years ago in St. John's, Antigua. He was the youngest of twelve children. He went to school in St. John's and left when he was thirteen."

Irving looked at Carrington.

"The year after he left school," Hope went on, "he was

83

apprehended in the act of trying to steal a camera from an American tourist in High Street, St. John's. No charges were pressed by the tourist, and the police decided not to pursue the matter."

Irving was tapping his desk impatiently with a pen.

"The following year he was again apprehended, this time on the beach in Halcyon Cove."

"Halcyon . . . ?" Irving interrupted.

"Halcyon Cove. A beach resort north of St. John's where there are many tourist hotels," said Hope.

"Go on, Sergeant," said Irving.

"He was apprehended on the beach in Halcyon Cove, this time in one of the beach-front hotel bedrooms. He was arrested, charged, and got the benefit of probation. He then was given a job in the kitchen of an Italian restaurant in St. John's."

Irving barely tried to conceal an immense yawn.

"This job lasted for two years," continued Hope, "until it was discovered that he had been systematically stealing food and drink from the restaurant and selling it in St. John's. He was fired. Charges were not pressed."

Irving nodded slightly, Carrington lighted another cigarette.

Hope continued: "Wilson spent the next couple of years without employment in Antigua, mainly working the beaches, selling jewelry to tourists, helping on ski boats, the diving boats, that sort of thing. A number of incidents occurred, incidents of petty larceny. Wilson was held under suspicion twice, but nothing could be proved. It was around this time that he went to Miami. His older brother had lived there for a number of years, married to an American. Wilson's brother offered him a job in a liquor store, but soon after his arrival Wilson disappeared. His brother only knew of his existence following his arrest by Miami police a year later."

Irving nodded. "Yes, that's when he first came on our files. That was two years ago. He was working credit cards, got busted by Miami." He looked down at the papers on his desk. "Convicted, sent down for six months as a first offense, released after three. Six months later he's back in for the same offense, this time in New York. Sent down for two years, out after nine months. That was six months ago." Irving removed his glasses. He had spoken rapidly. He put his glasses on again.

"He'd moved to stay with his sister. I interviewed her last week. Your sister-in-law, I do believe."

"Yes, sir," said Hope. "Last month, April twentieth to be exact, Ernest Wilson returned to Antigua and Barbuda on vacation. We suspect he pulled off some burglaries when he was home. He returned to New York on May first."

There was silence in the little office. The sound of a typewriter in the outer duty room could be heard.

"So, that's it?" asked Irving.

"That is all," said Hope.

Irving shook his head slowly.

"Never busted for drugs, Sergeant?"

Irving and Carrington exchanged glances.

"Was he running drugs?" asked Hope.

Irving returned his gaze to his desk and replied in a matter-of-fact tone.

"We have him coming in through Kennedy on May first. He goes back to his sister's uptown. A few days later he starts to fence some fancy rocks, classy stuff. That's his speciality, he's good at it. He shifts it all in about four days. Estimated pay-out—two to three big ones. He's also got some plastic which he starts trying to work on Fifth Avenue. He has a close one when a store tries to check him out with American Express. The stupid mother then tries to buy a glass giraffe at Steuben's—over a grand. He splits when they phone up MasterCharge. The next day he trades the plastic for three hundred dollars cash to a small-time hoodlum called Paolo Fusco. This Fusco's strictly a nickel-and-dime guy. He's run a couple of very minor jobs for the mob. After that we lose Wilson until he floats up here a week ago. We've picked up

Fusco, but he's not talking. He's scared of his shit. Now you're here."

This guy knows sweet nothing, Irving thought. He looked at his watch. He had a precinct meeting in eight minutes.

He put his glasses down.

"Sergeant Hope, the case is one of petty crime, a small-time criminal. I'm trying to close the file as quickly as I possibly can. It's my case because the stiff was found in my precinct. Unfortunately. The jewelry is standard stuff. Probably wasn't even stolen here from what you say. The card thing he was on won't even be investigated. A con in New York can work the same store with the same card every day for two weeks, and no one will even bother their ass to go along and pick him up for questioning. It's a matter of priorities."

Carrington nodded his agreement.

"The problem I have here," said Irving, "is with the body. I don't know if Mr. Carrington here has gone into this?"

Carrington shook his head.

"A problem?" asked Hope.

"Sergeant," said Irving, "I don't know if you are familiar with the—uh—procedures used by organized crime in this country to punish their opponents or to make an example of one of their own people who has betrayed them?"

Irving looked down at his papers.

"Well I will not take up your time," he continued, "with any details not relevant to the case at hand except to say that certain—uh—executions carried out in certain ways carry the hallmarks of particular families."

Carrington shifted uneasily in his seat.

"In this case, Sergeant," said Irving, "there were injuries on the body consistent with methods we have seen used before."

"Methods?" asked Hope.

Irving bit his lip.

"You see," he said, "the report from the Chief Medical Examiner's office says that they tied him up in a squatting position. Then they got probably a two-handled kitchen pot

86

and strapped it to his anus. There was one, maybe two rats in the pot. The rats have to eat their way out."

There was total silence.

"It is our belief that at some point he escaped," Irving continued. "The report says death was by drowning. When my boys discovered him in the East River half his ass was gone, and there were the hindquarters of a drowned rat protruding from it."

SERGEANT HOPE SAT there trying to absorb the tale of brutality. It was far beyond his experience.

"I would be pretty sure, Sergeant," Irving was saying, "that the mob is involved here, almost certainly the Vincenti family. But from our discussion this morning I can think of absolutely no reason whatsoever for their wanting to execute Ernest Wilson. O.K., Wilson was a two-bit plastic con. Everything is going all right until he meets Fusco. That's the obvious connection. He's picked up almost immediately. Now what did he do? Maybe he's working mob territory. O.K., let's say that's true. But no matter how much they want him off their patch they're not going to snuff a West Indian—excuse me, Sergeant—small-time hood in the manner reserved for the Godfather."

Irving spread his hands. He looked at his watch and at the two men in front of him.

"So none of us knows anything," he said.

Carrington nodded.

"That would seem to be the case, Detective," he agreed.

Irving again reverted to pinching his eyes. He remained as if deep in thought for fifteen seconds. Suddenly he sat up.

"O.K., Mr. Carrington, Sergeant Hope," he said in a plausible tone, "we have all got, I am sure you will agree, our fair share of problems. I suggest from the facts here we may be trying to invent a problem. There are no drugs around. We've got a messy murder, a dead West Indian, stolen credit cards, jewelry. So, what's new? The guy fouled his lines, some nut thinks he's the Marquis de Sade, so what? This is New York. I am, in the absence of any other evidence, putting this case on ice."

He closed the file in front of him symbolically. Carrington doubted if it would ever be opened again.

Then Irving leaned across his desk and spoke in a voice that precluded discussion.

"At our meeting last Friday, Mr. Carrington," he said, "I may not have come over strongly enough regarding the suggestion made by you that a policeman from the Caribbean should try to involve himself in the affairs of the New York Police Department."

Carrington opened his mouth to protest but was cut off.

"Now I'll say this once, Mr. Carrington, so listen good. I want this man on the next available plane back down to Antigua. There are certain leads that my men are following. I do not want the investigation fucked up by some black Father Brown who has been dragged here on false pretenses."

He turned to Hope who had become most uneasy.

"I'm sorry about this, but we're going to do it our way. I think you heard what I said. If I find you on my turf tomorrow I'm going to arrest you as an unlawful immigrant." He stood up. "Good-bye, gentlemen."

Carrington led Hope back out to the Cadillac. They got in.

"I'm very sorry about what happened back there," said Carrington, "but I did warn your commissioner that a trip like this was most unusual."

"I thought the suggestion had come from Interpol," said Hope.

Carrington laughed. "Goodness, no," he said. "Your man is trying to demonstrate to our State Department that he's taking a serious line against drugs in Antigua. That's why he's sent you here. I spent an hour on the telephone trying to dissuade him. Unfortunately, I have no power in the matter."

Hope felt a knot in his stomach. The commissioner had been most specific about the results he expected.

"Can he arrest me like that?" he asked Carrington.

"I'm afraid that he can, Sergeant, and I'm afraid that he will. Look, I'm out on a bit of a limb myself over this. You have a return ticket, haven't you?"

Hope nodded.

"Well, my advice is use it. Say good-bye to your sister-in-law and get out of here. Today. You've been set up, my friend."

They had reached Times Square, and the car pulled in to the curb. Carrington held out his hand.

"Do as I suggest," he said. He looked at his watch. "I would invite you to lunch, but . . ." His voice trailed off.

A moment later Hope was standing on the sidewalk on Forty-second Street watching the back of the big Cadillac until it became lost in the traffic.

He walked uptown on Seventh Avenue for twenty minutes, passing movie theaters, porn shops, and massage parlors. He had been landed in it by Commissioner Richardson all right; the old man must have been desperate to send him to New York against Interpol's advice. He weighed in his mind the reception waiting for him in St. John's when he returned empty-handed against the risk of being deported by the New York police. He had come now to Carnegie Hall and turned right on Fifty-sixth Street, walking in the direction of Fifth Avenue. He looked in wonderment at the shops, their mannequins dressed in clothes that would cost him two years' salary.

He strolled down Fifth Avenue with the wild hope that something might appear that he could associate with the dead man; after all, it was here that Wilson had worked his stolen credit cards and finally sold them.

All he saw were elegantly dressed people walking purposefully in and out of large stores, boutiques, jewelers' shops, beauty salons. He stared at the magnificent glass ornaments in the huge windows of Steuben's. Every animal that one could imagine was represented there, watched over by gimlet-eyed, middle-aged women. He paused at Rockefeller Center now bedecked in summer flowers and lively awnings. It was hopeless. He would telephone the commissioner and ask for instructions; he would do it from the apartment. Constanza had left him a spare key—she and her husband were going out that afternoon to look at furniture. It was after three when he turned into a fast food restaurant for his lunch.

HOPE TOOK THE express subway to 125th Street and walked to the apartment house. As he entered the lobby the caretaker gave him a funny look. He rode the elevator to the sixth floor and took out his key. A second before he put it in the door he froze. He pushed the door gently and it swung open, unlocked. He stepped inside. The apartment had not yet been tidied. Today it was going to take not just Constanza, but a team of carpenters and interior decorators to do so.

It was completely ransacked. The settee and armchairs had been knife-slashed, both backs and seats. Their springs stood oddly erect from their bases. The back of the TV lay in front of its shattered screen. Some floorboards had been pried up.

Hope went to his bedroom. His few personal items were scattered everywhere. His suitcase lay in tatters by the window. The mattress had been filleted, and all its stuffing lay in a heap on the bed base. The wardrobe was a mound of splintered debris. Wilson's suitcase had suffered the same fate as his own. Sergeant Hope moved on to the bathroom. Here the side of the bath had been pried off and the work-top area beside the wash-basin smashed. His sister-in-law's bedroom was equally devastated, the bed ripped, the furniture in bits.

Hope realized that all this was no act of simple, wanton destruction. What he was looking at was the result of a professionally executed search.

He left the apartment, forgetting about his plan to telephone St. John's, Antigua. He walked to the subway, a sense of mounting rage replacing his earlier bewilderment.

Since he had arrived in New York he had seen just one thing

that might be a clue. He was glad now that he had not shared it with the obnoxious precinct detective or the Interpol agent. He put his hand in his pocket and fingered it, then withdrew it and looked at it again. The cover of the book of matches looked back at him, the name "Les Petits Fours" embossed in red. He flipped open the cover. Inside it said "Haute French Cuisine." There were many unsolved questions in the case, but this one he could answer right away. Haute French Cuisine was just not Ernest Wilson.

IT WAS 7:30 P.M. when Hope paid the yellow cab and turned toward the restaurant. Outside in a glass-fronted frame was a menu, which he studied. The prices were astronomical. There was no chance that Ernest Wilson had ever eaten here. But how had the matches come to be among his possessions? Had he worked here?

A frock-coated doorman appeared. Having finished with the menu, Hope was peering into the lobby.

"Move along, pal," the doorman said.

Hope briefly considered engaging him in conversation, decided against it, and continued on up First Avenue. At the intersection of First Avenue and Fifty-third Street he crossed over and walked back down First Avenue until he was opposite Les Petits Fours.

Even by the standards of the other restaurants in the block, it was particularly lavish. Large, black limousines waited at the curb, their chauffeurs chatting in small groups. Hope stared across. He looked suspicious as he hunched up and down the block, his hands in his pockets. A group of young blacks on the corner of the block were watching him. Now they began to approach. Hope decided it was time to move. He would go around the back and find the service entrance.

He stepped off the curb to cross over. As he did so two men emerged from the restaurant. Hope froze rigid where he stood. Sir Tristram Hoare had left Les Petits Fours and was walking down First Avenue.

Hope ran out on to the wide avenue, hardly conscious of the screeching brakes. He weaved through the traffic and arrived at the door of the restaurant just in time to see Hoare disappear into a yellow cab. The cab pulled away from the curb and passed Hope. The face of the Englishman was clearly visible in the back.

Hope looked about him frantically. There were no other free cabs at the curb nor on First Avenue. Hoare's cab was now pulled up at the lights at Fifty-third Street.

Hope began to run, feverishly looking backward to see if a free cab had appeared. He was running flat out, sidestepping around people on the sidewalk. The lights turned green, and the cab pulled slowly away, still going up First. Hope ran like a man possessed, his heart pounding hugely. As he leaped across Fifty-third Street at the intersection of First Avenue, cars that were turning left had to swerve violently to avoid him. At one point the fender of a large Buick was almost upon him. Hope made a desperate jump into the air and landed with a rolling crash on the north sidewalk of Fifty-third Street.

He scrambled madly to his feet and charged on. The cab was a good hundred yards away now. Hope redoubled his efforts. His chest, suddenly deprived of air, hurt mightily. His head was down like a bull, and he sprinted like a man pursued by demons.

By some miracle the traffic lights at the intersection of First Avenue and Fifty-fourth Street were not correctly synchronized. They were still red. Hope was able to make a few valuable yards. He was oblivious to the protests of the pedestrians as he crashed his way through them. Up ahead he saw a woman getting out of a cab. A couple who had been waiting on the sidewalk prepared to get in. The next moment he dived through the cab door and landed with a resounding crash on the back seat. The cab driver turned around angrily. His jaw dropped. He saw a wild-eyed black man waving some sort of identity card at him.

"Follow that cab, man, now!" said Sergeant Hope of the Antigua and Barbuda police force. The order was given with such urgency and vehemence that the cab driver obeyed without a word of protest.

THE CAB CARRYING Hoare turned left into Fifty-fifth Street.

Hope's cab followed, thirty yards back. They crossed Second Avenue, Third Avenue, and then Lexington and Park Avenues. They crossed Madison Avenue, the vital cab now just ahead of them.

Hoare's cab pulled in to the left curb. From where he sat Hope could see they had arrived at a large hotel with "St. Regis" emblazoned over the door. Hoare was now walking up the hotel steps. Hope quickly paid the driver and followed. At the top of the steps a party of at least twelve blue-rinsed women were making a noisy exit. Excusing himself, Hope desperately tried to elbow his way in.

The lobby of the hotel gave the impression of substantial wealth on the loose. Expensive-looking people sat on gilded reproduction furniture. Heavy chandeliers twinkled down on columns of white marble, which supported the high ceiling and made arches into other areas.

Hope's eyes swept around. At the far end was another door through which people were entering and leaving. Beside him a gilded elevator hummed open and guests poured out. Hope stood on his toes. His heart sank. Nowhere in the crowd could Hoare be seen. Hope shoved his way through. The number of people made it impossible.

"Good evening, Sir Tristram."

Hope froze.

"Good evening," said an English voice.

Hope was standing immediately beside Sir Tristram Hoare who was facing the reception desk away from him.

"Could you have my account ready in about an hour," Hoare was saying. "I'm going to England tonight. Do you think you could arrange a car? You're very kind."

Hope was intently studying a gold-framed notice board where details of church services were inscribed. Now Hoare was moving to the elevator.

Hope followed his movements out of the corner of his eye. His mind raced. Hoare had not asked for a key. The elevator opened, and Hoare stepped in. Then the door closed, and he was gone.

Hope straightened himself and then walked to a glass jewelry case beside the elevators. He watched the flashing light. Hoare had been alone in the elevator. The lights stopped at the sixteenth floor. In the reflection of the glass case Hope saw the receptionist hit a little desk bell with her hand.

"Captain," she said.

The elevator was now on its way down. Hope saw a uniformed porter walk to the desk.

"Limousine to Kennedy for Sir Tristram Hoare, suite sixteen ten, one hour," said the receptionist.

The elevator had arrived back down at the ground floor.

The doors opened. Sergeant Hope stepped in and hit the button for the sixteenth floor.

THE CORRIDOR OF the sixteenth floor was completely quiet. The deep carpet muffled Hope's footsteps as he walked toward suite ten. There was an air of unreality about the whole thing. Hope felt a jab of pain in his stomach as he thought briefly of the consequences of being caught in what he was about to do. He put the thought aside and went on.

All the suites appeared to have two doors, about a dozen feet apart. On the first of these the number of the suite was shown. Hope had arrived outside suite ten. He listened intently. He could hear nothing.

Suddenly the door of suite eleven was opened, and a small man and a woman in a fur coat emerged. Hope dropped to one knee and began to tie his shoelace. The couple walked past without a glance and went to the elevator. Hope stayed in his position, regarding them furtively. Eventually an elevator arrived, and they stepped in. Hope stood up. He took a rectangular strip of plastic from his pocket and without difficulty opened the door to suite eleven.

IT WAS PITCH dark. It took some moments for his eyes to adjust. Then he began slowly to explore the suite. It took him five minutes of the most painstaking investigation before he was completely satisfied that the rooms were unoccupied. Then he turned on the lights.

He was standing in a small sitting room, which had two comfortable armchairs and a sofa arranged around a walnut coffee table. To the left, a door opened into a large bedroom. He went in. To the right of the bed there was a door ajar revealing a bathroom with heavy marble fittings. To the left was another door. It was covered in thick padded material. Hope concluded that this was the connecting door to suite ten.

He tried the handle noiselessly. The door was open. Hope released the handle. He put out all the lights in suite eleven before returning to the heavy connecting door. He turned the handle again, silently, and then began to open the door inch by inch. It was pitch dark. The door was about a foot open, and Hope could see absolutely nothing. He opened the door halfway, now stretching his hand into the void. His fingers came abruptly into contact with something. It was moments before he realized that he was touching the leather-upholstered surface of another identical door some two feet away. He stepped into the tiny space. His hand found a handle similar to that on the first door. He turned it gently. It was locked. He leaned upright against the door, but it held firm. He put his hand in his pocket and took out his key ring. There was a tiny penknife attached to it. He eased open a small blade and feeling his way in the total darkness, prodded the blade into the lock. He revolved the knife in the lock while, at the same time, keeping his weight on the door. For half a minute nothing happened.

Then all at once there was a deafening crash, and he fell into the sitting room of suite ten. He was sure that his entry had been heard. He looked around him—but there was no one to be seen. A small table lamp was on, giving the room all its light. The door to the bedroom was closed. Kicking the connecting door shut behind him, Hope half ran, half stumbled behind the plump sofa and crouched there.

He stayed in this position for two or three minutes, the blood pounding so hard in his arteries that his ears roared with the sound. Then he became slowly aware of noises coming from the bedroom. He raised himself slightly from his crouched position so that he could observe the room. There were documents on the walnut coffee table. Hope darted out from behind the sofa and went over to it. He saw sheets of typed paper with lists of names and figures that meant nothing to him. There was an orange-colored folder lying to one side. Hope opened it. Inside there was a map of an island. He saw the words Irish Republic. There were a number of arrows penciled in on the west coastline. He flicked it over. There was a photograph of some guns lying on a white sheet. Another photograph showed what looked like grenades and mortars. Under this he saw more sheets of typed paper. Then there was a cardboard calendar of the sort that showed all the months of the year together arranged in three neat rows. Someone had made a bright red circle around one date. Hope looked closer. It was June 3.

He hurried on. At the bottom of the file was a final photograph. Hope even in his hurry paused when he saw it. Looking at him from the photograph was the very pale face of a young man with black, curly hair. His gaze had the look of the most predatory evil that Hope had ever seen.

HOPE WENT TO the bedroom door and listened. There was a soft female moaning coming from the other room. Suddenly he heard Hoare speak.

"Oh it's no good. Let's give it five minutes."

There were sounds of footsteps approaching the door.

Hope dived back to his position behind the sofa. The door opened. From where he lay, Hope could see out through the barest crack where the cover of the sofa met the floor. A man's thick ankles with blond hairs were visible.

"I've got nearly an hour anyway," he heard Hoare say.

Another pair of ankles had now appeared. They were slim and dark. There was a sound of springs being depressed as someone sat on the sofa.

"Let's see if this will do the trick," said Hoare from the far side of the room.

"Uh huh," said a soft female voice. There was the sound of a liquor cabinet being opened. By stretching his hand under the sofa and raising its cover a tiny fraction from the floor, Hope was able to improve his view. Immediately opposite to where he was located, a full-length, gilt mirror hung on the wall. In the dim light of the room Hope was able to get a sort of fish-eye view of the sofa which he was now virtually under.

The girl on the sofa was startlingly beautiful. She was completely naked. She had smooth, coffee-colored skin and rich, dark hair that fell about her shoulders in abundance. She had a strong face of straight, clean lines. Her mouth was blood red. Her body was firm and desirable. She now lay full length on the sofa, slowly massaging her nipples with the palms of her hands. There was a loud popping sound. Hoare came into view. He was holding a frothing bottle of champagne in one hand and two tulip-shaped glasses in the other. He was also stark naked. He made his way to within an inch of Hope's peephole and sat down heavily. This additional weight caused the sofa to subside considerably and blocked Hope's view.

"Why are you so unhappy tonight?" the girl was saying.

There was the sound of two glasses being filled.

"Come and lie here," she said softly. "Mama will open her long legs and let her little boy lie between them."

There was the sound of shifting about on the sofa.

"You're so kind, so very kind," Hoare said in a strange voice.

The bottle of champagne was placed on the carpet with a thud. Hope heard Hoare groan with pleasure.

"God, I hate to leave you," he said.

"Mama's legs are long and strong," the girl crooned. "They gonna squeeze her little weak boy."

Hoare was moaning.

"Mama's gonna wrap her long legs around her little boy," the girl said in her soft, soothing tone.

Hoare moaned more loudly. The sofa had started to creak rhythmically.

"Mama's gonna rub her strong toes on her little boy's dirty thing," she crooned.

"Oh God, oh God, oh my God," wailed Hoare. The sofa was now almost bouncing.

The girl continued, her voice more urgent. "Mama's gonna hurt her little boy."

"I'm sorry, I'm sorry," cried Hoare.

"She's gonna hurt his dirty big thing," she said with guttural vehemence. The sofa was crashing up and down.

"Oh Jesus, oh Jesus, I'm sorry!" Hoare screamed. Then he let out a long, piercing wail as he climaxed, his body knifing up and then back down with a slapping sound onto the girl. She slowly rocked him back and forth, crooning softly as she did so.

"Oh my God," gasped Hoare. "Oh what pleasure. Oh my God."

Hope shut his eyes. Sweat poured down his face. The girl was speaking again. Now her voice was more matter-of-fact.

"Why are you so unhappy these last times?" she was asking. Hoare gave a long sigh.

"This business is so difficult," he said.

"Do you want to tell me about why it's so difficult?" the girl asked.

"Oh you're so strong," said Hoare. "Every time they get me in a corner, I think of you and how strong you are."

"When are we going to Brazil?" asked the girl.

"Oh soon, darling Annette, soon," said Hoare. His voice had a tremor in it. Suddenly he began to sob.

"Jesus I'm so fucking frightened," he said choking.

"Poor little boy," said the girl in her soft voice. "Poor little man. Soon we will be away and Mama will look after her poor little man."

Hoare's sobs were coming in large gulps.

"They're mad, you know," he cried pitifully. "They're absolutely mad."

"Tell Mama who's mad, honey," said the girl. She was again rocking her body forward and back. "Tell me, honey. You'll feel better."

Hoare continued to cry like a child. "Oh the Irish, of course," he sobbed, "the fucking Irish."

"Tell Mama why they're mad, honey," said the girl.

Hoare stopped sobbing for a moment. "Oh, I can't, I really can't," he wailed.

"That's O.K., honey. That's O.K.," she crooned. "Mama's strong. She's gonna look after her little boy."

Hoare started to cry anew.

"Oh my God," he sobbed, "they've used me, used my knowledge, my position. If it ever got out, I'd be lynched in the streets of my own country."

"Poor boy, poor boy."

"Do you know what they're going to do?"

"Tell me, honey," said the girl, "tell me what they're going to do."

Hoare took a long choking breath. "The bastards are going to kill the Queen," he said.

IN THE GLOOM of the little space between the sofa and the curtain, Hope thought his head would burst open.

CHAPTER
SEVEN

THE LIMOUSINE SPED out of the tollgate on the Triborough Bridge heading for Kennedy. In the deep back seat Tristram Hoare put a match to a very long Havana cigar and looked for a moment at the receding Manhattan skyline. The pungent taste of the tobacco was satisfying, calming after the tension of completing a deal that size. It had damn near fallen through; Quorn had completely overreacted about the Antigua incident.

Still, the consignment was on its way. Everything was in order; he had counted them himself and landfall was scheduled for nine days' time. You could never be careful enough with the Mafia, he thought; mistakes were not tolerated. And this had been his first real mistake.

They were in the fast lane of Grand Central Parkway now. Hoare thought of the girl. She understood his tensions and fears. He was serious about taking her to Brazil, just as soon as he tidied a few things up.

For some reason his head began to reverberate with the echo of a booming voice, his father's, heard nearly fifty years before.

"Tristram wants to start right at the top," the old man had said to his wife, their skinny son sniveling in front of the great fireplace. He had tried to shirk his duty—beating pheasants out of a wood with some laborers from the estate.

"Watch out," said Sir Charles. "You start at the top and the only way is down."

Hoare shook his graying head. Incredible how a thing like that could come back after so long. Must be this wretched business. He had never really got a fair break. He had inherited the estate to find it could not pay its way—far too many debts, barely covered by the proceeds of the auction.

It was fortunate that he had been a career soldier, a field officer in ballistics in the mid-fifties, right when they were trying to build up a new, ultramodern army. He had been good on armaments, had always shown an interest, even as a child in the gunroom, breaking his father's twelve-bore down into its three pieces and oiling them with loving care. But it had always come back to money.

Careers change in unexpected ways. He had been six months married when he was posted to Cyprus, just when EOKA was at its most vicious. There was the evening in the nightclub in Famagusta—he'd been short as usual. The offer had been simple: guns for money. It was only two rifles and a pistol to one of Digenes's men. He was sure no one had seen him or overheard. Yet he was quickly posted home. No accusations, no charges, just a change in attitude that only a fool would ignore. He quietly demobbed.

But then to his horror, gone also was the partnership in Rennick Galloway, so fondly promised by Peggy Hoare's father a year before. The old bastard was ex-Guards. He knew all right although other compelling reasons were given. All of a sudden, Tristram Hoare could not even arrange a lunch in the City.

Fuck them—he'd show them what success was. He returned privately to Cyprus and made contact. He had never looked back.

Now thirty years later, the biggest one of the lot under his belt, he should have been happy; yet he felt like a bull's-eye on a rifle range.

It was the Newmarket stable business that was the mistake. But what could he do? You did not refuse men like that. It had been worth an extra ten thousand in cash to place their awful little man with his mad eyes. And the way Hoare had done it was a stroke of the purest genius.

As an ex-steward of the Jockey Club he could not walk up to a trainer, hand him the photograph of a terrorist, and ask that he be given a job.

Then Hoare had thought of Fardan—Fardan, who sometimes fronted for the Libyans, sometimes for the PLO. He had done good business with Fardan long before the greasy, fat Arab had become even vaguely respectable. Now he was the undisputed arms dealer to North Africa and the Middle East, flying around the world in his own 707.

But at bottom Fardan was a man of the desert. He was sure to know the new Arab prince everyone was talking about, the one with the horse that had cost all the money. It was a calculated risk: Hoare had taken the photograph with him from Ireland promising that all would be arranged.

His luck held up. Fardan said such a small favor was not a problem—he had not even asked for a fee. The whole thing had been arranged in ten days; Hoare knew that Fardan would never tell the prince his name. Whatever happened, he would be safe. Anyway the fools were sure to be caught; at times he found himself praying that they would be . . .

Now they were on the Van Wyck Expressway. It would be good to get back to England. Despite everything it was the country he loved. It was going to be very hard to leave, but the risks in staying had become gigantic.

He allowed himself a slight smile. He had made it at last. With his money spread so widely that no one would ever find it, the world was, as his father used to say, his very own oyster.

As the limousine pulled into the British Airways terminal,

Sir Tristram Hoare realized with a certain sadness that this was probably the last time he would ever take a flight to London.

CHAPTER
EIGHT

THE COMMISSIONER'S BAD tempers were legendary affairs, but never before had Sergeant Hope been at the epicenter of one.

The old man hurled his great frame up and down his office, pausing every now and then to pound the palm of his left hand with his massive right fist. His rage was stoked with disappointment and frustration. Not only had the mission been a complete failure, but Sergeant Hope's behavior—unlawfully breaking and entering a New York hotel—could have made them look the fools of the Caribbean. There was no guarantee that there would not be further repercussions at a time when all the problems of Antigua seemed to be turned toward the commissioner for a solution.

And as for the fantastic story that the man had brought home with him . . .

"Who else has seen this?" he bellowed at Hope, picking up the typed report prepared by the sergeant.

"No one but you, sir."

"Are you completely certain?"

"Before God, sir, you are the only one to hear of this."

The commissioner snorted and threw the report back on the table.

"I ask you to go on a simple trip, to try and find out some background on your murdered, criminal brother-in-law, to try and help Antigua in her fight against drugs. In a little over a day you are virtually thrown out of the United States, you break into a famous hotel," he paused for breath, "and you then come back here and tell me a ridiculous story about a plot to kill the Queen of England."

Hope shook his head. Now back in Antigua, he had difficulty himself in believing what he had seen and heard in New York two days before. He should have anticipated this reaction.

The commissioner's rage continued unchecked.

"Here we had an opportunity—for the first time in years—to try and turn something to our advantage. I sent you to New York to do a straightforward job—and what do I get back?" he shouted. "I get this!"

He snatched up the report and ripped it in two. The torn pieces fluttered down to his wastebasket. The action of resolving at least one small part of the problem seemed to calm him.

Hope coughed.

"With respect, sir," he said uncomfortably, "and I know it sounds farfetched, but there are a number of strange coincidences in this whole business."

The commissioner stood with his back to the high window and glared at him.

"Take the obvious one," Hope went on. "This Englishman, Sir Tristram, is robbed here in Antigua, probably by Ernest Wilson. Wilson is murdered in New York, probably by the Mafia. Wilson has some connection with this fancy restaurant, as yet unclear. I go there, and the first person I see is Sir Tristram. Quite apart from what occurred afterward, sir, the chances of what happened actually taking place must be extremely remote."

Richardson shook his head emphatically. "Circumstantial evidence, Sergeant, all circumstantial evidence," he said.

"But surely warranting further investigation, sir."

"A series of . . . of trivial coincidences," fumed the old man. "I have far greater things on my mind."

"A man has been murdered, sir."

"Don't treat me like a fool!" shouted the commissioner. "I know someone was murdered. Who was it who told you in the first place?"

"I'm sorry, sir," said Hope. "It's just that everything seems to me to point to a certain course of action."

Richardson walked slowly around the desk until he was standing directly over Hope.

"Which course of action?" he asked more quietly, his eyes narrowed.

"To . . . to get on to the police, probably in Scotland Yard, sir," said Hope, "and to brief them on what we may have discovered."

Richardson took a deep breath. He walked back around his desk, sat down, and leaned across it.

"Of course, you are right, Sergeant," he said slowly. "I am sorry that I shouted at you just now. I lost my temper."

"I understand, sir."

The commissioner was observing Hope closely. "I . . . I have a lot on my mind," said the commissioner. "This came as a shock, understandably. I hope you will agree."

"Yes, sir."

Richardson joined his big hands on the desk in front of him and composed his face in what he believed to be a friendly smile.

"Scotland Yard will have to be told immediately," he said. "Leave it to me. Obviously, Sergeant," he went on, "you have, ah, stumbled on a plot of truly international proportions." He paused and looked Hope straight in the eye. "We have to be very careful, Sergeant Hope."

"Yes, sir," said Hope.

"I want you to do exactly as I say, Sergeant. Am I clear?"

"Yes, sir."

"You are to return to your normal duties at the Dockyard," said Richardson. "You and I never discussed Ernest Wilson, you never came to my office last week. Do you understand?"

"Completely, sir."

"You are to erase this business from your mind."

Hope nodded.

"You never went to New York, Sergeant, or to the United States. I hope that you obeyed my initial instructions to tell no one where you were going."

"Yes, sir," said Hope, "but . . ."

"But what?" glowered the commissioner.

"My wife's sister in New York, sir, and her husband. I think they blame my visit for what happened to their apartment."

"Leave them to me, Sergeant. You are not to worry. Leave them to me." The commissioner smiled in his expansive, fatherly way. "They cannot blame you if you were never there, Sergeant Hope, can they?" He chortled heartily.

Hope nodded warily. The commissioner was standing up, and Hope too rose. The head of Antigua's police came around the desk and placed an enormous hand on each of Hope's shoulders.

"Goodbye, Winston," he said. "Remember this is between the two of us. Leave it completely to me. You have done your duty, and done it well."

Hope nodded again and attempted a smile. Then biting his lip he left the office, passing a uniformed policeman who was just entering with a mug of steaming coffee.

"A nice hot coffee, Mr. Commissioner."

It had long been Constable King's role to calm his master's rage. An old hand at Police HQ, it was often said that he made a lot of the decisions when the commissioner foundered out of his depth.

"I'll just put it down here," he said brightly, giving no indication that from his desk immediately outside the door his eardrums had nearly been shattered by Commissioner Richardson's recent outburst.

The commissioner glowered darkly at his secretary and then sat down and nodded as the mug was placed on a small mat before him.

"Thank you," he growled. At least some people could always be relied upon. Constable King was useful and did not have to be told everything. The commissioner even managed a small smile of approval as the efficient policeman left the room silently, carrying the Commissioner's brimming wastebasket.

As soon as the door closed Richardson got up and began to pace up and down, his coffee forgotten. What had appeared as a solution to one problem had begot another. God only knew what else had happened up there. The man was a fool, out of his depth, bordering on the insane to come back with such a story. Richardson stopped in mid-stride. What if there was even a grain of truth in Hope's report? What then? He shook his head. A plot to assassinate the Queen of England! The thing was incredible. He could imagine the patronizing reception he would receive in London with such a wild story. And the report would have to go through official Antiguan government channels as well. Not only would Hope's antics in New York be told, but it would come out that the commissioner himself had dispatched the sergeant to the United States against specific Interpol advice. Against the wishes of the New York Police Department. The disastrous escapade would not be seen as Hope's fault at all, but his.

God Almighty! With the PM in his present mood the consequences were unthinkable. He pounded his fist with frustration and fear. He was due to report to a select committee on drugs in less than a week. Any chances of his looking good had been truly destroyed by Sergeant Hope.

PART TWO

May 26-June 3

CHAPTER
NINE

IT WAS ONE-THIRTY in the morning, still over two hours before the false dawn. By the dark waters of Lough Swilly, above the town of Letterkenny, a 35-cwt Bedford van sat in a pull-off by the roadside. Normally used by sightseers and truck drivers it was now empty except for the van, which had been stolen in Belfast three weeks before. Its time since had been spent in a small garage off the Falls Road having new tires fitted, the engine serviced, and body resprayed. The license plates it carried were those of a car stolen in Dublin the previous year.

The engine suddenly burst into life, and dimmed headlights came on. Two figures in dark clothes got out and made their way in silence to the front. Each had a roll of thick, black adhesive tape that he began to apply carefully to the headlights of the vehicle, progressively reducing the effective light-sphere as he did so. Eventually, the headlights had an area of only one square inch at their center. The task concluded, the men got back into the van where two other men sat smoking. One of these, the driver, checked his watch and, with a nod to his associates, drove slowly out of the lay-by and on northward by the shores of the lough.

Soon they would be through Letterkenny and into the villages of Ramelton, Milford, and Carrigart, driving always northwest until the very land itself came to an end. The driver was so familiar with the road he could have driven it blindfolded. As it was, their passage through the night was close upon invisible.

THIRTY MILES TO the north of Letterkenny, the peninsula of Melmore Head juts into the Atlantic. It is a fiercely remote place of great beauty, at the very northern tip of Ireland. A narrow road—the Atlantic Drive—clings to the side of the hill giving a breathtaking view of Tranarossan Strand below and the peak of Gornalughoge towering behind.

A blue Avenger sedan was pulled tightly into the hillside road, a man and woman in the back.

"What time is it?" she whispered.

Seamus O'Neill, a full colonel in the Irish National Liberation Army, held up his wrist so that the woman could see the illuminated dial. It was 3:00 A.M. A thick, persistent mist clung to the mountain. Please God it won't lift, he thought. He was in his late twenties, well built with strong shoulders and a broad chest. A shock of black hair covered his head, and a bushy mustache made him appear older than his years.

Abruptly, the lights of a car burst through the mist, starkly illuminating the inside of the Avenger. Seamus grabbed the woman in a tight embrace, his mouth buried in the red hair that fell to her neck.

The car passed slowly, its only occupant paying little attention to the couple in the parked car. Seamus's heart beat hugely. He remained in the same position, listening intently as the noise of the car's engine gradually receded. Eventually everything was pitch-dark and quiet once more. He became aware of the perfume on the woman's hair. Her name was Delaney. She had graduated to her present role as Seamus's assistant by luring off-duty British soldiers out of Belfast pubs. With her glad eyes, she had been successful half a dozen times. The backs of her long, desirable legs had often been the last thing the soldier had seen before a steel garotte had, in an instant, choked off his life.

Now her body was warm and soft and, as she moved slightly under him, Seamus felt his desire surge. He sat up and opened the window slightly. There was plenty of time for that, but not here.

"I think it was a farmer," he said.

Although the Donegal hinterland was largely sympathetic to the cause, one could never be sure. The smallest slip, the most casual remark, could blow over six months of painstaking planning. The INLA's guerrilla operation was a treadmill that depended on savage violence for its success. Such violence relied on a steady supply of guns, explosives, and ammunition, which in turn had to be purchased for hard cash. But the cash and gun flows were beginning to dry up. The chief source, the United States, had succumbed to the weak panderings of the turncoat Free State Government. Organizations such as Noraid were having much more difficulty in getting arms to the North, and there had been a number of well-publicized finds. Even movement across the border into the South was more difficult these days since the Royal Ulster Constabulary had begun to talk to the *Garda Siochána*.

The INLA needed a major offensive. It was to Colonel O'Neill that the brief had been assigned. His established contacts on both sides of the border allowed him to move with ease among the safe houses, those Republican allies who still opened their doors to men on the run. He thanked God that they had friends left, not just in the United States but among those foreign governments with embassies in Dublin who could always be relied on when the going got rough. The mission that was now reaching its climax would give the movement enough firepower to become the flagbearers of Ireland's Republican cause.

He got quietly out of the car and walked to the small stone wall, below which was sheer cliff. The mist outside had turned into a steady drizzle. Below and to his right he could hear the waves beating on the rocks. A small stream trickled busily down from the hill behind their position. He took out a British Army pocketscope—a device for night surveillance— and scanned the area below him. Nothing could be seen. Seamus checked his watch again. It was three-twenty. He stared into the night, wishing it was all over.

He had not always been a terrorist.

IN THE MID-SIXTIES he had been a schoolboy, a bright young lad, and the center forward on his school's football team. He left school at sixteen. His father was a mechanic who ran a small automobile repair shop in a side street behind his house off Belfast's Falls Road. Seamus O'Neill became apprenticed to his father.

This was Northern Ireland before the troubles. The civil rights marches, which would soon ignite the powder keg, still existed only in the minds of a few idealists. The Catholics, although representing over one-third of the population, were largely excluded by the ruling Protestants from any participation in the running of the Province. The minority looked increasingly for inspiration to the Catholic Republic to the south.

Seamus O'Neill had loved working under the watchful eye of his father.

"You'll be a good wee mechanic," John O'Neill said.

On Sundays, the whole family went to Mass together. Afterward, in the spring or summer, they often drove into the countryside for a picnic at the side of a quiet lane or in a field. There were few complaints. Seamus O'Neill came into early manhood with the security of one who has grown up in a tightly knit, working-class, Northern Irish Catholic family.

The O'Neills' neighbors, the Tanseys, were unexceptional people. Tim Tansey worked in a bottling plant off the Falls. At election times, he became involved in canvassing votes for Nationalist candidates, but for the most part he was a moderate. Tansey, his wife, and three children had lived all their lives beside the O'Neills in the same street of identical small houses.

On a Friday evening in August of 1969, Tim Tansey came into O'Neill's, where the family had just finished their supper. He held a mimeographed circular in his hand, and his eyes were bright with excitement.

"What do you think of that?" he asked and handed John O'Neill the leaflet. It gave the details of a march to be held the next afternoon, a march in support of civil rights in which Catholics would demonstrate in numbers that they could no longer be ignored. John O'Neill shook his head.

"Oh no! Oh no!" he said. "No way."

Tim Tansey looked crestfallen.

"It's a peaceful march, John," he said. "What can be wrong with that?"

The neighbors debated for a few more minutes, but it was obvious that John O'Neill was not marching anywhere.

"Well, you're a right one," said Tim Tansey, "and I always thought you were a bit of a Fenian."

John O'Neill chuckled as Tansey turned to leave.

"I'll go."

Everyone in the room turned to where the voice had come from. Seamus had been sitting quietly, listening to the two men. His mother was the first to react. She was on her feet at once and began to deal noisily with some saucepans in the sink.

"You'll do nothing of the sort," she said with surprising venom. "Now Tim Tansey, get out. I'll not stand for that sort of thing in this house." She continued at her saucepans, an old, yet familiar fear in her stomach. "Don't let me ever catch you getting into company like that," she hissed at Seamus with a ferocity that was completely new.

The next afternoon was hot. The crowds from the many streets leading to the Falls set off, their numbers swelling as they joined together on their march to the city center. Their eyes blazed in exhilaration at the triumph of it all as they waved their banners defiantly at the closed eyes of the Protestant city. The disenfranchised Catholics of Belfast were on the move, a pipe band played a rousing tune. The moment was briefly theirs.

Seamus had slipped out of the house quietly and made his way up to the Falls where he watched the marchers file past, banners saying "Equal Rights for Catholics" held high. Toward the end of the crowd he saw Tim Tansey. As he walked past, Seamus joined him. Tansey winked and smiled.

"Don't worry, lad," he said cheerfully, "not a word."

TOWARD THE BACK of the march they knew that something had happened. Everything had stopped, but they were still a long way from the city center. The pipe band stopped playing. Seamus made his way toward the front. A phalanx of riot police was blocking their way.

One of the organizers went foward, and a senior police officer emerged from the barricade to meet him. A heated discussion took place. Seamus could see the police officer shake his head vehemently and then walk back into his ranks.

Suddenly he heard a *whizz whizz* sound overhead. From the back of the crowd rocks were being hurled over the heads of the marchers into the ranks of the police.

People began to run, some forward trying to get through the police barriers, some back the way they had come. One of the march organizers, a tall young man with curly hair, shouted into a megaphone: "Please! Everybody, please be calm!"

His words were drowned out by the crowd noise, which had now swelled to a roar. The air overhead was thick with stones flying toward the entrenched Royal Ulster Constabulary.

There was the sound of shattering glass; some of the marchers had begun to break the windows of cars parked by the roadside. Seamus saw a man take a small jerry can of gasoline from under his coat and splash it through a broken windshield. The man then tossed a lighted match and ran, as did all the people nearby. There was a resounding *woomp*, and the car burst into flames. Then a greater explosion followed as its fuel tank went up, sending glass spinning viciously through the air.

Seamus began to make his way back to where he had left Tim Tansey. More cars had erupted in flames, and a large, green Ulsterbus was blazing. Other marchers had also decided to get out, but many were standing their ground, jeering at the RUC and hurling stones and bottles. Then there was a *pop pop* sound. It came from the direction of the police. All at once the air was thick with a choking smoke that caused the eyes to stream mercilessly. Everyone was now running back, handkerchiefs to their eyes. Some people had fallen to the ground and were being trampled by the blindly retreating marchers.

Seamus made his way back without much difficulty. There were shouts behind him. RUC squads, their gas masks giving them a ghoulish appearance, had rushed into the crowd and were dragging away their token captives. Seamus sprinted as hard as he could. He reached a point five hundred yards back along the route they had come half an hour before. There he paused for breath and looked at what had recently been a colorful street scene. A black pall of smoke and tear gas hung in the air denying the sun to the afternoon. Cars and buses blazed on both sides of the road, while stones, broken bottles, and tear-gas canisters littered the surface. The body of a man lay in the middle of the debris, his neck at a peculiar angle.

Seamus felt a hand on his shoulder. He spun around. Tim Tansey gave him a fatherly squeeze.

"Let's go home, lad," he said.

Seamus saw their reflection in a shop window as they went past. Their faces were black, their clothes stained with smut from the flames. He would have some serious cleaning to do before he faced his mother.

THAT NIGHT THE B Specials came. At first Seamus, lying in bed with his two younger brothers, could not identify the noise. It was the dull thud of wood on wood, like a mallet striking a peg. The noise was repeated incessantly and was drawing nearer. He got out of bed and went to the window where, by stretching his neck, he could just make out car lights and activity at the top of their street. He thought he saw smoke.

He hurriedly dressed himself and went downstairs. His father was already up and piling heavy furniture inside their front door.

"It's the Bs," his father said. "Get that chair there, hurry!"

They barricaded their door with most of the furniture in the house, right up to the small fanlight. They also blocked up the window of the front room, which looked out on the street.

The B Specials were closing, the noise that had awoken Seamus coming from the heavy, wooden butts of their rifles beating on the doors of the terraced houses. They were also breaking windows. Seamus had heard of the B Specials, Northern Ireland's dreaded auxiliary police force, but he had yet to see them in action. He ran back upstairs to get a better view from the bedroom window.

"No lights!" his father whispered urgently.

By now all the family were out of bed, the children crying and rubbing their eyes. Mrs. O'Neill had taken them into the kitchen.

Up the street, groups of people in their nightclothes stood in the open. Two houses were on fire. There was the sound of women crying. The B Specials were now so close that Seamus could make out their features. He saw a sheen of sweat glinting on the forehead of the man in front, whose mouth was partially open in a strange smile. They were coming down both sides of the street, a group of about twenty on each side, lashing out with their gun butts at windows and doors, swaggering with the air of conquerors.

Their leaders had a list that they consulted; it was checked against the house numbers as they went along. The group on

O'Neill's side were nearly level now, and the man with the list raised his hand. Tansey's! The B Special raised his boot and kicked the door powerfully. It held firm. The whole group then surrounded it and pushed with their combined strength. Slowly the barricades that Tim Tansey had erected gave way, and the squad of B Specials burst into his home.

From his position Seamus could hear Tansey's wife screaming. There was a continuous crashing and smashing sound coming from the house, and then Tim Tansey himself was dragged out into the street by two B Specials, while a third beat him methodically about the legs with the butt of his gun. A wisp of smoke came from the house, and Tansey's wife and young family came running into the street, wailing and crying.

Seamus rushed downstairs.

"They're burning Tansey's!" he shouted.

His father looked at him for an instant in disbelief. Then he ran upstairs to see for himself. The B Special was holding his rifle by the barrel and swinging it vigorously at the lower part of Tim Tansey's body.

John O'Neill rushed downstairs and started to pull back the furniture from his front door.

"They're killing Tim Tansey," he shouted.

His wife ran from the kitchen and caught his arm. "No, John! No!" she cried. Tears streamed from her eyes, which were wild with fear. "For the love of God, no!" The children in the kitchen were now crying uncontrollably.

John O'Neill shook her hands away from him.

"For the love of Christ, I can't let the man be killed," he cried. "I'll try and reason with them."

She continued to weep as he dragged the last of the furniture away and opened the door.

Seamus had come downstairs. "I'll go with him," he said. "You go back to the wee-uns in the kitchen."

The street was dense with smoke. There was pandemonium in the wake of the holocaust that was moving through. The B Special who had been beating Tim Tansey was now exhausted and was being replaced by another. Two of them held Tansey by the shoulders. "Fenian scum," Seamus heard one of them say.

John O'Neill ran out into the street. His son stood outside their closed door.

"Please stop, sir," John said to the man with the raised gun as he ran the short distance from his house.

The B special pivoted toward the man running at him. His two hands holding the barrel of the gun descended in a backhand blur, the tip of the gun butt traveling at five times the speed of his arm. It caught John O'Neill on the right-hand side of his face, high up on the cheek just under his eye. There was the sound of bone shattering, and O'Neill went down in a heap. Seamus rushed to his prostrate father. Abruptly, the B Specials dropped Tim Tansey to the ground and continued on their way down the street, hammering the doors as they went.

THE CASUALTY DEPARTMENT of the Royal Victoria Hospital, right on the Falls, was busy that night. All of West Belfast was in chaos, streets impassable with barricades, fire engines and ambulances unable to get through. Seamus had organized a group of neighbors to help carry his father and Tim Tansey to the hospital. Tansey was conscious but could not walk. John O'Neill appeared to be dead. They eventually had made it, barely dodging another B Special patrol.

Seamus was asked to sit in the waiting room of the hospital. He sat for over three and a half hours, trying to keep awake, numb to the tide of human misery swirling about him. Throughout the night, families of the injured called at the hospital.

Eventually a young, harassed looking casualty officer came into the waiting room. Fatigue lines were embedded in his face from the long night. He looked down at a clipboard.

"John O'Neill?" he asked the room generally.

Seamus stood up. "Yes?" he said.

The doctor came over. Seamus could not tell by his face whether or not he was about to hear the worst.

122

"Is he dead?" he asked.

The doctor motioned to Seamus to follow him. They went into a small office, and the doctor sat beside him.

"You're his son?"

Seamus nodded. His mouth was dry; he could not speak.

"Your father is still unconscious. He has sustained a very severe blow to his head." The young doctor spoke slowly.

"How did it happen?"

"The B's . . ." Seamus blurted. A great sob rose in his throat. The doctor shook his head and continued in his quiet tone.

"I'm just reporting for the consultant in charge," he said, "but I can tell you that your father's orbit—in plain terms the structure surrounding his right eye—has been shattered. We have had to remove the eye as its globe was completely burst, but that is something he will get over. Are you all right?"

Seamus was very pale and had begun to sway. The doctor rose and poured a glass of water from a sink in the corner. Seamus gulped from the glass and began to focus again. The doctor sat down beside him.

"We have another problem," he said gently. Seamus looked at him. "The blow has fractured your father's skull in a line extending up from the cheekbone, up the side of his head to above the tip of his right ear." The doctor drew a line with his finger up along his head. Seamus saw that the doctor wore a gold ring on his finger. He was amazed that he noticed such a trivial detail. The doctor was speaking again.

"He is bleeding inside his skull," he said, "which means they will have to operate."

Seamus shook his head in absolute disbelief. Fifteen hours ago they had all been sitting in the kitchen reading the Sunday papers.

"We're hopeful of a good result," the doctor said, "but there may be permanent damage."

"Can I see him?" Seamus asked.

The doctor nodded. He led him through the hospital until they came to a large elevator that took them high up in the building. White-coated doctors and nurses hurried about.

Patients were wheeled in and out of wards. There was a strong smell of antiseptic. The doctor gave Seamus a mask, and they both entered a room marked "No Admittance."

Seamus barely recognized his father, one of a number of patients. His entire head and part of his face seemed to have been replaced by an enormous bandage. He was the color of death. A drip was connected to each of his arms, one of blood, the other containing a clear substance.

This is not my father, thought Seamus. This is not my father. He bent down.

"You'll be all right," he whispered to the white-linened head. "You'll do fine."

There was no reaction from the figure in the bed. His eyes glistening with tears, Seamus straightened up. The doctor brought him downstairs and showed him to the street door.

"Good luck," the doctor said, "and I mean it."

Seamus walked through Belfast for nearly two hours, dreading the prospect of going home, of having to meet his mother. He walked through streets strewn with glass and stones and past the burned-out shells of terraced houses. The blackened remains of cars lay smoldering at every turn. Eventually, when he crept in, it was nearly five o'clock, the sky clearly marked with the promise of a new day.

His mother was still in the kitchen, asleep in a chair by the range, which had long gone out. She awoke when he came in. One look at his face told her everything she had dreaded, that she had prayed so hard would not be. She embraced her son for a long time, knowing that now everything was changed fundamentally, that life for them would never again be the same.

That night Seamus O'Neill became a terrorist.

HE TOOK OVER the garage the next day.

After three and a half months, when his father at last came home, he was an invalid who could neither talk nor walk. Each morning Seamus and his mother carried him downstairs and sat him up in his favorite chair beside the fire. There, they and the rest of the family spoke to him in normal conversational tones as if nothing had happened. It did not matter to them that he could not reply, they were not going to treat him any differently. Occasionally he tried to make a word, but all that came out was an enraged groan that made him shake violently; someone had to hold his shoulders until the spasm passed.

Seamus began to frequent the Republican Clubs in West Belfast, the cells from which the men of violence were emerging. Etched into his brain so that only death could remove the memory was the picture of Tim Tansey dangling like a puppet from the B Specials' hold while they shattered his legs with their blows. Curiously, that was where the memory ended. He had no precise recollection of what had happened to his father, but although he knew he must have seen it, his brain stubbornly refused to release the picture.

It was almost as if his father had always been the now old man with extensive paralysis sitting vacantly by the fire in the kitchen. What exactly had caused it was a total blank, never discussed among them. All that remained for Seamus was a white-hot hatred of such burning intensity that only violence would provide the salve to cool it.

FINDING VIOLENCE WAS no problem in Northern Ireland in the early seventies. Three years had passed since the first civil rights march, and Belfast, with a standing garrison of fifteen thousand British troops, truly resembled a war zone. Seamus O'Neill in the Provisional IRA was hijacking cars that could be used by the Republican cause. His knowledge as a mechanic was being fully employed.

One night he was cruising through Andersonstown, driving a stolen Ford Cortina with four other men as passengers. On the floor behind his seat was a Colt Armalite rifle and ten rounds of ammunition. As they rounded a corner, they suddenly found themselves confronted by a British Army patrol.

Three armored trucks and a six-wheeled Saracen personnel carrier blocked the road. The soldiers were paratroopers in full camouflage smocks and webbing. Cars were being stopped for questioning and search.

Seamus swung the wheel of the Cortina hard right, at the same time ramming the gearshift into first and slamming the accelerator to the floor. It was a mistake. The car screeched in a tight arc, almost overturning as it did so, and smashed the front fender of a car parked by the side of the road. There were shouts from the Army blockade. The car's back wheels spun furiously as they sought the grip to propel it away. Then the vicious throbbing of a Sterling submachine gun could be heard. The car's back window imploded abruptly with a loud pop, and the whole front of the car was sprayed with a mixture of broken glass, blood, and fragments of flesh and bone. With his view obscured, Seamus lost all control, and the car spun around wildly until it came to a crashing halt against the front of a house.

The soldiers dragged the dazed occupants out of the wreckage and slammed them up against a wall. They did not bother with the corpse in the back seat that now lacked a forehead.

They brought Seamus to the infamous Barracks of Castlereagh outside Belfast where he was questioned for hours at a time. When he refused to answer, he was hooded and then made to stand upright against a wall, his feet kicked apart and backward so that the weight of his body fell mainly on the tips of his outstretched fingers. It was like an eternity; the disorientation in the pitch-blackness was complete. Sleep was impossible as the eerie quiet was spasmodically shattered by the screech of a high-speed drill, activated with terrifying unpredictability close to his head.

After nearly one and a half days, so drunk with fatigue and sore with pain that his very name was a mystery to him, Seamus O'Neill scrawled his signature at the bottom of a page and was led away to a prison cell with a bed.

Within a month he had been sentenced to eight years' imprisonment by a judge sitting without a jury, convicted on his own written confession, one more terrorist off the streets of Northern Ireland.

FOR THE REMAINDER of his adolescence and early manhood he was sent into the compounds of Long Kesh. Hastily constructed on the site of an old airfield outside Belfast, the temporary prison camp at Long Kesh, with its compounds of up to one hundred prisoners, was more like an enclosed military training school than a prison. The discipline imposed by the compound leaders on their men was tight. Special concessions were given by the authorities, who allowed them to behave like prisoners of war, wearing their own clothes and grouping according to their paramilitary allegiance.

Seamus attracted the attention of the compound officer in charge of the Irish National Liberation Army squadron, the military wing of the old IRA. Their defined, violent aim was to make the province of Northern Ireland so ungovernable that the British would have to pull out.

Seamus sat during the long summer evenings on the clay of the compounds listening to lectures on history: how the Greek Cypriots of EOKA had succeeded in getting the Brits to withdraw through a campaign of unremitting violence; the history of resistance and triumph in Palestine; the guerrilla war in Vietnam; the revolution of 1916 in Dublin.

Everything pointed to the success of pressure against the superior forces of colonization and oppression. The numbers of British soldiers killed had doubled since the year before, off-duty members of the security forces had been blown to pieces, even an army helicopter had almost been brought down with a Russian-made bazooka.

"We'll push the Brits into Belfast Lough," they shouted with growing assurance.

And as the summer afternoons grew shorter and the weather changed and icicles formed on the barbed wire of

Long Kesh, the lessons they learned were not confined to history. There were lectures on guerrilla tactics, how to live off the land, the art of constructing homemade incendiary devices, and more.

Seamus learned what it was to have confidence in oneself regardless of how awesome the odds. He was taught that the large numbers of British soldiers were a help rather than a threat. Soldiers over an optimum number hindered the operations of the security forces, tempted their commanders to use men needlessly, hampered the collection of information to be used against the terrorists, and cost a small fortune. Large numbers of soldiers in guerrilla wars, he was told, are an inefficient weapon, put there solely for purposes of propaganda.

"England is spending a billion pounds sterling a year to stay in the North," one speaker said. "Ask yourself, in its financial condition, how long can that last?"

But as they sat behind the compound wire, under the eyes of soldiers in observation towers that could have been taken from Auschwitz, Seamus and his companions were able to see that the money had not run out quite yet. A series of long, concrete buildings were appearing on the flat land behind the compounds. Crews of men with a mass of machinery worked night and day to complete these structures, most of which had the shape of a giant "H."

The prisoner-of-war-life days in the compounds were numbered: the H-Blocks were rising.

TWO MONTHS LATER Seamus was shown into his new cell by a neatly uniformed screw and handed a set of prison clothing. At first he refused to put it on, but his OC ordered him to comply. With remission for good behavior, O'Neill could be out in the foreseeable future. He was far more valuable to the INLA outside than in.

The long hours of solitude nurtured the seed of his hate. He was in no doubt now as to his mission in life. He remorselessly pumped his colleagues for information during their free time, drawing on the breadth of their experience to supplement his own. He became a model prisoner who read avidly, mainly the history of oppressed peoples and the works of Marx.

As the years of his sentence dragged by, he slowly became convinced that the random assassination of security forces, although desirable, was essentially futile because they were expendable. The key to Northern Ireland lay in the place from where it was controlled: England. It was when the English decided to pull out, and only then, that Ireland would be left in peace. And the English largely ignored Northern Ireland, rather like a terminally ill relative for whom one has paid to be permanently hospitalized. A gigantic jolt to their complacency was needed, an outrage to crown all outrages.

The dim outline of a plan was conceived in Seamus O'Neill's head.

THE SHOUTS FROM the neighboring H-Block confirmed the protest that had been going on there for over four months. The prisoners, many of them lifers from the old compound, were refusing to wear the prison clothes allotted to them. Deprived of visits, parcels, and regular food, they had lived naked in their cells for months, painting the walls with the slop of their own excrement. During the day their bed mattresses were removed, leaving them with a bucket and a Bible as furniture. The feces-smeared walls incubated and hatched out great swarms of white maggots that crawled freely in the prisoners' hair and noses and eyes when they eventually slept. The men were regularly removed from their cells by the screws to be forcibly searched for any now-forbidden items, such as cigarettes. A screw's finger explored a prisoner's anus for a hidden object and, without being wiped or washed, then searched under his tongue and behind his gums. Beatings were commonplace. Seamus yearned to get out for his revenge.

Still the days crawled, and he studied and read. The other

prisoners passed the time by shouting Gaelic lessons to each other across the hollow corridors. O'Neill heard them but his mind was far away.

ONE DAY THE cell door was opened to admit a youth of about eighteen. He had a very pale complexion and a paten of black curls. One of his eyes was slightly cast. His body was broad and strong.

"How're ye?" asked Seamus.

There was no reply. Seamus shrugged and returned to his book. As the afternoon wore on, he observed his new cell-mate, squatting on his haunches, slowly tracing a circle on the cell floor. Seamus left his bunk and walked over until he stood over the newcomer.

"Did ye just come in?" he asked him.

There was no reply.

"Hey you, I'm talking to you," said Seamus. Still the bent figure made no movement to suggest he had heard anything. Coming from a new prisoner this was insolence of the highest order. Seamus poked the unresponsive back with the toe of his shoe.

"Hey you!" he said hotly.

There was an explosion of activity. The youth's right arm snaked around his back and Seamus felt his ankle caught in a vicelike grip. Simultaneously, the crouched figure sprang upright jerking the captured leg high in the air. As he fell heavily backward to the ground, a small but powerfully squat torso launched itself on his breathless, outstretched body. He felt a knee on his chest. Then all air was summarily cut off as a strong thumb and forefinger proceeded to crush his windpipe. He looked at the face now but inches from his own. All color had left it; only a waxlike tinge remained. But the eyes were the most alarming. In his rapidly fading vision, his whole system now screaming for survival, he clearly saw the edge of madness in the two eyes of the man who was now taking his life.

That was his final memory before the blackness engulfed him.

"HIS NAME IS Patsy Kelly," said Francis O'Hara, as he and Seamus shared the butt of a cigarette at recreation. "He's as strong as a wee bull."

"You needn't tell me," said Seamus rubbing his bruised larynx.

O'Hara laughed. "It took four screws to get him off you," he said.

Seamus respected Francis O'Hara. He was in his early thirties, had spent most of his adult life in prison, and if the judge who sat at his trial had his way, would still be there in old age. Francis O'Hara was an expert in homemade explosives. He had been convicted of driving a car packed with them to the back of a Loyalist Club in Londonderry on a Saturday night. No warning was given. Seven people were killed and over twenty injured, many of them mutilated, their useful lives at an end. O'Hara firmly believed that he would soon be freed as part of a general amnesty.

"Where is he from?" asked Seamus.

"He's from Derry," said O'Hara. "I've spoken to some of the lads he came in with. He's a tough nut, I'll tell you that. He'll be a handy man to have."

Seamus thought of the look he had seen in Kelly's eyes.

"What's his story?" he asked.

O'Hara looked around him. Small groups of men conversed quietly. Tension was building every hour in the prison. A prisoner had gone on a hunger strike that morning for the right to wear his own clothes. O'Hara spoke in a voice barely above a whisper.

"He's from the Turf Lodge area. His father died when he was a wee-un. He's the eldest of four. The Brits were doing a search one night. This lad was out somewhere—only his mother and his two sisters were in the house." O'Hara again checked around him briefly, then continued.

"The Brits went in, four of them. First they started messing with one sister. She was having none of it, so two of them dragged her upstairs and raped her. The mother was kept downstairs and she was kicking up something dreadful, so the two Brits downstairs raped her and then beat her up. This was what was going on when our friend came in."

"What happened then?" asked Seamus.

"Well, he flipped his lid completely. The first Brit he saw was trying to get up on his mother again. He broke his neck. The Brit died as he was, with his trousers down around his ankles. Bad cess to the bastard, may he burn in Hell. The other soldier jumped on Kelly, and they were rolling around the floor when the two Brits upstairs came down. He put up a hell of a fight, but they took him away and beat him within an inch of his life. They broke both his arms."

Seamus thought of his own experience. He did not doubt that O'Hara's story was true. Atrocities by both sides were part of everyday life in Northern Ireland.

"He's in here for four years," said O'Hara. "There was an outcry when he got the sentence. The Loyalists wanted him down for life, but the judge heard evidence from his mother and sisters and decided that there was unnatural provocation. His doctor also testified that your man had become unbalanced after all this and that he wasn't fit to stand trial."

Seamus remembered Patsy Kelly's wild eyes again.

"I'd agree with that," he said.

Back in his cell Seamus went about his daily routine as if Patsy was not there. There was plenty of time. The dim plan in his mind received another spurt of growth.

The next ten weeks would remain in the memories of everyone in the H-Blocks for the rest of their lives. With each day that passed, the hunger strikers grew weaker in body but stronger in spirit.

The whole world began to focus on the drama being played out in the northeastern corner of Ireland. Appeals were being made to the British Government to accede to the prisoners' fundamental requests: their right, as political prisoners, to wear their own clothes. Appeals also were made to the hunger strikers themselves to give up their suicidal course and to rest with the victory of worldwide publicity and sympathy that they already had.

And there was the euphoria of the night when one of the men in the H-Blocks, soon to die from self-starvation, was elected by 30,000 people in West Belfast to represent them in the British House of Commons.

Rumors were rampant. One was that the special emissary of the Pope had been in the H-Blocks to dissuade the hunger strikers from the mortally sinful taking of their own lives. Some said the strike was over, some were not sure.

"They mustn't stop now!"

Seamus stared at Patsy to make sure it was the young man now standing at the cell door who had spoken. He could not remember having heard Patsy speak before.

"Jesus, don't let them give in now." Patsy spoke again, more an intonation than a statement to anyone in particular. His powerful fists were clenched white at his sides, the muscles in his jaw working relentlessly.

"They won't, I know they won't," said Seamus.

Patsy looked at him suspiciously.

"Why do you say that?"

"I know the lads," replied Seamus. "They'll not give in until they get what's theirs by right, what's all of ours by right."

Patsy seemed to relax a little. He left the door and sat down on the steel bunk beside Seamus.

"They say he'll not last tonight," said Patsy, referring to a man now in his fifty-third day without food.

"I heard his family are there the whole time," said Seamus. "He was anointed this morning."

"Anointed with the blood of martyrs," said Patsy in his flat tone.

Seamus saw that the young man had almost no expression in his face, in fact the only life to it seemed to be in the eyes, which now shone with unrestrained fervor.

Seamus sensed his opportunity.

"Do you want to help to get even?" he asked.

Patsy's head turned to him. He really was built like a little bull.

"How d'you mean?" he asked in a voice barely above a whisper.

"I know your story, what happened to your mother and your sister," said Seamus and instantly sensed the surge of hostility that swept up into the other man, his thick arms contorted by the force with which he now gripped the sides of the bunk.

"I have a story too," Seamus went on quickly, "about someone who meant everything to me."

Patsy's eyes blazed with a mad intensity and hurt. Seamus felt the other was just about to spring on him. I must control this force, he thought as he raced on to explain the story of his father's accident, the marches, the burnings and atrocities, his own operations with the Provos, gradually diffusing as he did so, the reflexive animal anger of the man beside him.

"We've got to be cleverer than them," said Seamus finally, "and work together for the cause. Our only chance is to work together as an organization."

Patsy said nothing for a while. He looked down at the floor, his arms resting on his knees.

"What do you want me to do?" he asked at last in such a low voice that Seamus had to bend forward to catch his words.

"I want you to learn," said Seamus, "to learn and to listen. Do as I say and I'll see you get your chance."

That night Seamus slept soundly, happy in the knowledge that he had recruited a valuable new weapon for the army of liberation.

IN THE REMAINING eighteen months of his sentence Seamus worked hard on the education of Patsy Kelly. Seeing the pale face with its unsettling, slightly off focus stare, Seamus realized that here he had a rare asset, someone whose dedication to revenge put him firmly on the side of the psychotics, but who otherwise appeared to act and behave normally. Patsy could absorb complicated instructions without difficulty and, when Seamus tutored him in the principles of explosives, he recited back what he had learned without a fault.

As one by one, the hunger strikers died, Seamus used the emotion released by their deaths to forge further the venomous human weapon who had nearly become a creature of his own making.

The day Seamus O'Neill walked out of Long Kesh, his sentence completed, the last prisoner he saw was Patsy Kelly, who was due to be released the following year.

"Blow up some of the bastards for me," whispered Patsy.

"You know where to come when you get out?" asked Seamus.

"I'll be there," answered Patsy.

NOW AS HE sat on the Atlantic Drive, the first tinges of dawn making their way into the May morning sky, Seamus reflected on how effective Patsy had been for them. It was his ruthlessness that was so remarkable. He simply wanted to kill. And in killing he was quite unconcerned for his own personal safety. It did not matter whether it was British soldiers, Reservists, or RUC men who died; each new strike was another notch in the man's relentless personal war of hatred against the Northern Ireland establishment.

Seamus could see that Patsy's blood thirst was like a drug to him. He wanted to kill because he liked it, actually took pleasure in it. His experience all those years ago had severely and permanently unbalanced him but had given the INLA a unique killing machine.

IT WAS IN early March that the INLA war council had made the decision to put the first part of Seamus's plan in motion.

In April Patsy left a misty Southern Ireland port as a deckhand on a cattle ship to Libya. Before he left, Seamus had spent a full week in the Antrim hills with him, planning and explaining. Once the outline plan had been formed, it was easy to fill in the details. The Englishman had been particularly helpful—his knowledge was invaluable and available to the highest bidder. An ex-steward of the Jockey Club, no less. Kelly's placing in the stable had been achieved with ridiculous ease.

He raised the pocketscope to his eye again, smiling as he did so at the thought of Patsy still asleep in Newmarket, the very heart of the sport of British Kings. There would be the greatest outcry that the world had ever known, and the British people would at last insist that their Government quit Ulster for all time.

The sense of power that Seamus felt with this thought was quite dizzying. That Patsy would never survive it was a detail of little interest to him. Patsy was simply the instrument that was being used for the execution, and he had been honored to accept the assignment that would cause his name to go down in history, one of the great martyrs for the cause.

Seamus could see the headlines: "INLA CLAIM RE-SPONSIBILITY." Ballads would be sung about them down the years.

The thick drizzle allowed him to see very little with the night viewer. His attention was directed by a distinct sound that was again repeated. It was the soft splash of oars on water in the bay below, barely discernible over the crash of the surf. Almost simultaneously he discerned two needle points of light pulling up to the head of the beach and then being quickly extinguished.

"They're here," he said to the woman now at his side.

The first light of dawn was touching the peak of the mountaintop opposite them, but the bay below was still in darkness. The drizzle stopped, and all at once visibility improved. Through the pocketscope he could make out figures leaving the van and walking down the beach to the water line. There was a high tide, a detail that Seamus had not overlooked. His eyes swept the bay through the instrument. His heart beat mightily in his chest. There in the center of the Tranarossan Bay a squat fishing trawler bobbed with the swell of the sea.

He could now make out the outline of the dory whose oars he had heard moments before. It was larger than the usual tender, about sixteen feet, with built-up sides designed to hold the utmost cargo. The dark shape of stacked rectangular boxes, their weight pressing the dory well down in the water, was also visible. He could see two figures in the small craft, one sitting on the stern, the other rowing smoothly. The largest ever gunrun was about to land in Ireland.

Seamus handed the pocketscope to Delaney. With every passing moment, morning was spreading into the sky and down the sides of the mountain. A lark suddenly burst into song on the hill behind them.

"Damnation!" he hissed through clenched teeth, grabbing back the instrument, "why can't they hurry it?"

He looked in desperation at the dawn. It was going to be a lovely morning. The bow of the dory had now touched the beach. The oarsman and his companion jumped out into the tide and with the help of the waiting men dragged the long boat up onto the sand. It took them all their strength to get the heavy craft out of the reach of the water. Immediately, they began to offload the weighty boxes, carrying them rapidly, two men to a box, up the beach to the van, which was parked on a flat, grassy area behind the sand dunes.

Seamus was following the operations on the strand with such concentration that he almost missed the sound. It took about three seconds for his brain to retrieve the noise it had heard, analyze and identify it. On the far hillside someone had snapped shut the bolt of a rifle.

Seamus lowered the pocketscope with a jerk. His heart beat wildly, and the blood boomed in his ears. He gripped his companion's arm and, pointing his finger sharply toward the bay, dragged her down below the low stone wall that stood between them and the steep, sloping cliff. He strained his pounding ears but could discern no further noise above the crashing surf.

First daylight was now established in the valley. He raised his head fractionally over the wall and with his naked eye saw the men below him on the beach continuing with their task of unloading, their gray forms just visible. He was sure of what he had heard, but now he began to try to find other excuses for the sound. A beast breaking a branch, perhaps, as it walked the hill. Or a stone, dislodged by a sheep, falling to the rocks. The task underneath was nearing completion. He could see the boat clearly. About four crates remained to be taken to the van. He tried to contain his anxiety. He began to search the surrounding countryside, straining his eyes to their limit, until they began to water. His entire body was one large antenna, rigid from the intense effort of trying to collate any other shred of noise that would confirm the original danger.

Then his eardrums exploded. The figures on the beach froze like statues. A rifle shot rang out over the valley. A staccato voice drilled into his head.

"You are completely surrounded! You cannot escape! Raise your hands immediately or we will open fire!"

The effect on the beach party was electric. They broke into two groups. The four men from the van dropped the crates they were carrying and began to run up the beach to their vehicle. The two men who had been offloading the dory grabbed what was the remaining box and threw it heavily over the side onto the sand. As it fell it split open, and a quantity of hand grenades rolled down the beach into the tide. The two men caught the sides of the boat and pulled it toward the water, their legs pumping like pistons with the effort in the sand. At the same time a metallic clanking sound came from the bay as the trawler began to haul anchor.

Heavy gunfire blasted from the far hillside. Although nearly day, the flame from the rifles could be seen. Their target was the van. Before the running figures had reached it, the van was completely immobilized, its tires in ribbons. The wail and flash of police sirens suddenly erupted on the green plain behind the beach. The men with the boat had reached the water. One of them was frantically maneuvering a seventy-horsepower Evinrude into place at the stern and was furiously pulling the starting rope. All at once the morning was alive with activity.

At least a hundred blue-uniformed *Gardai* had surrounded the van and overpowered its four occupants without a struggle. Soldiers in camouflage battledress were pouring down from the hillside and the surrounding sand dunes onto the beach, some digging in at strategic positions, others running on to back up the police.

A lone *Garda* ran along the sand into the water. He grabbed for the boat just as the outboard engine burst into life. A single shot rang out, and the *Garda's* hands grasped at his head as he fell backward into the knee-high surf. The bow leaped from the water as the man at the helm gave the engine full throttle. A fusillade of gunfire opened up and the figure at the outboard arched into the air, his body riddled with bullets, and then slumped backward, his dead weight crashing down on the handle of the Evinrude. The dory began to circle wildly, still at full speed. The other man desperately pulled at the fallen body, trying to drag it off the controls. Another barrage of shots rang out, and his head snapped upward and back. He was dead long before he hit the bottom of the boat, which still continued its maniacal circles.

With a great roar the engines of the trawler burst into life. It leaped forward, clearing the head of the bay in a matter of seconds. At the same time the gray shadow of a naval frigate rounded the point, her deck guns firing a cannon fusillade across the trawler's bows; she did not give way but headed for open sea. Another blast from the frigate holed her just above her water line. The trawler's engines died. It was all over.

Seamus O'Neill observed the nightmare enfolding below him with disbelief. Then abruptly his survival instincts took over. He rushed back to the car and, throwing himself to the ground, began to claw under the chassis where he had, five hours previously, taped a SIG-Sauer pistol. The sticky adhesive tape was stubbornly attached to the metal. He wrenched at it desperately, and at last it came free. He scrambled to his feet and jumped into the passenger seat. Delaney was behind the wheel with the engine running. They screeched off up the cliff road away from the beach and toward the village of Doagh. Seamus tore the clinging tape from the gun and checked the chambers. He looked ahead. Miraculously, no police or army patrol had bothered to circle that high up the cliff. The Avenger sped down the steep road and rounded a bend.

Two uniformed *Gardai* were standing in the roadway. They wore luminous orange jackets. As far as Seamus could see they were not armed. They were speaking into small walkie-talkies. One of them stepped forward to block the Avenger's route, and the other approached the driver's window as Delaney rolled it down. The *Garda* put his head in and Seamus shot him in the mouth. The force of the blast from the pistol caused the policeman's head to disintegrate backward in a halo of blood. Delaney stood on the accelerator. The hood of the Avenger caught the other *Garda* full in the stomach. He hurtled upward and bounced from the windshield to the road.

AS THEY DROVE away at top speed Seamus pounded the car seat with his clenched fists and swore viciously. His anger scarcely abated during their long drive down the northwest coast of Ireland, through the Glenties Pass, by brooding Ben Bulben, to the seaside town of Bundoran. They drove without rest, stopping only once for gasoline, down to the town of Carrick on Shannon and then in a long, curving loop eastward, through the Irish north midlands. Gradually his anger was replaced by a sense of loss and acute depression.

"They knew," he kept saying. "They knew from start to finish. They knew."

Delaney did not offer an opinion.

By the time they reached Drogheda and started to climb northward again toward Belfast, only one burning thought remained to him for consolation. He still had his best card left to play—and play it he would, at Epsom in the County of Surrey on the third of June.

CHAPTER
TEN

THE BEDSIDE PHONE rang softly. The dark-skinned man reached for it with long-practised reflex, automatically checking the luminous clock dial as he did so although he was barely awake. It was 4:00 A.M. New Jersey time. He put the receiver to his ear and grunted. He listened for a few moments.

"Fuck!" he said with feeling and swung his legs onto the floor. He was wide-awake now. The caller was still talking. Beside him in the bed, his wife shifted.

"Emilio?" she said drowsily.

He gestured to her to be quiet. He was listening intently.

"Jesus Christ!" he said, this time more loudly. "Holy Jesus!"

The caller hung up, and Emilio stared at the phone for a few moments before replacing it.

"It's nothing, go back to sleep," he said to his wife. He padded out of the bedroom and downstairs. As she drifted back to sleep she could hear him begin to telephone.

QUORN LAY IN the king-size marble bath, his eyes wide open and fixed on a spot in the bathroom ceiling. It was four-thirty, and he had been in that position for the fifteen minutes that had elapsed since he had got the call.

He was calm. He had always known that something like this might happen. He was subconsciously prepared for the event. Now he knew what he must do.

In a way he blamed himself for not acting a week ago. Still, it had been worth running with. The money was in O.K., but the position was now unstable. It could start fraying at any moment. The facts were only a trickle, but they would begin to flood in during the day. Every passing hour meant increased danger for everyone.

He toweled himself slowly, the water dripping from his large, hairy frame onto the cork-tiled surface of the floor. His mind had already jumped twelve hours ahead, working out the logistics of the plan. He walked to the bedroom and, still thinking deeply, dropped to the floor as he did every morning and began his pushups. His body knifed up and down rhythmically, the powerful arms moving like perfectly tuned hydraulics. He passed one hundred, his mind still adjusting, adapting, sorting out the loose ends. After one hundred and fifty, he stopped and stood up. He was not even hot.

He walked to a built-in wardrobe unit and pressed a concealed latch in its floor. The bottom clicked open to reveal a small aperture from which he withdrew a package. He went to the bed and unwrapped it carefully.

There was a faint smell of oil. The 9mm ASP rolled out of the rag onto the covers. It had started off as a standard Smith and Wesson 39. Its barrel had been shortened to just over three inches; the grips had been replaced with specially lightened models; a new trigger guard with a forward hook had been fitted so that the gun could be steadied in both hands for firing in combat mode. Quorn ejected the pistol's magazine, checked the safety catch, recoil spring, and breech, reloaded the gun, and wrapped it back in the rag.

Then, still with a towel around his waist, he went to the telephone and punched a number. It took less than a minute to book himself on that morning's British Airways Concorde to London, leaving JFK at 08:30 hours.

He lay down on the floor and began his regular series of situps.

HIS DAY HAD just begun.

CHAPTER
ELEVEN

SERGEANT HOPE SAT in the outer office, high in the brick building on American Road. He held a file on his knees, which he now opened, and looked again at the newspaper clipping. It was the foreign news page from the previous day's *Nation's Voice*, May 27.

The center story was of a spectacular gunrunning operation to Ireland that had been foiled two days previously by the security forces. Four people had died including two Irish policemen. The shipment was described as "one of the biggest ever peacetime hauls of illegal arms and ammunition."

The Reuters story was surmounted with a map, and it was this that had initially caught Hope's eye, for there was a map of Ireland, just as he had seen in New York, with an arrow pointing to a spot on the northwest coastline where the attempt to land the guns had failed. It was startling. The information they had given Scotland Yard had been acted upon without delay, and the terrorists had been foiled.

Yet the commissioner had not called.

THE DOOR BESIDE Hope opened, and the efficient-looking constable in shirt sleeves, whom he had seen on his last visit, smiled and beckoned him in.

Commissioner Richardson was smoking his indispensable pipe, a sheaf of paper in his hands. He put them down and waved briefly to a chair.

"Thank you for seeing me so quickly, sir," said Hope.

"I had not expected to see you again so soon, Sergeant," said the big man, puffing industriously. He paused for several moments, looking at Hope's profile with a mixture of interest and apprehension.

"Well, Sergeant," he said, "you wanted to see me."

"Yes, sir," said Hope putting the file on the desk. "It's about my . . . ah, visit to New York, sir."

Richardson frowned.

"I thought we had agreed," he said cautiously, "that your visit to New York was to be forgotten."

"Yes, sir," replied Hope. "But when I read this . . ." he pointed to the file.

Richardson's frown deepened. He turned Hope's file to him and read the clipping.

"They must be very happy in Scotland Yard," Hope was saying, "that you were able to give them the tip off, sir."

Richardson's heart had quickened a beat. This was the first time he had read the paper in front of him. Nothing further had been heard from New York, and he had dared to hope that the matter might be at an end although each time the telephone rang he expected Interpol to be on the line. Now here was this fool on the loose again, jabbering his head off. Hope was becoming the sole danger. He had to be handled.

"Of course they are, Sergeant," said Richardson carefully. "They are very happy."

He looked again at the article and then at Hope.

He had no recollection of Hope mentioning anything about gunrunning to—where was it?—Ireland? The earlier madness had been about someone wanting to kill the Queen. It now seemed that the sergeant was inventing things as they cropped up, probably the shock of the disastrous New York trip. If the matter kept on like this it could end up with a Commission of Inquiry.

"I am very pleased with your work, Sergeant," he said.

"Thank you, sir," said Hope. "It is an amazing story, isn't it?"

Richardson turned the file back to Hope.

"Amazing," he said. He looked at the station sergeant closely. "What do you think will happen now, Sergeant?" he asked.

"It's hard to believe, sir, but the whole business must be true. These Irish terrorists are going to try to kill the Queen."

Richardson composed himself with the calm countenance of someone who is pacifying a dangerous lunatic.

"But the authorities would appear to have the situation under control over there," he said, "following my report."

"Of course, sir," replied Hope. "Have they questioned Hoare yet?"

Richardson stared at him.

"Who?"

Hope felt a strange twinge in his chest.

"Sir Tristram Hoare, sir. The man whose room I heard it all in. In New York."

"I, ah, I haven't heard, Sergeant," replied Richardson.

"Sir Tristram Hoare knows the identity of the terrorists," said Hope. "I am sure of it, and this news is the proof."

Richardson's frown deepened further.

"Please go on, Sergeant," he said.

"I'm sure they will require me in London, sir, to identify him and to give evidence." Hope fished in his file. "I have written another report of the incident," he said, "to help you brief Scotland Yard before I go. Time may be running out."

Richardson took the offered document.

"Thank you, Sergeant," he said, smiling.

"I have prepared myself to leave immediately, sir," said Hope. "My usual man will take over in the Dockyard."

Richardson kept smiling.

"Very good, Sergeant," he said, fighting to restrain the urge to shout at this imbecile. He leaned back in his chair and contemplated the ceiling for a moment.

"As you know, Sergeant," he said, "like ourselves, the British have special sections to deal with things like this, matters of such vital national importance."

Hope nodded.

"Of course, sir. I completely understand."

"It's very necessary when taking up a matter as delicate as this to do so with the right section."

Hope nodded again.

"This is just what I have done. Now it is up to them to come back to us. They have their ways of doing things."

"It's essential they pick up Hoare, sir," said Hope. "Hoare is the key. He knows the identity of the assassin and the place where the attempt will be made. I'm sure of it."

Richardson rose from his chair and walked around the desk until he rested his enormous frame in front of Hope.

"What comes through all of this," said Richardson, "is the excellent work which you have done, Sergeant, work which will be indispensable," he lowered his voice, "to the Yard as they move to stop the attempt."

Hope looked at his superior.

"Your loyalty is a credit to you, Sergeant."

"Thank you, sir."

"I don't have to tell you," said Richardson, "what the newspapers would do if they got hold of something like this."

Hope nodded grimly.

"There's no copy I hope?" asked Richardson, indicating Hope's report.

"No, sir."

Richardson stood up. "As a matter of fact just before you arrived, Sergeant, I was about to ring London to ask them exactly when, in the light of this," he waved toward the file, "they wanted you over to talk about . . ."

"Hoare."

". . . thank you, yes, about Hoare."

He moved toward the door, and Hope stood up.

"As soon as a specific request is received," said Richardson, "I will let you know myself and see that you are cleared to go to London straightaway."

They were at the door, which Richardson opened.

"Otherwise," he patted Hope's back, "I think that the greater interests of everyone, and I am sure you know who I mean, Sergeant, are best served by keeping absolutely quiet."

"I completely understand, sir," Hope said. "You may rest assured that I will stand by until I hear from you."

Richardson grasped his hand and shook it warmly.

"Good man," he said. "Well done. And remember. I will call you."

A MINUTE LATER back behind his desk, the big man shook his head slowly from side to side in disbelief. The report he was reading was the stuff of a cheap thriller. If the prime minister should ever find out what had gone on in New York, how they had risked Washington's displeasure . . .

Violently he shredded the report into tiny pieces, cursing Hope as he did so. Richardson scooped the pieces into an ashtray, lighted a match, and put it to the mound of paper. One could never be too careful.

Sergeant Hope was proving too difficult. Richardson bit his lip. Perhaps there was another way. Over the years it had been suggested that Antigua should have a permanent presence on the island of Redonda, a volcanic rock thirty-five miles northeast of Antigua whose area ran to half a square mile of bird guano. Stationed on Redonda, Hope would be out of harm's way and, more important, uncontactable.

Richardson began to feel better following his idea. Sitting down he packed some tobacco into his pipe bowl and began to write a memo to his head of personnel.

CHAPTER
TWELVE

SIR TRISTRAM HOARE walked slowly up the thickly carpeted steps from the Savoy's River Restaurant, past the antlered deer, out of the great hotel's doors to the Strand. He had just finished a two-hour lunch bought by his stockbroker, who a week previously had turned all of Hoare's investments into cash. Turning left, he strolled in the direction of St. James's, the remains of a Montecristo Number One clamped between his teeth.

There had been no further word from Quorn. The thing had gone off the boil, Hoare's carelessness in Antigua forgotten as everyone counted his money. He looked at his watch. By now the shipment should be well in, spread out among a hundred different Irish cottages.

He walked slowly, savoring the warm May scents in the air, a transitory feeling of well-being flooding his whole body. He ran a hand through his graying, blond hair. This would be his last May in London for some time, perhaps ever, but he had known the likely consequences of his actions when he had exchanged his knowledge for money. He had justified it to himself on the basis that they were unlikely to succeed. He had had long practice in self-justification; now it came easily.

At Charing Cross station he paused for the traffic. A newsvendor selling the *Evening Standard* was directly opposite, a loud headline emblazoned on his stand. A steam hammer hit Sir Tristram Hoare in the solar plexus. He rushed across to the newsstand, fumbling for change. A car swerved violently to avoid his charging figure. He could scarcely breathe.

It was all there. The largest arms find ever, lists of guns, two Irish policemen murdered, two unidentified gunrunners dead. There was a picture of the trawler holed by the Irish Navy and another of the Irish *Taoiseach* congratulating the security forces for having foiled such an important terrorist operation.

Hoare's head buzzed as he reread the paper with incredulity. It was impossible. The whole operation had been a complete failure. Somebody was going to pay.

A feeling of utter dread now replaced his recent euphoria as he realized that the narrow path between safety and peril that he had taken for so long had suddenly dissolved. His wet cigar butt was still in his mouth as he clambered into a taxi and directed it to his home.

He had a plan. Now he had to put it into immediate effect. As his taxi sat jammed in traffic at Marble Arch, he tried to bring his racing mind to concentrate on his predicament. He knew where the dangers were going to come from. First the Irish, if they felt that they had been shopped, might mobilize some of their cells in London in a wild reflex of revenge. Their method would most likely be a bomb under the car. Then the Cosa Nostra would be incensed about a deal of that magnitude going wrong. They would know that his carelessness had put them at risk. Last there was Quorn.

Hoare considered calling New York and sounding out the situation, but then he rejected such a move. The die was irretrievably cast and he had to make his own way out. Quorn would have spoken to his Mafia contacts.

It was possible that Quorn himself might make for London —unlikely, but just possible. He looked at his watch. It was nearly 3:00 P.M. Still only 10:00 A.M. in New York. By the time any of them over there woke up and heard the news, it would be evening in London. Even if he wanted to, the soonest Quorn could get across would be tomorrow morning; that was May 29. Hoare now shuddered despite the warm afternoon. He tried again to concentrate on his plan.

He had to get out—fast. He had a false passport specifically for this purpose. All his personal effects, papers, files, and diaries, had been meticulously microfilmed and then destroyed. He would literally vanish.

He would fly to Schiphol that night and then connect through to São Paulo, Brazil. There was enough cash to see him through until he could arrange transfers from his bank accounts elsewhere. When the heat was off, he would send for Annette in New York. The thought of her made him feel better. He might call her now if he had a moment. The idea of life without his wife was appealing. He looked again at his watch.

The taxi pulled up to the entrance of Wilton Towers, and Hoare hurried in, nodding briefly to the uniformed doorman. He pressed the elevator button, stepped through the gilt-colored doors and then lay back against the mirrored wall. He felt like a wet rag, utterly exhausted. What he needed now was to lie down for an hour. Sleep would clear his mind and relax his body. He would awaken refreshed and ready.

He inserted the key in the door of his apartment. He stepped into the small hall, swinging the door shut behind him. At that instant he caught a movement out of the corner of his eye. He spun around reflexively, bringing his left arm down heavily on the glinting steel.

Raw pain exploded in the severed muscle of his forearm. His assailant had kicked the door shut. He was crouched low and was now beginning another feint with the knife. Hoare had barely time to make out the dark, olive-skinned face, the

155

yellow tinge to the eyes. He was hypnotized by the long, shining weapon, rather like a knitting needle only thicker and razor-sharp on two sides.

Something sticky was on his left hand. He looked down at his own blood seeping onto the rug of the small vestibule. He shouted wildly and backed away.

The knife, held straight-armed, was traveling at speed for his chest. Hoare lunged wildly at a tall vase standing on the hall table where he normally left his mail. He scooped the heavy ornament with his right arm toward his attacker. The man easily sidestepped the falling vase, but the diversion had given Hoare a precious moment to retreat into the large living room.

Hoare looked frantically around, shouting as he did so. What he needed was to attract someone's attention. He ducked behind the sofa where an array of liquor bottles was set out on a sideboard. Although he was bleeding badly he was not in any pain now. It can't be too bad, he thought. He grasped a bottle and flung it at his assailant, who was nearly on top of him again. This time the missile caught the man in the chest. He grunted slightly. Hoare now grabbed a heavy cut-glass brandy decanter and, turning slightly away from his tormentor, launched the now blood-stained decanter with all his strength at the center of the large picture window of the apartment, which overlooked Hyde Park. The window shattered in a great explosion of glass. Hoare turned back to face the knife and felt an extraordinary, white-hot sensation below his right armpit. With horror he looked down and saw the steel being withdrawn at an almost leisurely pace from above the side of his rib cage. He gulped with fright, and a new pain filled his chest. Still he was able to move. If I can only make the window, he thought.

He began to throw anything that he could lift at the knife man. And he began to scream. A loud, wailing cry of pain and terror. He was faintly aware of the traffic noise five floors below. Surely somebody . . .

The knife was coming again, this time with almost deliberate slowness. The urgency seemed to have gone from the dark man's movements as he closed on his bleeding quarry. Hoare's right hand made contact with something. It was a heavy, brass floor lamp just in front of the shattered window. With a strength he never knew he possessed, he lifted the lamp over his head with both hands. This movement, for an instant, presented the dark-skinned man with a broad, unprotected target area of waistcoated chest and stomach. He did not squander his opportunity. With the grace of a world-class fencer he flexed his knees and then, in a movement so fast that it was over even before it could be seen to have begun, he plunged the long steel weapon into the heaving depths of Sir Tristram Hoare's abdomen, twisted it, and withdrew.

In utter disbelief, Hoare witnessed what had undoubtedly happened to him. Although it had taken only a fraction of a second he found himself, brass lamp still raised overhead, trying to analyze his predicament. And then the pain came, a jagged, searing tearing of such impossible ferocity that it made the dull throbbing in his arm and shoulder seem a luxury. He tottered slowly backward toward the splintered window, his life's blood now oozing out from a point over the top of his trousers down onto the carpet. There was a sickening swell in his throat. For some reason his arms remained rigidly upright, his sticky hands still grasping the lamp that he had intended to launch in his own defense. A low, moaning gurgle came from his throat. The backs of his legs came in contact with the jagged glass and cut them deeply, but the pain barely registered in his agony-swamped brain.

In amazement he saw his executioner wipe his blood from the blade of the knife with a scarf of his wife's that had been lying on a chair. And then he began to fall, backward, everything suddenly subordinated to the law of gravity, into the London rush-hour traffic.

THE SUPERSONIC PLANE screeched onto Heathrow's runway

number one at 18:00 hours exactly, ten minutes ahead of schedule. The man at Immigration ushered Quorn through without a murmur. He walked to a pay phone in the baggage area and dialed a number. When Hoare answered Quorn would say he was calling from New York.

"Hello, yes?"

A man's voice on the other end. Not Hoare's.

Quorn replaced the receiver quickly. He claimed his suitcase from the carousel and walked briskly through the green Customs channel out into Terminal Three. It took him less than ten minutes to go to the men's toilet, transfer the 9mm ASP from its compartment in the suitcase to the snug underarm leather holster, check his bag into the Left Luggage, and board a black London taxi for the West End.

He alighted at Marble Arch and walked the last three blocks to Hoare's home. As he approached Wilton Towers he could see that something was happening. A large area of the road in front of the apartment house was cordoned off with red, police tape, allowing only a single line of cars to trickle through. A crowd of about a hundred were gathered around. Two television crews were shooting footage and interviewing inside the cordon. Quorn joined the crowd. The area of road and pavement next to the building was strewn with broken glass, which glinted in the reflection of the television crews' arc lights. A heavy, brass floor lamp, badly bent, lay incongruously by the curb. Dull brown stains spattered the ground. The man in front of Quorn turned around to go. Quorn met his eye.

"What's going on here?" he asked affably.

The man shrugged his shoulders.

"Somebody broke into a flat up there," he said. "Threw the bloke who lives there right out the window, they did. Bloody marvelous isn't it?"

The man shook his head and walked away. Quorn observed the scene for a few more minutes. He was late.

A TV crew was packing up, its report completed. Quorn

walked around the back of the crowd to the van. A technician was loading equipment.

"Hi," said Quorn with a friendly smile. "I thought we only got this sort of thing in New York."

The technician laughed. He was a young man with a beard, blue jeans, and tennis shoes.

"That's what you think, mate," he said. "We've got everything in this bleeding country now, from Arab terrorists to bloody race riots."

Quorn laughed convivially and offered the technician a cigarette.

"Someone said he was thrown, is that right?" asked Quorn.

"Yes, they pushed him right out of his front window. Poor bloke hadn't a chance, it seems."

"How come all the publicity?" asked Quorn. "Was he famous?"

"I don't think really famous," said the young man. "I'd never heard of him. Hey Bill!" He turned to a man who was lifting a large camera into the van. "What was the bloke's name what fell?"

Bill thought for a second.

"Sir Tristram Hoare," he said.

"Yes, that's it," said the technician. "Bit of a tongue twister." He shrugged. "Means nothing to me."

"Who do they think did it?" Quorn asked the younger man.

"Some burglar, I think," he replied. "Sir what's-his-name must have disturbed him."

The television crew had now loaded up and were preparing to leave.

"What a way to go," said Quorn and smiling, bade the technician good-bye.

"He's not dead you know," said the younger man as he climbed into the van. "He landed on a passing car—it broke his fall."

Quorn stood riveted to the spot, the smile still on his lips. The van drew away from the scene, and the crowd of onlookers began to disperse. Quorn made his way to a telephone booth in the next street and opened the Yellow Pages under "Hospitals."

THE AMBULANCE DRIVER made for University College Hospital, Gower Street. Despite the insistent, flashing siren and two police outriders, traffic was slow to let them through. Behind the driver, two male nurses did what they could for the man whom they had recently scraped from the road near Hyde Park. One of them inserted an airway down his throat to assist his erratic, labored breathing while the other attempted to stem the blood that was leaking from what seemed to be a multiplicity of apertures.

The houseman in the Accident and Emergency Department had come on duty within the past minute and a half. No one had alerted him that a major accident case was coming in, and so he sat, with a copy of *The Times* on his knee, picking some lunch out of an eyetooth with his left fingernail, and wondering what his chances were with the Australian nurse he had just seen in the staff dining room. He looked up abruptly as the ambulance party made its entrance, complete with two helmeted, jodhpured and jackbooted policemen. He stood up.

The figure that lay on the ambulance trolley resembled more a carcass of freshly slaughtered meat than anything else. Blood, dried and fresh, covered everything. It was not possible to tell what color the hair had been due to matted blood. Blood dripped down onto the trolley's wheels leaving two blotchy-red tracks running into the building from the ambulance.

"Sister!" yelled the houseman. "Is he or she alive?" he asked the ambulance men.

"Just about," came the reply

A blue-uniformed, middle-aged woman appeared at the door of an office, her eyebrows raised in surprise at her unaccustomed summoning.

"Sister, get the on-take surgical team, fast!" shouted the young doctor. "Over here," he cried to the ambulance men and grabbed some curved bandage scissors with which he began to cut the clothes from the body, which he was quite sure was dead. The bloodstained face was very pale; the tongue that protruded grotesquely from under the temporary airway had a distinctly bluish tinge.

"They're on their way," said the sister, now at the houseman's elbow. The upper part of the body was bared, and the doctor could see bubbles of air foaming at the mouth of a wound high in the man's upper chest.

"Pneumothorax," he said. "Get me a chest drain."

The sister disappeared.

"Do we know who he is?' he asked one of the policemen standing at the back of the room.

"No, sir," replied one of them, "but the CID are on their way here."

"Where did all this happen?"

"Hyde Park," said the policeman.

"Hyde Park?" said the houseman. "Christ, what next?"

The doors of the room leading from casualty burst open, and an older man hurried in followed by two nurses.

"Well, Harper?" he asked the houseman.

"I've got a very faint pulse in the neck," replied the houseman.

The registrar's eyes scanned the mess.

The houseman went on: "He's got a pneumothorax as you can see. I'm putting in a chest drain."

The registrar turned to the nurse behind him, who happened to be the subject of the houseman's recent admiration.

"Get me a liter of Haemeccel. We'll put in a CVP line," he said. He turned to the other nurse who had arrived with him. "Get some blood by emergency cross-match," he said. "This chap's nearly gone."

The door opened again, and a white-coated, female anesthetist entered the casualty room.

"Evening, Maud," said the registrar. "Rather a messy one here, I'm afraid."

"So I can see," said the woman. "Is he breathing?" She had moved directly to the in-house oxygen supply.

"Barely."

"Better intubate," she said. "Who is he, anyone know?"

"He's from Hyde Park," said the houseman.

"Hyde Park?" said the anesthetist as she removed the temporary airway from the patient's mouth and inserted a long, blue tube into his trachea. "I jog in Hyde Park."

She began to squeeze a small respirator bag gently. Beside her the nurse from the surgical team had quietly erected a drip, which was now connected to the patient's lower right arm. The nurse from Australia had sponged all the encrusted blood from the white, naked body and was blocking the puncture wounds with swabs.

"George," said the registrar to the houseman, "get in a bladder catheter, would you?" He turned to the sister. "Get those ECG electrodes strapped on."

The door opened, and a porter came in.

"Two more policemen outside, sir," he said to the registrar. "Want to know if they can talk to the patient."

"Get me a needle and syringe," said the registrar, turning to the nurse. "I'm sure there's a lot of internal bleeding. Poor bugger. I'd give him two chances."

The Australian nurse passed the registrar a plastic syringe with a three-inch steel needle. With a movement that to Sir Tristram Hoare would not have been entirely unfamiliar, the registrar drove the needle straight into the dying man's abdomen.

"What shall I tell them, sir?" asked the porter.

"Tell whom?" asked the registrar.

"The policemen, sir."

"Tell them he'll be out to them just as soon as he's freshened up a little in here," said the registrar, slowly drawing back the plunger of his syringe.

The two traffic policemen quietly left the room.

"Mr. Johns is scrubbing up in theater," said the registrar to no one in particular. "Just give him a buzz, someone please, and say that we are almost stable down here. We'll be on our way in a moment." He then surveyed the scene. The newly arrived, compatible blood seemed to be going into the man's body at a faster rate than his bleeding.

"All right, let's go," cried the registrar.

The trolley, pulled by a porter, bashed through the double doors and sped down the corridor toward the elevator that would bring it up to the operating room. The anesthetist ran on one side, continuing to hand-ventilate while the sister ran on the other side holding the suction apparatus connected to the chest drain. At Hoare's head ran the Australian nurse holding the supply of blood, followed by the houseman (who was admiring the movement of her firm buttocks beneath her thin cotton dress), the registrar, two further nurses, and finally a porter, whose job it was to push.

In a room off the theater, a consultant surgeon and two of his assistants completed scrubbing up; they entered the brightly lit operating area as the trolley was pushed in.

They had five tough hours ahead of them.

IT WAS TWO in the morning, and the main buildings of University College Hospital, Gower Street, were dark, their doors bolted. Only the Accident and Emergency Department across the road still bustled with activity, the lights shining out from its modern structure into the night.

The tall figure of a man, walking briskly, rounded the corner from the direction of Tottenham Court Road. He wore a white, starched coat, the ends of a stethoscope protruding from one pocket. He entered Accident and Emergency and walked straight to the blue doors of an elevator in the main reception area. The nurse and houseman at the reception desk to his right were busy taking details from a youth with blood pouring from a gash in his head.

The steel-blue doors opened, and the tall man stepped in. He took it to the basement and from there, still walking briskly, made his way through the underground passage that runs under Gower Street until he came to the basement of the main hospital. He entered another elevator and pressed the button for the fifth floor. When the doors opened he went unhesitatingly to a door with a sign saying "Intensive Care." A blue-uniformed sister half rose from the desk in her small office as he entered. He hit her considerately with a chop to the side of the neck, and she folded soundlessly across her desk.

There was the sound of shoes outside on the brittle floor surface. The man stepped behind the door, his hand on the butt of the gun in his pocket. A young nurse with blond hair and a white uniform entered. She drew in her breath sharply on seeing the prostrate body. A second later she was beside the sister, lying in the opposite direction.

The man listened intently. There was no further noise for the moment. A list lay on the desk, and he withdrew it gently from under the sister's head. Thirty seconds later, with the door of the office locked, he walked down the corridor until he found the room he wanted.

A pretty, black nurse sat by the bedside. She smiled up at the doctor as the door opened. The descending blow intended for her neck was deflected by her arm, which she raised reflexively to defend herself. She opened her mouth to cry out, but the man with the funny face moved like a cat. He leaped on her, one large knee thrust forward, his entire weight behind the battering ram, which hit the girl at the top of her abdomen where her stomach ended and her rib cage began. All the wind was expelled from her lungs, and she went into immediate spasm, writhing speechlessly on the floor, her eyes bulging as her whole system fought to cope with the sudden cut off of oxygen.

The large man was on his feet and had turned his attention to the patient in the bed. The very ashen face of Sir Tristram

Hoare lay on the pillow, the eyes closed, the cheeks, even the lips drained of any color. A thick tube ran from beneath the bedclothes to a white, steel, mechanical respirator, parked beside the bed, on its own trolley. It was itself connected by two tubes to an inbuilt supply of air and oxygen in the wall. A further tube stuck from his mouth.

The white-coated man examined the machine. A red light shone from it, above a metal switch that was in the "on" position.

He heard a noise from the bed. Hoare, the effects of the massive anesthetic receding, had momentarily regained consciousness. His eyes opened, and he tried to comprehend his surroundings. The man with the funny jaw looking down at him was so familiar. The man was smiling. Everything was going to be all right. He was safe. He tried to speak, but something was blocking his throat. He wanted, desperately, to ask how he had been saved. The man must have seen his efforts, for now he was bending over him and removing something from his mouth. Hoare felt a raw tearing in his throat. The man was now saying something and had gone slightly out of view. Hoare heard a metallic click. Then the face reappeared. A frightful feeling of suffocation suddenly engulfed Hoare, and at that instant he recognized the face hovering over him.

A flood tide of dread spread through him.

"Quorn," he gasped.

It was the last word he ever spoke.

CHAPTER
THIRTEEN

THE HORSES MADE their way at a brisk gallop around the curving, left-hand turn at the base of the hill. As they straightened out and began to climb the undulating turf, two of them spurted in front, their nostrils shooting sharp jets of breath into the cool morning air. Their pace quickened even more as they made their ascent toward the small group of onlookers at the hilltop. One of the horses, a superbly made colt, gradually began to put daylight between himself and the horse beside him, the latter straining his neck and head with every stride in an effort to keep abreast. The rider on the leading colt was perched motionless, the cloth beneath the saddle flapping back against his knees in the wind. About three hundred yards of the rising ground remained. The rider clicked his tongue and, in an almost imperceptible move, nudged his wrists and knees simultaneously into the horse's neck and withers. With a great surge of power the colt lengthened his stride and devoured the remaining yards to the top of the hill in a streak of speed.

Jeremy Carvill clicked the stopwatch in his hand and noted with satisfaction the distance by which Noble Lord had beaten the four-year-old Ormus; only Jeremy knew that Noble Lord's saddle cloth carried ten pounds of heavy racing lead.

He watched Stroker Roche, now standing almost upright in the stirrups as he tried to pull the colt up. This would be the last piece of serious work for Noble Lord before the Derby in five days' time. Stroker jogged the colt back to Jeremy. The animal was sweating very slightly but scarcely blowing after his exertions. Stroker jumped to the ground in a smooth, fluid motion.

"He'll do," he said to Jeremy as he handed the horse's reins to a thickset, swarthy stable lad with black curly hair and a drooping mustache who had been waiting beside the trainer.

"He's sure to get the trip, I think," said Jeremy.

He was referring to the Derby distance of one and a half miles, a distance over which Noble Lord had not yet been asked to race.

"He'll get it," said Stroker. "It's not a true mile and a half at Epsom anyway. If he comes down the hill all right he'll walk it."

The two men turned to watch the animal, which the bookmakers had made their clear favorite for the world's most famous thoroughbred horse race, being led around in a circle by the lad. The horse moved with the grace and elegance of the highborn. The ripple of satin skin over muscular limbs hinted at the potency underneath. The very depth of chest and girth was a live testimony to the inner powerhouse that drove the elegant legs faster than any other horse of his time.

"He's never looked better," said Jeremy.

As much as this horse had transformed his life and his finances, a win next Wednesday would set Jeremy Carvill up for life. By arrangement with Yaw, Jeremy had acquired five percent of the colt following his success in the Two Thousand Guineas. By any reckoning, with his pedigree and looks and his unblemished record to date, if he won the Epsom Derby,

Noble Lord's worth as a stallion would be not less than fifty million dollars. It was not difficult to work out Jeremy's share of that.

Already he had begun to get requests from the elite of the racing world to train horses for them. Two days previously, the great Portuguese shipping magnate, Antonio Batista, had phoned him from Lisbon to say that six two year olds currently being trained elsewhere in Newmarket would be arriving at Jeremy's stable yard the following morning. With owners like Batista, Jeremy could become one of the great trainers of his day—and on his own terms. Money, a commodity he had never had, was now beginning to flow in, and with the money came recognition, the hallmark of success.

Jeremy and his jockey continued to watch the colt walking a circle, on every stride rolling out the toe of his foreleg in a movement of fluent liquidity and perfection. Each hoof was placed in its turn on the green turf with all the delicate precision and deftness of a great dancer.

"All right, that will do, Zeid," said Jeremy.

The stable lad with the sullen face nodded briefly and began his walk back to the stables leading Noble Lord. Jeremy climbed into the red Porsche 928S—a recent purchase—and with Stroker beside him, the Master of Ritchbridgeton made his way back across the green rolling fields to breakfast.

Zeid walked slowly with the horse, pausing to light a cigarette only when Jeremy was out of sight. The other horses and their work riders were ahead of him, their first lot for the day completed.

He marveled, not for the first time, at Seamus O'Neill's meticulous planning, which had got him where he was. Even his name, Jean Zeid, now fitted him better than the one he had been born with. His well-worn passport showed him to be the national of a tiny Gulf state, the son of an Arab and his French wife. He wondered where Seamus was now.

It was at the meeting in Belfast that the plan had been revealed to him. Audacious, breathtaking, yet like all master strategies it was extremely simple. That he had been chosen as the instrument to carry out a mission of such devastating importance filled him with an inner peace that he had not known since childhood. He unquestioningly accepted the plan and his elite part in it.

How Seamus had managed to learn so much about English racing, he would never know. They had spent a full week together until Patsy Kelly understood everything in minute detail. Then there was the sea trip with the cattle, disembarking at nightfall in a starlit Tripoli.

He was brought straight to the desert training camp at Al Fuqaha, where for three weeks under the eye of his American instructor—a renegade CIA man—all his guerrilla fighter's instincts had been honed and improved and refined. He had particularly excelled at unarmed combat, a fact that could be confirmed by some of the PLO recruits unlucky enough to draw him for practice.

And he had been taught to ride a horse, a skill to which his short, stocky body easily and quickly adapted. Soon he was delighting his Arab instructor by the natural ease with which he controlled the most fractious stallion in the stables. He had also been instructed in the ways of animal husbandry, shown how to groom his mount, how to pull unwanted hairs from its mane and tail, to pick compacted stable straw and stones from its hooves, to feed and water it and to clean and care for the endless bridles, bits, headcollars, girths, saddles and straps that make up the everyday part of a horse's livery.

He had arrived in Jeremy Carvill's stables in mid-May, employed at the direct request of Prince al-Fahd. Not even the prince, immersed all his life in the intrigues of the Gulf, could have begun to guess at the course of action he had just set in motion as a favor to his friend Fardan.

Zeid reached the yard. Chalkie Charlesworth was waiting there, holding open the door of Noble Lord's stable.

"I hear he trounced Ormus," he said proudly.

Zeid nodded and led the horse into the stable. Chalkie's

pride in his charge was lessened by this churlish stable lad with whom he had been recently burdened. He was a robot who went about his stable tasks in total silence. Chalkie had at first put it down to homesickness. On the third morning after first lot he had gone into the tackroom where Zeid was busily applying leather oil to a bridle, his back to the door.

"Cheer up, lad, it's not that bad," Chalkie had said, giving the broad back a hearty slap.

In a whirl of action Zeid swiveled around, the calloused edge of his rigid right hand descending in an arc toward Chalkie's neck. The ex-jockey was still nimble enough on his feet. He instinctively moved inside the blow, closer to Zeid, so that the sweeping projection of the chopping arm caught him painfully on the shoulder. He fell back with a crash into a stack of tin buckets by the wall. Before he knew it Zeid was on him, one knee on his chest, both hands grasping the open collars of his work jacket with constrictive tightness.

"Jesus," gasped Chalkie as he felt the air being squeezed from his body, "I was only . . ."

The dark face was now not two inches away from his own. The black eyes in it were quite mad.

"Listen you British bastard," Zeid's voice hissed, "touch me again, and I'll kill you."

Then he shook Chalkie like a terrier and threw him back into the debris on the floor.

Of course, Chalkie had reported the whole incident to Jeremy, but to no avail. The prince wanted Zeid in the yard, probably to have an independent report about Noble Lord, and, until Derby Day, that was that. Such an arrangement was highly irregular and a source of considerable irritation to Jeremy. But until June 3 had passed, Jeremy was not going to let a minor incident distract him from the main job at hand. There was too much at stake to risk the prince's displeasure for the sake of two weeks.

Now, with five days to go, Zeid stood at Noble Lord's head as Chalkie adjusted a light stable rug on the colt's back.

"We'll show them, laddie, won't we?" crooned Chalkie as he fastened the breast strap. "That's my boy."

Zeid also looked at the magnificent horse with satisfaction but for a completely different reason. He did not care if the horse ever ran another race in his life. But it was Noble Lord that was going to give him the passport he needed to get into the parade ring for the Epsom Derby.

After the horses had been groomed and fed, the lads had a half-hour break. There was a canteen area in the yard, and it was here that they gathered for their tea and a smoke. The atmosphere was electric with excitement, reflecting the stable's enviable position less than a week before the Derby. Most of the lads had been wagering on Noble Lord's Derby prospects since the previous autumn, using their knowledge of the colt's ability at home to bet at bookmaker's odds considerably more generous than those today. The Derby favorite's impressive morning workout had notched their ebullience to a new peak.

"—He was never out of a canter."

"—Stroker never stirred on him."

"—Did you see poor old Ormus?"

"—Ormus won the Royal Hunt at Ascot by three lengths you know."

"—God, he's some horse."

"—He's gone evens in this morning's *Life!*"

"—Evens! I 'ave him at twenties!"

The swell of their excited conversation drifted up from the canteen to the stable lads' flats overhead. In one flat, the door securely bolted, Zeid sat on the side of a narrow bed, his whole being absorbed by the object laid out in front of him. With the dedication of the psychopathic killer, he was closing on his prey with meticulous care.

The Type-64 silenced pistol manufactured by the Chinese State Arsenal is unique. It seems to have only one function in life, that of assassination. Its appearance, that of a bulbous, cumbersome weapon, is caused by the integral silencer whose

172

casing surrounds the barrel and extends in front of the muzzle. It achieves almost total silence both from this arrangement and because it has been designed to fire only rimless bullets, which travel at subsonic velocity. When fired, no gases escape from the body of the gun. They are prevented from following the bullet by a number of rubber discs built into the barrel.

To Zeid, the weapon was perfection itself. Its silence, combined with its deadly accuracy, gave him a very real chance of carrying out his mission successfully and getting away in the ensuing chaos although the latter consideration was of no importance to him. He had an absolute lack of any concern for his own survival.

The gun that he now oiled was as familiar to him as his left hand. For long hours in the hot North African sun he had practiced until his unfailing accuracy had become almost monotonous. Particularly, he had perfected the left-handed snapshot carried out at walking pace, an extremely difficult piece of marksmanship at thirty yards, but one of which he was now the accomplished master.

Seamus had thought of everything.

"The horses walk around the parade ring in a clockwise direction," he had explained, using a pencil and paper to illustrate. They were sitting in a deserted cottage, high in the Antrim hills.

"The owners and trainers of the horses stand in the center, the lads leading the horses walk on the left side of the horse's head, leading with their right hand so that the horse's head and body is between them and the people in the center."

He had drawn it out precisely for Zeid to see.

"Therefore you must shoot under the horse's neck, a shot that has to be taken left-handed."

Zeid now understood perfectly that to shoot right-handed would mean a radical change in movement that would not only attract attention but would risk exciting the highly bred racehorse and spoil his chances of a direct hit.

"Your only danger," Seamus explained, "is being seen by

the spectators who will be on your left. You will have to drape a cloth or something like it over your arm, and that of course will make the shot all the more difficult."

Grueling days of practice in the Libyan camp had seen that Zeid was just as accurate firing from within the shelter of a blanket folded on his arm.

There had been no question of risking the gun on his trip from Libya to Newmarket. Instead, a week after his arrival to work in Jeremy Carvill's yard, Zeid had gone to London on a day off. There, in the seclusion of a pub toilet in Shepherd Market a small, wrapped package had been passed to him by a man who left without uttering a word.

The Chinese murder gun, fresh from its journey in the diplomatic bag, had arrived in England.

THE SOUND OF the lads' voices told Zeid that the work break was over. He wrapped the pistol back in its oiled paper, and then in a dark cloth. Prying up a floorboard under the bed, he returned the gun to its hiding place. Then he skipped downstairs, bouncing lightly on the balls of his feet, to continue with his chores for the morning.

CHAPTER
FOURTEEN

ONCE THE LONDON residence of Lord Palmerston, the Naval and Military Club in Piccadilly offers a splendid oasis to its members from the bustling West End life that trundles ceaselessly past its high, wrought-iron gates. The Club is set back from the street outside, separated from Piccadilly by its own courtyard. The lofted ceilings of its halls and the elegant lengths of its portrait-hung corridors lead to an enclosed paved garden, where goldfish as big as mackerel splash in their pool, oblivious to the busy pace of life one hundred yards away.

On the first Monday in June, which was also the first day of the month, two men in their mid-fifties sipped comfortable snifters of vintage brandy, savoring its taste in the early afternoon heat. They were seated on two iron garden seats—supplemented by ample cushions—and appeared in no hurry to move.

"First-class lunch, Charles, first-class," said the shorter of the two, a man with clear blue eyes and the generous complexion of a Norfolk farmer. Jim Abbott had been a policeman all his life. His jovial features belied the razor-sharp brain that had guaranteed his successive promotions to his present position: Assistant Commissioner of "C" Department (AC "C" for short) in London's Metropolitan Police—in other words, the head of the CID. Under his direct command came all criminal investigations, the Special Branch, liaison with Interpol, the Anti-terrorist Branch (known as C.13) and the Royalty and Diplomatic Protection Department.

The man whom he addressed was his opposite as far as personal features went. Sir Charles Lowther was a very tall man—over six foot three inches—and built like a reed. He looked sparse and ascetic. His position in the misty upper echelons of the Foreign Office produced occasional items of joint interest on security that led Abbott and himself to meet.

Their lunchtime chat had been a very general one, requested that morning by Lowther. Abbott had to get back to the Yard. He felt it was time to provoke the Foreign Office man to show his hand. After all, a lunch was no more free in their business than any other.

"Really first-class," said Abbott again.

"The old 'In and Out' isn't at all bad, is it?" asked Lowther, giving the Club its famous nickname. "I rather enjoyed my fish."

As if to support his remark a large goldfish with white streaks on its body jumped salmonlike in the small pool. Lowther took a sip from his brandy.

"Anything from Ireland?" he asked casually.

Here we go, thought Abbott. He considered the question for a moment.

"Nothing too unusual," he eventually replied. "No increase in movements, for example."

Lowther's hooded eyes were expressionless.

"Hmm," he said.

"Why, should there be?"

"I'm not sure," replied Lowther.

Abbott scratched his head. He began to analyze the situation vis-à-vis Ireland, as up-to-date as when he had left his office at 12:15 that day.

176

"Well it's essentially either the IRA or the INLA," he said. "It's the wrong time of the year for the IRA to try anything. As you know, they're Christmas shopping specialists. The bomb in Harrods is an example. And we generally know when they're on the move. Different thing to try and stop them, of course, but we do know when they're about. And at the moment we think they're not." He paused to raise the deep amber brandy to his lips. Lowther was absorbing his every word.

"Now the INLA are another matter," Abbott continued, "more extreme, no warnings given, much more to the left. However two things mitigate, in my view, against their affecting anything in my sphere of operations—which is essentially London—and they are, one, they haven't tried anything here since they murdered Airey Neave, and two, they were caught red-handed, over a week ago, trying to bring an extremely large arms consignment in through Donegal. I should think that both cash and morale are pretty low after that adventure. So I'm ruling out anything from them just for the time being."

He finished his drink in a gulp. He was satisfied that his summary of the situation reflected all the information known to the Metropolitan Police. "But obviously there's more," he concluded, giving Lowther a wary look.

Lowther recrossed his long legs. "Just a few straws in the wind," he said distantly. He was used to dispensing information in tiny drops, watching it spread out slowly in the intended direction eventually to accomplish the objective, his hand long forgotten. Abbott waited. He knew the rules by which the man played.

"One of our Caribbean chaps," Lowther continued, almost to himself, "got wind of something local there about ten days ago. Wild sort of thing. Seemed a bit unlikely at the time so no one paid much attention. However, part of it was about a possible gunrun into Ireland so we passed it on. They had some ideas of their own over there anyway, but our chap turned out to be right on the button. As you say, they nabbed the lot of them, almost the same day."

Abbott nodded.

Lowther went on: "Naturally we had a second look at our man's report, since another part of it—a sort of footnote—involved mention of a rather explicit threat to one of our VIPs"

Abbott raised his eyebrows.

"Yes," said Lowther, "very odd, I agree." There was a pause.

"When you say 'something local' . . . ?"

Lowther pursed his lips. "Let's just say that what we have is a copy of a private interdepartmental report in the government of a, ah, former colony," he said precisely.

"And VIP?" asked Abbott.

"Nothing more, just that," replied Lowther.

"Government, royalty, business, could he not say?"

Lowther rubbed his ear. "His impression was somebody close to the top, perhaps in the royal family," he said.

The two men sat in silence for a moment. The sun had gone behind one of the Naval and Military's high chimneys, throwing a brief shadow on the meeting below.

"Very tedious," Lowther sighed. "The information about the gunrun was far too correct. Makes the stock of the whole thing rise, rather, don't you think?"

A bloody bull market if I'm not mistaken, thought Abbott. What the hell have I got now? He wondered. Lowther had uncrossed his storklike legs and was examining his wrist watch.

"Well, I'm afraid I've got to get back," he said, rising to his feet.

The two men made their way up the steps and past the reading room, where several old naval or military gentlemen were snoring soundly from the depths of large leather armchairs. They walked down a long, silent corridor toward the front hall. Lowther stopped suddenly as if something had just occurred to him.

"Did you get involved in the Tristram Hoare thing last week?" he asked.

Abbott was familiar with the details, but the question surprised him.

"Not personally. Bloody messy from what I've heard," he said.

Lowther's hands were behind his back and he spoke in the manner of someone recalling a long-distance memory.

"I could never really tolerate Tristram Hoare," he said. "Peculiar bird by all accounts. We were in the same house at Eton. Ah well."

He unclasped his hands and they made their way through the hall and out onto Piccadilly. As he walked into Green Park, Abbott could see Lowther making his way up Piccadilly, his tall head bobbing, until he was lost in the shadowy portals of the Ritz.

Ten minutes later in his office in New Scotland Yard, Abbott brushed aside his secretary's attempts to give him his messages and walked straight to a large bookcase behind the desk. There he took down a weighty *Who's Who* and turned the pages rapidly until he reached the entry he wanted. He read quickly, nodding his head as he did so, in confirmation of what he had suspected.

The entry gave its subject's secondary education quite clearly: Harrow 1937-42. The name at the head of the section was also clear: it was Sir Charles Radcliff Lowther.

CHAPTER
FIFTEEN

THE AC "C" took off his glasses and rubbed his eyes with his knuckles. It was five o'clock on Monday afternoon, and the streets, sixteen floors below Abbott's office, were busy with rush-hour traffic. Abbott's desk was littered with papers, and four other men sat at the long table that stretched out in front of it. To Abbott's left was David Marriot, one of Abbott's two Deputy Assistant Commissioners (DACs). Beside Marriot was Commander John Wallace, head of the Special Branch, who had been promoted to the position when Abbott was made an Assistant Commissioner. On Abbott's right sat Ted Lamont, whose title was Commander (Protection) of the recently formed Royalty and Diplomatic Protection Department, a selection that Abbott had made personally. A section of this department deals solely with the protection of the immediate royal family and is known as the RPG. To Lamont's right sat the totally bald and fit figure of Sandy McKechnie, the Commander of the Anti-terrorist Branch which is also known as C.13.

"So there you have it," said Abbott, "a twofold rumor from the Caribbean, part one of which has been deadly accurate.

We have got to, by any yardstick, take part two as being equally serious."

"Can't we learn any more information from our informant out there?" asked Marriot. "I mean, what has the Caribbean got to do with it? How do they get involved in the first place?"

Abbott shook his head.

"If the FO wanted us to know any more they would have told us," he said. "It is possible they just do not know any more themselves. One way or the other we are stuck with what we have."

Lamont leaned forward. The head of the RPG was in his mid-forties, a no-nonsense policeman who had shown a flair for organization early in his career, which had led to his present appointment. His special responsibility was for the security of the royal palaces; now he spoke in a calm, assured voice.

"If you don't mind, sir," he said, "in view of what I have heard, I would like to make a quick telephone call."

Abbott nodded and Lamont left the room. The assistant commissioner was in no doubt that leave was just about to be canceled for all RPG officers and that royalty protection would be quietly doubled within the hour.

He looked to Wallace.

"What do you think, John?" he asked.

Wallace leaned back in his chair. He was a very tall man with thinning gray hair and a sharp face. His rise in the Special Branch had been along the traditional lines, from sergeant, through inspector, chief inspector, and chief superintendent to the position he now held. Wallace was a very hard worker and a first-class CID man.

"As you already know, sir," he said, "the Irish problem—and I assume we are all agreed that this is what we have here—well, the Irish problem has been going our way for the last few months. Very little activity to report on this side. The Donegal business, whilst we were not directly involved, was very welcome news and a bit of a feather in the cap for the Irish government, courtesy of the CIA, I would say at a guess."

Abbott listened intently as his Special Branch head spoke. A very large part of Commander Wallace's time was spent trying to keep one step ahead of the IRA in Great Britain. The "Irish" heritage of the Special Branch, going back nearly one hundred years, had basically not changed all that much. To the Special Branch fell the onerous job—without the benefit of passport control—of trying to keep England safe from an influx of IRA bombers.

"From what I have heard, I propose, effective now," said Wallace, "to put all our people at points of entry on immediate special alert and to double surveillance at those points. The trouble there is that we do not really know what we are looking for. I will get on to Northern Ireland and talk to the RUC and British Army Intelligence and see if they know anything, if there has been any unusual movement, if anyone is missing who should not be, and so on. I will also give the Special Branch in Dublin a call and see if any of the blokes they picked up in Donegal had anything worthwhile to say although, in fairness, if there had been something, I think Dublin would have let us know."

The door opened and Lamont came back in.

"John is just going over his side of it," said Abbott. Lamont nodded and sat down.

"I shall get the word out this evening," continued Wallace, "to our fellows on the ground here in London to do a head count of all our Irish friends. We will see if anything unusual is going on. We will get Liverpool, Birmingham, and Manchester involved as well. At least when we are finished they will know somebody's taking a special interest in them."

"Good," said Abbott. "Now, what about Hoare?"

At the beginning of the meeting Abbott had explained Sir Charles Lowther's clear trail marking at lunchtime.

"I shall assign somebody full-time to the Hoare case straight away, sir," said Wallace. "Hopefully something will come out of it that might bring us a little nearer to finding out what's going on."

"Good," said Abbott. He turned to Lamont.

"Ted, could we have your views?"

"Thank you, sir," said Lamont. "As you might imagine, I have stepped up current protection, specifically for the Queen and immediate royal family. I have a full list of their engagements for the coming week, and after this meeting I shall go over it with Commander McKechnie to agree on a maximum protection approach."

Sandy McKechnie, the tough head of C.13, nodded.

"We are also going to review all our normal protection procedures in the light of this fairly specific threat and see how we think they measure up," Lamont went on. "As a precaution I have canceled all leave, and I am assigning extra protection to members of the government and the obvious diplomatic people."

"Thank you, Ted," said Abbott. "Sandy . . . ?"

McKechnie hunched forward characteristically. He had come to the police via the Royal Engineers Commando Unit. He had under his command an elite squad of tough anti-terrorist officers who were highly trained in the storming of hijacked aircraft, bomb disposal, and the rescue of hostages from embassies under siege. McKechnie was an uncompromising leader who exacted very high standards from his men. His personal courage under fire was the stuff legends are made from.

"I'll go over the program with Ted, sir, and we will come up with the best possible way to approach each situation," he said. "I will alert all my people that they may be needed. As we are dealing with a possible Irish terrorist threat I think it's reasonable to assume that we should give a high priority to explosives. I shall be working with that as a first assumption."

There was a murmur of assent from the men around the table. Abbott stood up.

"Thank you, gentlemen," he said. "We have all got quite a lot to do. We shall meet early tomorrow, time to be decided."

The four men picked up their papers. Abbott put on his jacket and made his way to the door with them. He had a meeting in five minutes with the Commissioner of the Metropolitan Police. It would be up to the boss to alert quietly the right person at the Palace that there was something on. With a bit of luck the Queen might be persuaded to curtail her schedule until this thing was out of the way. But as he entered the elevator, Abbott knew in his heart that such a development was most unlikely. Royalty would always refuse to be frightened into hiding.

COMMANDER WALLACE WALKED into his office. A youngish officer in plain clothes was waiting outside. He had a round, alert face and was going bald.

"Come in, Chief Inspector," said Wallace.

Chief Inspector John Dawson followed his commander into the office. Wallace had picked a good man in Dawson. Tough, shrewd, an intuitive investigator, he reminded the commander of the ambitious sort of young policeman he himself had been twenty years ago. Dawson looked like a man who played a lot of squash. He was well regarded in Special Branch and was an authorized shot, which meant that he could carry a Smith and Wesson .38.

Wallace outlined in detail to Dawson what had been discussed at the meeting with the assistant commissioner.

"I want to get the Hoare business clarified and out of the way without delay," said Wallace. "The fact that his murder has been mentioned in the same breath as the gunrunning is worrying. I know nothing about the man except that he was part of our establishment, a knight of the realm, an underwriter at Lloyds, an ex-steward of the Jockey Club, and so on. If these sort of chaps are now trying to knock off royalty, this country will look like Uganda before long."

"Very well, sir," said Dawson.

"I want to know everything there is to know about him," Wallace went on. "Bank accounts, investments, women, whether he took one spoon or two, the lot—and I want it before tomorrow morning."

"Right, sir," said Dawson. "As it's quite late, we are going to have some searching to find the people who know anything. I would like to bring in Inspector Henderson and Inspector Brabbs."

"Perhaps just as well not to go into too much detail with them at this point," said Wallace. "The fewer people who know about the royalty threat, the better. We do not want the media in on this."

"Understood, sir," said Dawson.

Wallace nodded and, as Dawson left, picked up one of the telephones on his desk. Within thirty minutes people arriving from the Irish Republic at U.K. air and sea ports would start experiencing increased delays as random requests by Special Branch men for personal identification was increased three-fold. Passengers on flights from Dublin to London would be requested, in mid-air, to complete special pink landing cards. Customs officials at all points of entry would be taking a special interest in luggage from Ireland.

Wallace asked the switchboard to put him through to a number in Belfast. As the call was connected, both he and the man on the other end pressed the switch on their automatic scrambling devices.

TEN MINUTES LATER Chief Inspector Dawson sat in his own office with Inspectors Henderson and Brabbs. Dawson outlined the sudden interest in Hoare, briefly stating the gunrunning connection. Brabbs had headed the initial inquiry into the Hoare case.

"Whoever set out to get him made bloody sure they did," said Brabbs. He was young for an inspector, in his late twenties, wore trendy clothes, and drove a sports car. He had an excellent record, particularly on narcotics.

"The poor bugger might just have pulled through the knife attack after falling five storys into Hyde Park, but they got him in the hospital."

"Was there no question of police protection?" asked Dawson.

186

"At that point we thought it was a rather exotic burglary," replied Brabbs. "The wounds were pretty unusual—done by a stiletto, according to our pathologist."

Dawson said nothing. At each step the smell from the case became worse.

"Do we know anything about Hoare's financial affairs?" he asked.

"Very little at this point, sir," replied Brabbs.

"What about his wife?"

"She was taken away under heavy sedation the day it happened. She is staying at her sister's house in Shropshire at the moment. I am due to go down there on Wednesday to question her."

"Do we not have bank statements, correspondence from stockbrokers, and so on?" asked Dawson.

"The flat was clean as a whistle, sir," said Brabbs. "After the hospital business, when we upgraded the case, I went through all the personal effects. I found nothing."

Dawson bit his lip. They were going to have to start at the beginning.

"Mervyn," he said to Brabbs, "you are going to talk to Lady Hoare today, now. Get on to our boys in Shropshire, and make sure she is at home. I want to know everything."

"Right away, sir," said Brabbs. This is bigger than the boss is letting on, he thought.

Dawson turned to Henderson.

"I want to find out everything there is about this man's finances. The information is out there. Get on to our contacts in the main clearing banks. Go right to the top if you have to. Hoare is sure to have had an account with one of them. Get his statements, returned checks, share certificates. Find out who his stockbroker was. I don't care if you keep the City of London up all night. We must know."

Inspector Brabbs was about to leave.

"What about Hoare's apartment?" Dawson asked him. "Have we got a key?"

"Yes, sir," said Brabbs. "Forensic have been all over the

place but came up with nothing. I will have the key sent up to you."

"Very good," said Dawson. "I want to know how you got on the minute you get back here."

Brabbs left the office, and Dawson began to read the official report of Sir Tristram Hoare's death the previous Thursday. The knife wounds were coldly listed—a one-inch-deep gash into the lower left arm five inches above the wrist, a stab wound one and a half inches deep in the right upper chest between the breast bone and shoulder. A stab wound, at least five and a half inches deep, in the center of the abdomen leading to immediate, massive hemorrhaging. There was a diagram of the apartment and some photographs showing the window through which Hoare had fallen. Then there was a further report detailing the romp through Gower Street Hospital that had finally put paid to Hoare's slim chance of survival.

Dawson made notes as he read through the file. He turned to a file of freshly compiled press clippings. They began with reports of the incident at the apartment, went on to Hoare's death in Gower Street, and then ended with a brief description of the funeral three days later. The general impression was that Hoare had come home after lunch, an assassin was waiting, and there had been a fight that ended with Hoare's ejection through his own picture window.

Whoever was out to get him had not given up easily, judging by what had happened in Gower Street Hospital. There was press speculation that hinted at a possible MI5 connection. The story had fizzled out by Saturday.

Dawson scratched his chin. Why would anyone want to murder Sir Tristram Hoare? Dawsons briefing by Commander Wallace pointed to a clear connection with the INLA.

He switched off his desk light, left the building, and drove the short distance to Hyde Park in fifteen minutes. The doorman made no attempt to challenge him as he walked into the apartment building and took the elevator to the fifth floor.

A good job of cleaning had been done, but there were still signs of the life-and-death struggle that had taken place. Large dark stains showed on the rugs, particularly around the window. Minute particles of glass twinkled near the baseboards, reflecting the overhead lights. And there was the unmistakable smell that is left by dried blood.

Dawson began a meticulous search. He firstly concentrated on the obvious, beginning with a large oak desk in the master bedroom. It was cluttered with bills and correspondence between Lady Hoare and the various charities and clubs she obviously supported. There were renewal subscriptions for Lady Hoare's magazines, her bank statements, which appeared fairly ordinary, her check book, postcards from her friends on holiday. Dawson moved on to the closets, first Tristram Hoare's. He frisked each suit in turn, exploring all the pockets, searching for any scrap of paper that might be left behind. There was nothing. He examined Lady Hoare's clothes in the same way with no results. Then he turned his attention to the bedside furniture, the light fixtures, and the bed itself, removing the mattress completely and probing the base of the bed for a hidden compartment. When this yielded nothing he moved on to the bathroom and then the kitchen. Zero.

He went to the hall and carefully removed each picture from its place on the wall, probing behind it for a concealed switch or hinge. He had been searching for over an hour now. He went back to the kitchen and filled the electric kettle, which he switched on. The dead man had been very careful. The apartment was clean, unnaturally clean. Brabbs was right. A visitor from outer space would find it very hard to know what Sir Tristram Hoare had done for a living; his clothes in the bedroom and his razor in the bathroom were the only evidence of his existence.

Dawson poured himself some black coffee—there was some expensive brew in a jar from Harrods beside the kettle—and tried to think of his next move. On a bookself beside him was a row of cookbooks, which he had already flicked through. Sitting on top of the books was an expensive camera in a leather case. He had already opened the case and checked the camera; it was empty. Beside the camera was a squat yellow box of 35 mm Kodak color film. He had opened it on his first visit to the kitchen. It contained a small plastic tub with new film inside. Dawson drank some coffee, savoring the taste as it slid down his throat. A small signal had been activated in his memory. He frowned and putting down his coffee, reached again for the Kodak box. The first time he had examined the box he had to break a paper seal on its top. Now he opened it again and removing the plastic tub flicked off the top to reveal the film inside, which he emptied on to his hand. He stared at it for a moment. The small cartridge lay there harmlessly. Then it dawned on him. The film cartridge had no tail, no piece of celluloid to connect to the ratchet teeth of the camera for loading. This was a used film in a new box. Unless it was special film for a new type of camera. He grabbed the Leica and opened its back. The mechanism for loading film was exactly as he thought, small, black notches protruding from a wheel.

Without bothering to finish his coffee, Dawson hurriedly shoved the film into his pocket and drove at speed to the Metropolitan Police forensic lab in Lambeth.

"HERE ARE YOUR pictures, Chief Inspector."

They were standing in the center of a room in the Forensic Science building. A friendly technician handed Dawson the prints, over a hundred in all. They were of pages of encoded lists and numbers, sheet after sheet of figures that would mean something only to their author, and further pages giving lists of guns followed by serial numbers. Ten prints were pictures of rifles, grenades, and boxes of ammunition laid out in neat rows. Two showed an arrestingly beautiful half-caste girl lying naked in a suggestive pose.

"Have you identified the guns, Chris?" asked Dawson.

"Yes, sir. Colt Armalites, most of them—nearly five hundred—a couple of hundred FN Snipers. Dozens of Heckler and Koch HK81s, a whole row of Kalashnikovs—nearly fifty —and then there's a ragbag of bits and pieces including pistols, rocket launchers, and mines. It's a very large consignment by any standards. There's also a lot of nasty ammunition, explosive bullets, KTW metal-piercing, French metal-piercing spire points and so on. To round it off there's sixty boxes of grenades and an assortment of pistols. Worth a fortune, the whole thing."

"Did you have a list made out?" asked Dawson.

"Yes, sir," said the technician, handing Dawson a sheet of paper. Within ten minutes the contents of the list would be in Dublin Castle.

"What are all these about?" asked Dawson, pointing to the pages of numbers.

"No idea, sir. We haven't managed to crack them yet."

"And who the hell is *she*?"

"Don't know, sir, but I wouldn't mind finding out," said the technician with a smile.

"Bloody lovely," said Dawson, shaking his head.

"What I can tell you is that this photograph was probably taken in New York."

"How do you know that?" asked Dawson.

"We magnified the shots twenty times greater," the technician replied. "In the corner of this one here," he pointed to a grayish smudge in the photograph, "we found this." He produced a very blurred blow-up that revealed part of a black letter on a white background. "My money says that's *The New York Times*," he said.

"Let's follow it up and see if you're right, Chris," said Dawson. "Can you get that photo off to New York right away? I'll ring them in thirty minutes and see if they have been able to dig up anything on her. Meanwhile I'll try and sort out those guns with Dublin."

He walked to the door.

"Thanks a lot," he said, "good work," and hurried to the elevator.

ELSEWHERE IN LONDON additional policemen from the RPG were unobtrusively strengthening their protection at locations where members of the royal family were in residence. Those officers protecting the homes of cabinet ministers and key diplomats to the Court of St. James were advised to be on special alert. Before midnight there was scarcely a member of the Metropolitan Police who did not know that something was going on.

Teams of men from C.13 with sniffer dogs and electronic detection devices began to double-check buildings that would be used by royalty over the next forty-eight hours. Extra guards were put on these locations and emergency ID passes issued to those using them.

And in Greater London, in the traditional Irish working-class areas, men who had been looking forward to a quiet Monday evening, found themselves being questioned in their front rooms by some of their old friends from the Special Branch.

The largest ever peacetime security operation to be mounted in England was lumbering into gear.

CHAPTER
SIXTEEN

THE STABLE OF a racehorse trainer before a big race is a place of notorious tension. Large fortunes and lifetime reputations hang in the balance. Before the Epsom Derby the weight of apprehension—particularly if the hot favorite for the race is in your care—is almost unbearable.

With two days to go, Jeremy Carvill had given up the idea of sleeping. Despite the fact that he had employed a top-notch security firm to patrol the stable yard twenty-four hours a day, one fully armed man at all times outside Noble Lord's stable, Jeremy himself spent most of the night near the horse.

There had been a few letters from cranks, threatening Jeremy, the colt, and the owner, but these were to be expected in the light of the huge publicity that now surrounded them all. The police had been told of the threats; they advised the precaution of the security guards. A famous horse might be mutilated in its stable by someone with a grudge whose mind has finally been tipped by the media attention. In Ireland a horse worth ten million dollars had disappeared one night without trace.

Jeremy had never experienced anything like the buildup that was going on. His photograph was featured every day in at least two national dailies. In the last week he had brought horses to compete at smaller tracks, Haydock and York, and at both places had given interviews on live nationwide TV. He had also been besieged by reporters, all looking for a special angle, or for further confirmation of the confidence Jeremy had in Noble Lord.

Jeremy had taken to supervising the colt's feeding times personally. Four times a day, beginning at 5:00 A.M., he got a full bucket of gleaming Canadian oats, which had been bruised under the wheels of a roller in Jeremy's feed room to make them digestible. To these were added and mixed light bran, the very husk of the wheat, a cupful of vitamin additive, soybean meal and a spoon of linseed oil—the latter for Noble Lord's coat. Jeremy personally examined the hay that had been isolated for the champion—the very best of first crop, purchased the summer before—and saw to it that the colt's bedding was deep and luxurious, built up from the floor of the stable to the sides at a gentle angle to prevent the great horse becoming cast against the wall if he decided to take a roll. A slip, the slightest oversight or carelessness in any of these areas could cost Jeremy—and his children and grandchildren— their seed corn.

It was 3:00 A.M. as Jeremy walked into the yard for the second time that night. It was June 2, and the night smelled of summer. The brightly lighted perimeter showed two patrolling guards. Each had a long truncheon and carried a flashlight. The area around the stables was illuminated in a more subdued way so as not to disturb the horses.

Jeremy saw the guard outside Noble Lord's box get up to stretch his legs.

"Everything all right?" he asked.

"Yes, sir, everything's fine," replied the guard. "He's munching away in there."

Jeremy smiled. Horses require very little sleep but a good

194

deal of rest. If Noble Lord was relaxed, then all was well. He decided not to look in on the horse but to leave him be. He turned to go back to the house. He almost fell over the figure standing directly behind him.

"'Night, guv." Chalkie Charlesworth's monkeylike face was grinning brightly as Jeremy wheeled around.

"Christ, you frightened me," he said.

"Sorry, guv, I just couldn't sleep either."

"Come on, let's get a cuppa," said Jeremy, and they walked toward the kitchen of the main house.

It had been quite a few weeks since Jeremy had had the opportunity to sit down alone with Chalkie, and now he was glad of this moment together. He could easily forget how much the whole operation depended on the skill and loyalty of this tiny, wizened man. They had come through thick and thin, Chalkie sticking with him when the prospects were appalling. If they pulled off the Derby on Wednesday, Jeremy intended to see that Chalkie would never want again. Chalkie, who normally lived with his wife and family about five miles from Jeremy's yard, had moved in ten days ago and was now sleeping in a box next to Noble Lord.

Jeremy poured two mugs of tea from an enamel pot and sat down at the kitchen table.

"Nerve-racking time," said Chalkie.

"I've never known the like of it," said Jeremy. "I spend half my time giving interviews to bloody reporters. Still, I shall be very surprised if he's not in the first three on Wednesday. He has to be."

Chalkie nodded his agreement. The two men knew the horse in their care better than anyone. Now they began to re-analyze Noble Lord's entire racing career to date, race by race, all the gallops he had done in preparation, the horse's habits, likes, and dislikes, the minutiae that are of such interest and fascination to people who are utterly absorbed in their work.

"Stroker will settle him down early on," said Jeremy. "If he doesn't meet with a mishap coming down the hill, we'll be in business."

"There's a lot of talk about this French horse," said Chalkie. "He's a nippy bugger—and he's won over a mile and a half, which is more than we have."

"Oh to hell, I'm not afraid of him," said Jeremy. "I saw him in Longchamps as a two year old—he's not half the horse our fellow is."

Jeremy took a swig of tea. "I'll tell you what I'm afraid of and that's the Irish horse," he said.

"Southern Cross? We had his measure at Newmarket."

"Yes, but over a mile and a half at Epsom, things might be different. You can never rule Reilly out."

"What about Pentle Bay?" asked Chalkie.

Jeremy shook his head. "He won't get the trip. I'd be keeping my eye on Pavarotti before him. He won his trial at Sandown very convincingly. But," he took a deep breath, "our fellow's the one they've all got to beat."

"He's as happy as a lamb out there," said Chalkie.

"What'll you run him in if he wins on Wednesday?"

"Don't even think of such a possibility," said Jeremy. Like many racing men there was a vein of superstition deep inside him.

"Sorry, boss," said Chalkie. "When is the prince showing up?" he asked, changing the subject.

"I've got to go up and meet him in London tomorrow."

"He must be over the moon," said the head lad.

Over anything he can lay his hands on, thought Jeremy. "Yes, he's very happy," he replied. He had spoken to Yaw the previous evening by telephone. The Arab was in Rome and planned to arrive at London's Ritz on Tuesday. Jeremy made a pledge to himself that if he won the Derby, he would be his own man from then on.

"There's just one thing," said Chalkie. Jeremy looked up from the form book that he had been reading.

"I know we've been through it before," said Chalkie, "but do I have to have Zeid on the box down to Epsom? Honestly, boss, the bastard really gives me the creeps."

Jeremy sighed. He could see Chalkie's point, but nonetheless, his instructions from the prince had been precise. He could not risk upsetting his owner at this stage. Zeid was now a fully accredited employee of the yard. His papers had come back from Racecourse Security Services a week ago.

"Sorry, Chalkie, but just this once he has to travel," said Jeremy. "Between you and me, these Arabs are bloody odd buggers. They trust no one. I'm pretty sure Zeid is reporting straight back to HQ on every move we make. But I promise you one thing. After Wednesday, win or lose, we are going to stand up and be heard. You're the head lad, and if you say he goes then out he goes, Thursday morning if you like. That's a promise."

Chalkie smiled grimly.

"If you say so," he said. "I've just got a rotten feeling about him. Call it intuition if you like. For one thing, I'm not even sure if he is a bleeding Arab. Have you noticed how pale he's become since he came here? And another thing, you call him, and half the time he doesn't hear. It's as if he's not used to the name 'Zeid.'"

"Oh, maybe the little bastard is deaf," said Jeremy.

"He's not deaf. He might have a screw loose, but he's not deaf."

Jeremy got up and stretched.

"Let's not make trouble, Chalkie," he said. "We've all got our problems. Now, what time will you leave?"

"Straight after breakfast," said Chalkie. "I'll stay with the horse in the back, and Zeid, or whoever he is, will travel up front. Tommy Wilson will drive. He can come back to Ritchbridgeton tonight. We'll give the horse a gentle walk when we arrive. Stroker said he'll come out and say hello."

"O.K.," said Jeremy. "You've got feed and tack organized?"

"No, I never thought of that," said Chalkie.

They both laughed and walked to the door. The tall trainer put his arm around Chalkie's diminutive shoulder.

"I'll see you all right, Chalkie," said Jeremy. "Wednesday will be our day."

"Wednesday's tomorrow," said Chalkie.

"Christ, so it is," said Jeremy.

It was 4:00 A.M. on Tuesday, June 2. It would be dawn in thirty minutes.

CHAPTER
SEVENTEEN

TO THE NORTH of Belfast, past Carrickfergus in northeast Ireland, sits the sleepy, comfortable town of Larne. Its principal feature is that to and from its port every day travel the ferries from the Firth of Clyde, and from Stanraer on the Scottish peninsula of The Rhins, whose southern tip juts down into the North Irish Sea and is known as the Mull of Galloway.

Larne is less than thirty-five miles from Stranraer as the crow flies, and traffic between the two ports, originating and ending within the United Kingdom, attracts no Customs or Immigration attention and minimal police surveillance.

On this Tuesday morning, the 2nd of June, a couple of extra policemen in Stranraer scanned the faces of the few dozen passengers who alighted from the ferry after its one-hour crossing. They paid little attention to the couple who walked confidently off the boat, chatting easily together, the man dark-haired with a mustache, a tan raincoat over his arm, the woman's pleated skirt showing her legs to advantage, her red hair glistening in the warm afternoon. The man carried a leather suitcase, the woman a smaller bag on a shoulder strap. They left the port terminal and made their way to a bus that was standing in the parking lot outside. The inside of the bus was hot. People were in their shirt sleeves, conversing good-humoredly. Summer had arrived at last.

The bus started up for its two-hour journey. It skirted Luce Bay and the town of Glenluce before crossing the moors to Newton Stewart. Then it turned a sharp right, making its way through the villages of Creetown, Gatehouse of Fleet, and Ringford before crossing the River Dee and entering Castle Douglas. The passengers in the bus observed the pleasant Scottish scenery, the rivers and bays, the occasional castle. The day was perfect for such a tour. They continued over the Urr Water into Crocketford and eventually down into the city of Dumfries. There the couple disembarked and walked the short distance to the railway station. They purchased one-way tickets and boarded the train standing at platform four. Thirty minutes later the train pulled out of Dumfries. It descended through the village of Annan, along the side of the Solway Firth with its breathtaking views. It stopped briefly at Gretna Green, and the dark-haired man allowed himself a grim smile. He was in England. Nothing could stop them now.

They settled back for the long journey south. They would pass through Carlisle and Penrith, Lancaster and Preston, through England's industrial heartland of Manchester and Nottingham, ever southward, each telegraph pole that flicked by like the teeth of a rake bringing them closer and closer. The man slept intermittently. Twice the red-haired woman went to the sandwich bar and returned with refreshments. She said nothing. If he wanted to talk he would. She crossed her legs and watched his face in repose; to her it was the face that represented everything: handsome, courageous, and soon legendary. His eyes flicked open and caught her. She felt herself glow as she looked away, out of the speeding window. Her hand strayed to his suitcase, laid on the seat beside her, where the faithful SIG-Sauer sat upright in a false compartment incorporated into the back of the binoculars case.

Colonel O'Neill of the Irish Liberation Army and his assistant were on their way to the Derby.

CHAPTER
EIGHTEEN

SERGEANT HOPE COULD not prevent his hand from trembling as he read the letter for the tenth time. It was a directive, effective immediately, transferring him to the island of Redonda. He was to leave by police boat; his replacement in the Dockyard was already on the way.

Since the arrival of the letter, Hope had tried continuously to speak to Commissioner Richardson but in all his efforts he had been unsuccessful. For it was not the unexpected transfer that distressed Hope—part of the job was to expect transfer without notice, and in this case it carried promotion to the rank of captain and an increased salary even though the location was thankless—it was the story in the morning newspaper, now lying open on his desk, that had caused Hope to try so desperately to contact the only other man in Antigua who shared his secret.

Sir Tristram Hoare, a prominent Englishman and a visitor to Antigua only two months previously, the paper said, had been savagely knifed and thrown from the window of his London flat by intruders. He had died shortly afterward in hospital. There was no suggested motive.

At his last meeting with the commissioner five days ago, Hope had handed over his fresh report, but since then he had heard absolutely nothing.

The old man had been clear: when they needed Sergeant Hope in London, he would be in immediate contact. But still Hope had heard nothing, and now, in the light of the Hoare story in front of him, the other appalling information in the newspaper was its date—it was June 2. Hope recalled once again the calendar that had been at the bottom of the file in Hoare's New York suite. There had been a bold, red circle around one date: it had been June 3.

Now Hope could not be totally sure whether or not he had emphasized the importance of the date in his last report of which he had, per instructions, kept no copy. It was of paramount urgency. What other possible significance could June 3 have, except the one to which everything now pointed? With the attempted arms importation to Ireland thwarted on May 27, there remained only one terrible possibility.

Had Scotland Yard contacted Hoare before his death? And if so had they managed to get to the bottom of the awful secret that had so haunted the dead man? The only person who could answer these questions was Commissioner Richardson.

Hope considered telephoning England direct—but Richardson had been adamant: Hope should speak to no one else about the matter.

And even if Hope did call Scotland Yard, a huge institution, who would he speak to? Hope made up his mind. Richardson had to be contacted. He reached again for the telephone, a feeling of impotence and fear spreading through him as the words of Sir Tristram Hoare—himself now murdered—came to him: "The bastards are going to kill the Queen."

"Police Headquarters," said the familiar voice of the telephonist.

"Sergeant Hope in Dockyard's again for the commissioner," he said.

"Sorry, Sergeant Hope. Commissioner Richardson has gone to a conference in Government Buildings."

"But did you not give him my message?" asked Hope. "I told you it was vitally important."

"I'm sorry," said the girl, "do you want me to give him the message again in the morning?"

"The *morning?*" Hope almost crushed the plastic receiver with his fist. "Look, where can he be reached in Government Buildings? Please, it's of the most extreme urgency."

"I'm sorry but that is classified information."

"This is an emergency!"

The telephonist hesitated.

"I'm not supposed to give this out," she said, "but he's in the prime minister's office."

"Thanks," shouted Hope.

In less than a minute he was speaking to a secretary in Government Buildings. A large knot had formed in the bottom of his stomach at the thought of the intrusion he was about to make.

"The commissioner is at a meeting in the prime minister's department with a number of other officials," said the secretary. "It would be most unusual to interrupt them."

"It's very important," said Hope, pressing on desperately. "Can you get a message to him?"

"It's all most irregular."

"Please."

"What is the message?"

He paused. "The message," he said slowly, "is that Sergeant Hope from Dockyard's is on the line and wants to know if the Commissioner has read this morning's paper." Commissioner Richardson was sure to be aware of the item; confirmation of the fact would put Hope's fears at rest.

"That's the message?" the secretary asked.

"Yes," replied Hope.

"Hold on, please. I'll see."

There was a clicking sound as he was put on hold and then a silence that lasted nearly three minutes.

"Sergeant Hope?"

It was the secretary again.

"Yes," he answered.

"I gave the commissioner your message," she said in a strange voice. "He has sent you this reply. He said to tell you," the girl went on, "that he has not had the time to read the paper today or in fact for several days. He also said to wish you well on your way to Redonda and that he will contact you there in July."

There was no sound from Hope's end.

"Did you get that, Sergeant? Do you understand it?"

"I think I do," said Hope as he replaced the telephone.

Slowly his gaze moved to the picture of the monarch that hung opposite his desk. It was an old portrait dating from the Coronation. The youthful, yet regal smile of the Sovereign never failed to fill Sergeant Hope with a very personal affection. They had gone through life together. She was omnipresent, on coins, on stamps, on all the notes of the East Caribbean dollar. He had been in London, in front of Buckingham Palace to join in the cheers when one of her children had been married. And when her sister, the princess, had come to Nelson's Dockyard in the sixties, young Constable Hope had stood within a foot of her.

Now he felt a huge anger rise in his chest. The facts were in the paper. In New York he had stumbled on a plot that would be executed tomorrow. By then he would be on a volcanic rock, thirty-five miles away from civilization and uncontactable.

The words of the Interpol man in New York now rang in his ears: "You've been set up, my friend." There was only one thing to be done.

Scribbling a note to Constable Tomkinson claiming sickness and telling him to contact the motor launch scheduled to transport him to Redonda, Hope walked from the quiet police station to his car. He drove into St. John's, and, withdrawing most of his savings from the bank, he walked across the street to the British Airways office and purchased a ticket to London.

LATE THAT NIGHT, as the red, white and blue 747 climbed east into the starlit sky over Antigua, the black man in the center aisle wondered why he had just jettisoned his career and pension prospects, not to mention all his money, on a mission that seemed so plainly stupid.

CHAPTER
NINETEEN

"GOOD DAY, GENTLEMEN."

Jim Abbott took his seat behind the desk. This time five other men sat down: Commander Wallace had brought along the chief inspector who was on the Hoare case. Abbott had listened to a brief résumé from Wallace just before the meeting; he had not liked one iota of what he had heard.

It was two o'clock, Tuesday afternoon, the second day of June and the sun was high in the sky, beating down on the tourists who were filing into nearby Westminster Abbey and the Houses of Parliament. For the men gathered in Assistant Commissioner Abbott's office it was day two in a security operation that would keep them going flat out for twenty-four hours.

"If you could lead off please, John," Abbott asked his head of Special Branch. There were dark rings around Wallace's eyes; Abbott guessed that the commander had worked right through the night.

"Thank you, sir," said Wallace, clearing his throat. "Our investigation essentially came under two headings. First, Sir Tristram Hoare and second, the IRA stroke INLA. To begin with, Hoare. Chief Inspector Dawson here has made some rather startling discoveries. He found a roll of film in Hoare's flat that, when developed, revealed photographs of, among other things, large quantities of guns and ammunition." He spread out the photographs on the table. "We sent a list of the guns in these shots to Dublin. The police there confirm that the weapons listed make up a large part of the Donegal arms shipment that they intercepted on May twenty-seventh."

"Hoare had these photographs?" asked David Marriot, one of Abbott's DACs. "That's extraordinary."

"There's more," said Wallace. "There were also two photographs of a woman." He placed the poses of the nude girl down in front of them. "Forensic reckoned they were taken in New York. Chief Inspector Dawson got on to the NYPD, and they identified her without difficulty as a Marie La Josne, a high-class prostitute who is well known to them. They picked her up last night. Chief Inspector Dawson will tell you the result."

"Thank you, sir," said Dawson. "Evidently when they first questioned this La Josne about Sir Tristram Hoare she completely denied any knowledge of him. It seems she didn't know he was dead. When they let her know this and put on the pressure, she caved in. She told them that she stayed with Hoare when he came to New York, that he was involved in illegally shipping guns to Ireland and the Lebanon but she thought that the business had mainly been to Ireland over the last twelve months. Hoare had salted the money away somewhere, South America, she thought, and had promised to bring her down there in the near future. She then told them that on his last trip, which was two weeks ago, Hoare had been very upset. He particularly mentioned that he had been used by the INLA in a plot which he could now do nothing to stop. That plot was to kill the Queen."

There was total silence in the room.

"Any information on how or when?" asked Sandy McKechnie eventually.

208

"Nothing, except that La Josne thought it was to be in early June," said Dawson. "They've held her overnight in New York and will question her again today. She's pretty frightened. Thinks someone might try to knock her off."

"Another of Chief Inspector Dawson's men has been to Shropshire," said Wallace, "to speak to Lady Hoare. She is staying with her unmarried sister and is still extremely distressed. Chief Inspector?"

"Yes, sir," said Dawson. "Inspector Brabbs interviewed her for over five hours last night. He came away with the impression that whatever it was the old boy was up to she certainly knew nothing about it. What we did build up, though, is a picture of Hoare's travels, which it seems were quite extensive.

"According to his wife, he was in the States at least three times this year, and yet his passport only shows one such visit. That suggests he traveled under aliases. He and Lady Hoare led quite separate lives although he did take her on holiday to Antigua in February. We have tried to check with the police in Antigua if anything unusual happened when they were there, but so far we've had no feedback."

"The Caribbean connection," murmured Abbott. The men around the table nodded.

"We found out that Hoare used an American Express card," said Dawson. "We have managed to get an analysis of the account from American Express in Brighton. There are quite a few payments to airlines, but two in particular which are of interest. They were made in November and December of last year: one is to British Airways for a trip to Belfast and the other to Irish Airlines for London-Dublin-London. Inspector Brabbs questioned Lady Hoare about these trips. She says she never knew he went to Ireland and that they know no one there."

"Why does she think he made any of those trips?" asked Abbott.

"She doesn't know, sir," replied Dawson. "She only saw him

about one week a month. She said he traveled around a great deal.

"As for his finances, all we could discover is that he recently sold off all his investments. But we can't find his bank account, and we don't know what he did with the cash."

There was silence. The sun now shone directly into the room. There was a discreet knock at the door, and a uniformed officer wheeled in a trolley with tea and biscuits. Abbott thanked him and stood up to administer.

"All right," he said. "It's all bloody ugly if you ask me. Here we have a bloke who, out of the blue, has photographs of guns used in the arms shipment of the decade. This is an English peer, a member of Society here, remember, with entrées all over the place. He's flying around the world God knows why, and at the end of last year makes two trips to Ireland in quick succession. We think he has a false passport. The Donegal arms shipment gets intercepted. The very next day Hoare is first knifed and later executed right here in London. He was supporting a floozie in New York. She now tells us that he was in a plot to kill the Queen. We are only learning about all this today. Other people know a lot more about this than we do: a hooker in New York, terrorists in Ireland, someone in the Caribbean. We need to move, gentlemen, fast. Great forces may be moving against us." He sat down again with his cup.

Commander Lamont nodded. DAC Marriot moved uneasily in his chair. The head of the Special Branch, John Wallace, spoke:

"Following our meeting yesterday afternoon, I had a long conversation with my counterpart in Dublin, a man called Wall who is always very helpful," he said. "They are pretty sure that the Donegal arms shipment attempt was masterminded by a Seamus O'Neill, a former Long Kesh internee. He is a very senior INLA man. Just after the arms shipment was intercepted, a man and a woman were stopped as they approached a roadblock about three miles from the beach where the action had taken place. One of the *Gardai* had his

210

head blown off—the *Gardai* were unarmed—but the other one had time to get a good look at the man before they tried to run him over. The description fits Seamus O'Neill. Here is the gentleman himself."

He produced a further number of photographs, which he spread out on the desk. There was the standard face and profile taken in police custody against a standard background. There were several other photographs, these taken by a hidden camera, one in a busy street, another at a rally. Finally there were enlargements from crowd scenes at what may have been a football match and a blurred shot in a car, probably at a checkpoint. They all showed a dark brooding face, a mass of black curly hair and, in the latter shots, a bushy mustache.

"I partially let Mr. Wall in Dublin into our problem as I knew it then," continued the head of Special Branch. "I told him there had been a threat to a member of the Government—and he came up with something very strange. He said it only occurred to him in the light of what I had said, but following the arms interception they had extensively questioned four of the captured men in Dublin Castle. One of them, who is alleged to have been close to Seamus O'Neill, made a remark—and remember here are Irish Republican terrorists talking to Republic of Ireland police—he made a remark as follows: 'We were unlucky today but the Brits' luck is going to run out in a big way very soon!' He refused to elaborate and is currently in prison in the Republic awaiting trial."

There was silence in the room.

"Another of these gunmen," Wallace went on, "alluded quite specifically to an Englishman being involved in the guns deal and in fact in previous deals. However he either would not or could not give a name. Neither did he give any further information about an assassination plot."

"Can't they find out any more over there in the light of our predicament?" asked McKechnie.

"They may try," replied Wallace, "but remember, these are hardened terrorists, criminals, call them what you will, who have all spent most of their adult lives in Northern Ireland prisons. They are not easily intimidated. Questioning over a longer period may produce something, but that's not much good to us. We need information now."

"What about extraditing them to the North, letting our boys there question them?" asked Marriot.

Abbott shook his head.

"I have already gone into that," he said. "At the moment there is a very sensitive RUC extradition request being processed in Dublin. If it goes through it will create a valuable precedent. We do not want to flood them with extraditions at the moment until that one is past the post."

"Because of all this," said Wallace, "we have tightened security at all points of entry into the United Kingdom, not just from Ireland, but everywhere—U.S. flights, Continental traffic, the lot."

A phone buzzed beside Abbott's desk. "It's for you, Chief Inspector Dawson," said Abbott. Dawson went behind the desk to take the call as Wallace went on:

"There's been no break on the ground here in London either," he said. "No unusual movement, no rumor that anything special is about to happen. If there is a plot, they're keeping it bloody tight."

There was the shuffle of papers around the table. Dawson, who had been speaking quietly into the telephone, returned to his chair.

"Chief Inspector?" asked Abbott; he knew that the call to the meeting must have been important.

"Yes, sir," said Dawson. "As Commander Wallace said, we have stepped up security at all points of entry. Commander Wallace was speaking with the RUC in Belfast last night and asked them to try and locate the current whereabouts of Seamus O'Neill."

"That's correct," said Wallace. "Either the RUC or the Army are sure to know if he is about. Go on, Chief Inspector."

"They sent us these photographs from Belfast, and we wired them out to all our Immigration people," said Dawson. "That was my man downstairs who is liaising with the officers in the field. He's just had a call from a police sergeant in Stranraer in Scotland. A man fitting O'Neill's description came in on the Larne ferry this morning. The ID is also supported by a bus conductor in Dumfries. He may have been accompanied by a woman, but we're not sure. We're following it up as best we can, but as of this moment I am afraid the trail is cold."

Abbott surveyed the men sitting in front of him. Eventually he spoke: "So we have a major problem," he said. "The Hoare business makes it particularly sinister. We have got to assume that Sir Tristram Hoare was plotting with the INLA, assisting them in the planning of an attempted assassination. Sounds incredible, but that is what we have to assume. You have done good work, Commander," he said to the head of Special Branch. "I have no doubt you will keep us abreast of any developments, particularly involving Mr. O'Neill."

He turned to McKechnie. "May we have your views?" he asked the chief of C.13.

McKechnie thrust his bald head forward. "I still think any attempt will be by explosives," he said. "However the involvement of Hoare is unique. It makes us look at the whole business in a new way. We have a fair idea how a terrorist might plan such a thing, but a knight of the realm, so to speak, casts the threat in a new light. I mean they could try and walk into a garden party at Buckingham Palace with a hand grenade for all we know."

"That's right," said Lamont. "And that is why Commander McKechnie and I have decided that until further notice we have got to increase protection to such a level as simply to rule out—as far as is humanly possible—any attempt. We have got to cover every possibility."

"On an indefinite basis?" asked Marriot.

"At least until we have nabbed Seamus O'Neill and found out more about this Caribbean plot," replied Lamont.

"Or they make their attempt," said Abbott. "I think this business has all the signs of coming to the boil fairly quickly. Everything has been quiet, and suddenly we have all this activity. My nose tells me that something will happen very shortly. Commander?"

Commander Lamont assembled his notes.

"Yes, sir," he said. "On that assumption we have been going over the royal schedule for the coming week. The Queen and the royal family returned to London last night. The first official engagement is a state dinner for the Australian prime minister, which takes place tonight. Then we have our first real nightmare, which is tomorrow, Wednesday, June third. The Queen and the royal family with about twenty guests go to Epsom for the Derby."

"What about the rest of the week?" asked Abbott.

"Thursday, the Queen goes to Portsmouth to inspect a new aircraft carrier," replied Lamont. "That's reasonably O.K. as the whole day will be spent in an enclosed naval dockyard. On Thursday night she flies directly from Portsmouth to Balmoral for the weekend."

"So Wednesday is our first main problem," said Abbott. He knew well the security dilemma presented by such an appearance. "The Epsom Derby, London's big day out," he said, "where our racing fraternity will all gather in style to see the horse of their choice romp over the Downs, sadly less, of course, one of their number this year, an ex-steward of their own Jockey Club, recently deceased in most unusual circumstances."

"Yes, I had not overlooked that, sir," said Lamont. "It makes Epsom all the more likely. I shall just run over the royal itinerary, if I may."

Abbott nodded. The fact that Hoare had been a Jockey Club steward raised unprecedented questions about security.

"The royal party go by special train from London Bridge station to Tattenham Corner," said Lamont. "They leave London Bridge at about noon, arriving at twelve-thirty. They transfer at Tattenham Corner station to the royal cars, which will be waiting there. They drive from the back of the station directly onto the racecourse, entering the course halfway down Tattenham Hill. The cars then parade down the hill, around the famous Tattenham Corner, taking the same route as the horses in the big race, up the straight a distance of about half a mile until they come to a halt in front of the winning post. There will be an estimated half a million people both out on the Downs and in the enclosures watching, on either side of this procession. At the winning post the Queen is received by the racecourse manager. The band of the Grenadier Guards plays the National Anthem, and the royal party walk off the course, through the Members enclosure, into the bottom of the grandstand, where there is a special lift to take them up to the Royal Chambers and the Royal Box. These are located at the top of the stands." Lamont paused to allow for any questions. There were none.

"Epsom, it seems, is unique," he went on, "in that the paddock is located over a quarter of a mile from the enclosures. The tradition is that the Queen and royal party leave their box before the Derby and are driven down to the paddock to see the horses being mounted. Having seen this completed a further tradition is then enacted when the Queen walks," he paused, "yes, *walks* up the center of the track and back to the enclosure to see the race."

The men in the room said nothing as they all took in the magnitude of the security task facing them. Abbott was the first to break the silence.

"You may be asking yourselves the obvious question," he said, "and the answer from the Palace is, no way. She will go no matter what, all the more so because of something like this."

"Could the walk from the paddock not be curtailed?" asked Dawson.

"I don't think so," replied Lamont. "Its tradition is a comparatively recent one, but it began about eight years ago when we had another scare following an IRA bombing in London. Everyone expected the Queen to drive back from the paddock, but she insisted on walking the whole way. The people loved her for it."

Abbott turned his attention to the commander of the antiterrorist squad.

"Sandy, there are the problems. What are the answers?" he asked.

The head of C.13 looked at all the men in the room in turn. "We are assuming," said McKechnie, "that there is a high probability that someone will try to kill the Queen tomorrow. We therefore propose to narrow the angle to a point that will make it very difficult, hopefully impossible, for them to succeed. We will assume further that normal security means that any attempt will take place when the Queen is out of Buckingham Palace. First the journey to Epsom.

"Working with Commander Lamont and the RPG, we are going over the royal railway carriage with a fine-toothed comb, literally taking it to pieces. It will then be guarded at all times until it is used tomorrow. We are sweeping the entire railway line between London Bridge and Tattenham Corner today and tomorrow morning. This operation will include dogs from the RPG and electronic detection equipment from C.13. If the INLA have mined the tracks we will know."

"What about someone taking a potshot at the train as it goes by?" asked Marriot.

"That's a difficult thing to do if you think about it," replied McKechnie, "with very little chance of success. Nonetheless, the carriage is being fitted with armor-plate glass windows, and the RPG and ourselves, in conjunction with local police along the way, will patrol the railway line at any point where there might be trouble."

Wallace nodded. He had seen McKechnie's men in action before. He doubted if an uninvited field mouse could cross the Epsom railway line with impunity on Wednesday morning.

"Now Tattenham Corner station itself," McKechnie went on. "We will of course search it with dogs and equipment well in advance. But Wednesday will see a huge influx of people through the station, so there is always the chance that an explosive of some sort could be put in place on the morning. Therefore we are closing the station to the public from 11:00 A.M. to allow us to do a final sweep."

"Won't that cause a huge traffic problem?" asked Dawson. "Won't the punters be trying to get out to the races on that line?"

"That's unfortunately true," replied Lamont, "but we have little option. We have spoken to British Rail, and they are going to put on extra trains to the two other local stations, Epsom Downs and Epsom town itself. We are liaising with the local police commander in Croydon who will arrange for buses to be available to take people from these stations to the races. And of course, as soon as the royal party leaves London Bridge, British Rail can run as many trains as they want to Tattenham Corner. It will still only be noon, and the first race does not start until two."

Dawson could see the enormous logistics problems that the security exercise would create. Commander Lamont's great talent was in organization; liaison between the many units that would be concerned with royal protection was his chief responsibility.

"Thank you, sir," said Dawson.

"From Tattenham Corner station," said McKechnie, "we have the royal procession down the course. There are seven Rolls-Royces involved, and they are all enclosed. The first three, which will carry the Queen and immediate royal family, are bombproof and bulletproof. They each weigh nearly three tons. Nevertheless we will sweep the actual track itself although we have spoken to the ground staff out in Epsom and they know every blade of grass there, so it's very doubtful if anyone could dig a hole in the track and put a bomb in it without being spotted. We have also doubled the number of uniformed officers who will watch the crowd on each side of the track for the procession."

"What about the air?" asked Abbott. "Won't a lot of people come by helicopter?"

"A good point, sir," said McKechnie. "The choppers will be like flies out there on Wednesday. What we've done is to ban all arrivals or departures from twelve-thirty to one. That's also going to create a stink, but I think it's necessary. We'll have two police choppers standing by for any possible interception that may be necessary. There will be the usual restriction on airspace below twenty thousand feet for the day—no planes pulling adverts or anything like that. We have also asked the RAF to stand by in case there is a violation."

"Very good," said Abbott. "So now she has arrived at the winning post, the entrance to the Members enclosure."

"That's right, sir," said McKechnie. "The Queen leaves her car, shakes hands with the manager, and the band strikes up the national anthem. This is our first real flashpoint, and we have had to take quite extreme measures, which I hope you will approve of. Firstly, everyone entering Epsom racecourse on Wednesday will be body-searched."

Abbott raised his eyebrows.

"That's going to be quite a job," he said.

"We see no alternative, sir," said McKechnie. "It will apply only to the people coming into the racecourse proper. Commander Lamont can make fifty officers available for this job, and they will be supplemented by local police. All hand luggage will be gone through including things like cases carrying binoculars. It will apply to everyone from racecourse staff to catering people. All catering supplies will be checked as well."

Abbott nodded his approval.

"Our second measure," said McKechnie, "will be to draft in up to six hundred police specifically to form a human wall around the Queen, firstly for the playing of the anthem. We will have further use for these men as you will see, but when she arrives they will completely surround her. Other officers will clean an area back to thirty yards from where she stands. The area of Epsom Downs on the opposite side of the course will also be vacated. Any VIPs who wish to be inside this circle for the anthem will have to preclear it with my staff. They will be issued with special ID permits. Following the anthem the same men will break to form a gangway leading under the stands. We will have over one hundred armed plainclothesmen mingling with the crowds in the immediate vicinity. There will also be sharpshooters on the roof of the stands."

"Any difficulty in getting adequate numbers of men, Commander?" asked Abbott.

"No, sir," replied Lamont. "They are assembling as we speak."

"We have every available explosives expert out in Epsom at this moment, sir," said McKechnie. "The buildings and stands are over seventy years old, but we should be able to prove them completely safe. As for the Royal Box and the lift leading to it, we are taking them apart literally, piece by piece. For example, all the wood paneling and the ceiling in the Royal Box are being removed, and the Jockey Club rooms underneath are getting the same treatment. We are even pulling apart the two television sets in the Royal Box. With these new radio detonators they could have planted a bomb six months ago and let it off tomorrow. The whole place will be sealed tighter than a drum from when we are finished this evening."

Abbott was making some notes.

"What about the kitchen staff and other staff in the Royal Box? What about the food?" he asked.

"All the staff are part of the Queen's household," said McKechnie. "They come out from London tomorrow morning and bring food and drink with them."

"As a matter of interest, why do they need two television sets in the Royal Box?" asked Abbott.

McKechnie smiled. "I understand it is because a senior member of the royal party likes to follow the cricket whilst the others have the racing on," he answered.

Abbott grinned. "Sensible man," he said.

"What about a bomb in a car outside the stand, on the roadside?" asked Marriot.

"First of all it won't be able to get near enough to do enough damage," said Lamont. "There is a thirty-foot open area and then a six-foot iron railing between the stand and the road. But just as a precaution we have closed the normal car park behind the stands and are moving cars back toward Tattenham Corner."

"It won't be a car bomb, I'm pretty sure," said McKechnie, "unless it's a kamikaze attempt—and that's not these boys' style. Even if they do try, it won't work."

"So what happens next?" asked Abbott.

"The next part is really the most crucial flashpoint and also the last one," said McKechnie. "The Queen and the royal party come down out of the box and are driven to the paddock to inspect the horses."

"That's quite a distance you say?" asked Dawson.

"Yes, nearly five hundred yards," said McKechnie. "The Queen will be driven down the track over the Langley Vale Road to the paddock. We shall strengthen police and plain-clothes presence in the same way as we did when she came up to the track two hours before. Obviously we shall double-check the road running under the track and have it clear. The paddock itself is an area surrounded by trees on one side and buildings on the other. All the buildings will have been swept at least three times before the Queen arrives. Any personnel such as TV crews who will overlook the paddock will have to be cleared by my staff."

"Good," said Abbott.

"The Queen enters the paddock," continued McKechnie. "A large wooden security rail runs around the entire perimeter of the paddock, and inside it there's a steel rail on a concrete base. Spectators will be ten or twelve deep outside these rails looking in at the horses and the royal party. There are a series of small concrete steps, fifteen blocks of them in all, around the outside of the paddock on which the spectators can stand.

We propose, sir, to have all our available uniformed men, up to six hundred of them, form a tunnel from the royal car into the paddock and then physically to ring the inside of the paddock itself. The Queen will be literally surrounded by a wall of police officers, as will the people associated with the Derby and, of course, the horses themselves."

"That will cause a bit of a comment, won't it?" asked Abbott.

McKechnie shrugged his wide shoulders. "The paddock area is wide open compared to the enclosures. There is no way we can be one hundred percent sure that someone will not slip in there from the Downs with a gun or maybe a hand grenade. If he takes his place beside the paddock rail he would have a potshot. I know what I am proposing sounds a bit siegelike, but I really do not see what choice we have. We will ask the TV people to try and record the event as sympathetically as possible, to try not to emphasize the police presence. I am sure they will help us out."

"These horsey people, the trainers and so on," said Wallace, "can we check them out?"

"We can, thankfully, rely somewhat on an outfit called Racecourse Security Services for that," said Lamont. "There are very strict procedures. Everyone associated with the horses must be checked out and registered with RSS first. Everyone to do with the horses has numbers and passes. Don't forget those horses out there tomorrow are worth a fortune—collectively tens of millions of pounds. The racing people have had to take their own security measures, and this gives us a bit of comfort in that regard. We will, of course, step up our surveillance."

"Best do a double check, just in case," said Abbott. "Hoare's involvement in this whole business could mean anything."

"What about the owners of the horses?" asked Dawson. "They will be in the ring as well."

"They will have come through the enclosure earlier," said McKechnie, "where they will have been body-searched."

"And then there is the walk back to the stands," said Abbott.

"Yes, sir," said McKechnie. "What we have in mind is that the men in the paddock will form, in effect, a mobile security ring around the royal party for the walk back up the course. In other words from the moment she steps into the paddock to the moment she arrives back in the enclosure the Queen will be completely surrounded by a wall of police officers."

"Rather defeats the purpose of the walk I should think," said Abbott. "I mean no one will even get a glimpse of her."

"I think the fact that it is done and reported to be done is what will be looked at, sir," said Lamont calmly.

"All right, any questions?" asked Abbott.

There were none. "I will not hold you," he said, "I have complete confidence in what I have heard—mind you, I would not have expected less."

The men stood up, gathering their papers and stretching their limbs.

"By the way," said Abbott, "anyone got any tips for tomorrow?"

"It seems there is only one horse in the Derby, sir," answered Dawson. "It's Roche's—he's even money."

"What's its name?" asked Abbott as they walked to the door of the office.

"Noble Lord, I think," said Dawson.

"I might have a quid on that if I get a moment," said Abbott. He looked at his watch. It was four o'clock. Another twenty-four hours and it would all be over.

TWO MILES AWAY to the northwest across Central London, Jeremy made his way through the heavily ornate lobby of the Ritz. Chubby pink cherubim smiled down at him from richly gilded cornices as he punched the button of the elevator. Jeremy shuddered. He had made his mind up when he left Penny an hour before: he was going to keep the relationship strictly professional. Damn it all, he thought, I'm training the favorite for the Derby. I'm not some sort of kept gigolo for this Arab poofter.

He knocked on the paneled door of the suite. The door was opened by a swarthy retainer whom Jeremy had not seen before. What he saw next took his breath away. The large living room of the suite had been completely transformed into an amazing desert tent or *majlis*. All the conventional furniture had been removed. Brilliantly colored silks billowed down from a central point in the ceiling to the sides of the room, leaving but a small aperture for entry. Muted lights glowed through the reds and ochers and yellows, into the sumptuously inviting interior, where mounds of satin-covered cushions were arranged in a comfortable circle. Delicate fragrances hung in the air. It was difficult to believe that this was the West End.

Jeremy removed his shoes and entered. Two further retainers left as he did so, bowing to a reclining figure who raised his hand as Jeremy entered.

"My friend," said Prince Abdullah bin Yasir al-Fahd. "Welcome."

"Hullo, Yaw," said Jeremy, "nice to see you."

Yaw motioned him to sit. Jeremy felt the Arab's eyes surveying him.

"Did you have a good trip?" he asked the Prince.

"Yes, good," came the reply. There was a slight pause.

"Very good," said Yaw again, laughing to himself.

"You were in Rome, I think you said?" Jeremy asked politely. "Enjoyable?"

Yaw opened his mouth to answer, then he appeared to change his mind and shut it again. Then he caught his nose between his thumb and forefinger; his face suddenly became purple and his whole body shook violently. With wonderment Jeremy realized that his principal patron was in the throes of a massive, uncontrollable fit of the giggles. After a minute the spasm passed, and the Arab began to breathe in and out very deeply as if following some well-practiced therapy.

"This time tomorrow it will all be over," said Jeremy discreetly.

Yaw sighed and wiped moisture from his eyes. "The horse is

good?" he asked with another slight snigger. It seemed that the effort of conversation was beyond him.

"He has never been better in his life," replied Jeremy cautiously. "He made the trip to Epsom this afternoon without a hitch. All we need now is some luck, and the race is ours."

As he spoke he noticed that Yaw had produced a small ivory box, which he now opened. He was pinching some white powder from it to the back of his hand. He then raised his hand to his nose and snorted vigorously, first into one nostril then the other.

"He will win the race?" asked the prince.

"You can never tell in a big race like the Derby," said Jeremy. "However everyone seems to think we have a major chance. We've done it once this year already."

The prince started his squeaky giggle again, shaking with merriment, lying back helplessly on the cushions, his freely watering eyes staring at the top of his tent. This time it took him nearly three minutes to compose himself. Then he sat up, muttering something in Arabic. He beckoned Jeremy to sit nearer and pinched up some powder on the closed back of his fist, which he offered to the trainer.

"I don't really think I should," said Jeremy.

"Sniff it," said the prince.

Jeremy did as he was told, two hits, and then lay back on the cushions. A feeling of lightheaded frivolity suddenly overcame him. He began to chortle. "I think I'm going to . . ." his sentence trailed off in a peal of laughter.

The Arab opened the box again and took a sturdy helping of the white dust. Jeremy reached over to help himself and then leaned back chuckling again. The whole, brilliant tent had assumed magical properties, and he was being transported on a flying carpet of exhilaration. The tensions of five minutes ago had evaporated—like the white powder he had inhaled. He tittered again. He was as high as a kite. This is the life, he thought. Nothing could bother him now. Not even the coffee-colored fingers that had begun to unbutton his shirt.

224

CHAPTER
TWENTY

HE WAS RUNNING for his life now down a road that he did not know. The voices of his pursuers were behind him, but it was pitch-dark and their faces could not be seen. The frame of the rectangular object that he was clutching dug painfully into his chest. He looked at it, and the girl smiled back at him from the picture. He looked at it again and saw her lips were moving, but there was no sound. He felt wet with fear. Now there were shouts behind him, and a voice boomed out his name. Clutching the picture more closely, he tried to increase his speed but was unable. He began to cry. Tears ran down his face onto the portrait. He looked at it again, and a blinding flash riveted his whole body. The girl was gone. In her place was the head of a pale-faced youth with black curly hair, intense hatred blazing from his small dark eyes. Sergeant Hope knew him well. He wanted to shout at him to go away, but no words came. The youth was laughing. He caught Hope painfully by the arm.

"Are you all right?"

He blinked his eyes and looked around him. The plane's engines hummed; in the darkened cabin a few lights were still on, illuminating books for those passengers who could not sleep. The 747 was no more than half full. The hand that had woken him from his troubled sleep had been withdrawn. A small, pretty face with a wrinkle of concern was observing him from the next seat. He was drenched in his own sweat. He licked his lips.

"That was a bad one, huh?" said the young woman.

She had blond hair, fastened on each side with two red clips. She wore denim shorts and a pink T-shirt that contrasted with her brown arms; a large, chunky, white coral bracelet encircled her wrist. She was very small and was sitting in the lotus position—a difficult accomplishment in an airplane— one taut brown knee and upper leg with tiny golden hairs nudging the space by Hope's right elbow.

"I'm sorry," he muttered. "Must have had a dream."

She gave him a bright smile.

"It's quite impossible to sleep comfortably in these planes," she said.

Hope nodded. He looked at his watch. There were still four hours flying time before they reached London.

"I hope I didn't wake you or . . ." said Hope. His voice was still thick, the images from his nightmare now spinning with lightning speed to the edge of his memory. The young woman was extremely attractive, her smell fresh and inviting.

"Don't worry," she was saying. She pressed the hostess call-bell. "You and I are going to have some coffee."

A sleepy hostess brought them coffee from the galley where she had been napping. The hot liquid made Hope feel better. The young woman raised the plastic cup.

"Cheers," she said with a laugh. "By the way, I'm Debbie."

Hope shook her small hand. It felt warm and firm, and he kept it in his for a short moment.

"Sergeant Hope," he said and instantly regretted it. "Winston Hope" he added.

"Oh, are you army?" she asked.

"No," he replied as he tried to think of a way to escape this line of questioning. Each minute that drew him closer to London increased his dread that the whole idea was a huge mistake. He began to perspire again; a feeling of panic was gathering itself in his belly.

Debbie was speaking again.

"Boy," she said softly. "I don't know what you've done or who you are, but you are one hell of a mess right now."

She reached for his hand, which was damp with sweat, and took it in both of hers. "Just try to relax," she said soothingly. "There's no need to talk if you don't want to, but if it would help, I'm a good listener."

She switched out the overhead light and, putting their empty coffee cups on the next unoccupied seat—the rest of the row was vacant—she slipped up the two tables. She held his hand in her lap and pressed it gently. It was an interesting hand, attractive, with long strong fingers, the hand of an artist perhaps, or a musician. It curled like a kitten in her lap as she stroked it. She began to talk soothingly to him, stroking his hand, telling him of how she had been born in San Francisco, had gone to school there, and how when she was nine her father had made her a gift of a camera. Ever since that day photography had become her all-consuming hobby and was now her full-time job.

She spoke softly, telling the man beside her about her career. First she had done it as a hobby, around the time of the anti-Vietnam War marches on Washington. Debbie had found herself in the direct line of a police baton charge. She snapped it, and next day the photograph was on the front page of a hundred U.S. newspapers.

She had gone to New York, working on various assignments with enough success to pay the rent. Three and a half years ago she had come to London on a job, liked it, and stayed. Now she was returning after a two-week break in Antigua.

Then Hope began to talk. At first the words came out jerkily. Debbie listened to his story with growing amazement. When he hesitated, she encouraged him. The flow of words became a torrent. When he had finally finished he lay back exhausted. They were both silent. She believed him.

"You must feel very much alone," she whispered. There

227

was no reply. It was almost completely dark in the cabin. Only the heat from his close body revealed that he was there.

She felt a movement as he withdrew his hand. The armrest between their seats was raised, and she suddenly felt the weight of his head in her lap. For a moment she did nothing, then gingerly, she put a hand on his head.

He adjusted his position slightly so that his face now looked upward. Then his left hand came to the soft base of her neck and pulled her down until his head was covered by her blond hair. She smelled like a bunch of flowers.

All at once, where minutes before he had felt insecurity and dread, the warm assurance of companionship now spread through him. With the warmth of her lap as his pillow, Hope drifted into an untroubled sleep.

As the plane's engines droned on, Debbie reached to the next seat for the thin airline blanket that lay there. She flicked it over them both. It would be at least another hour before breakfast was served.

CHAPTER
TWENTY-ONE

THE TRAFFIC BEGAN to arrive in earnest at 5:30 A.M. The cars poured in across the Downs in the summer morning light, making for favorite positions tried and tested years before. Open-topped buses arrived to take up their places along the rails of the straight, near Tattenham Corner. Even at that early hour one could see the makings of spirited parties from place to place: tables set up loaded with cases of beer, awnings attached to the sides of campers, fold-up chairs and hammocks appearing from the backs of cars, smoke wisping from freshly lighted barbecues.

From the police chopper that circled the area from first light the scene resembled the invasion of Epsom Downs by an army of ants. Growing lines of slowly moving cars waited patiently on the approach roads for their release onto the huge expanse of green, and when it came, scuttled swiftly in different directions.

The visitors in the cars and buses were not aware of the careful scrutiny with which they were regarded by the unusually large number of policemen. Uniformed men in charge of all the traffic points had a good look at each vehicle as it came onto the Downs. Special Branch men, dressed in jeans and jackets, mingled with the growing crowds, listening and watching, for the word out of place, the suspicious movement, the furtive glance. Only the pickpockets realized that the yield from their usual Derby Day harvest would be bad this year.

The plainclothesmen were particularly attentive to the high area at the very center of the Downs from where an expert marksman, given the right circumstances, could draw a bead on the Royal Box immediately opposite. This area had been closed by the police to any vehicles: all traffic had been diverted on down the track. A sniper, or a terrorist with a rocket launcher, would have had a first-class vantage point from the top of a bus parked on the hill.

MAJOR GATHORNE-HARDY was making his way to his office in the paddock at 5:45 A.M. when two uniformed policemen approached him.

"Can I help you, sir?"

"Gathorne-Hardy, clerk of the course," said the major.

"Your pass please, sir," said one of the men.

Gathorne-Hardy produced the special yellow security pass that the police had issued the day before.

"Thank you, sir," said the officer in charge. "Would you be so good as to wear it at all times?"

Gathorne-Hardy swallowed hard and made his way into his office. It was like being asked to wear ID at home. The last twenty-four hours had surpassed anything in his long experience as Epsom racetrack's effective stage manager. Police, hundreds of them, had swarmed all over the place since early the previous morning. There had been at least a dozen sniffer dogs probing every corner of the stands and enclosures. They had even dismantled the elevator leading to the Royal Box. And each member of Gathorne-Hardy's staff had been made to fill out a questionnaire to qualify for a security pass. That was what had really galled him; they worked here the whole year and then, for Derby Day, some bloody policeman was going to decide whether or not they got in. He had even to fill one out himself. The rumor was that the police expected an IRA bomb attack on the royal party. Even so it took a lot of the fun out of it to be treated like a bloody criminal. The major had spent nearly forty years giving his services to racing. His retirement was two years off. An ex-Blues man, he got on well with his colleagues in Portman Square. He picked up the telephone and dialed a single number.

OVER A MILE away, near the six-furlong chute up Tattenham Hill, the mobile telephone attached to Jimmy Flynn's belt buzzed.

"Morning, Flynn," he heard the familiar voice. "Anything to report?"

The head groundsman unclipped his phone.

"Morning, Major," he replied. "Nothing really, sir, except that I have never seen so many policemen in my life."

"Very irritating," said the clerk of the course's voice. "As long as we don't have to pay for them all."

"They have been up and down the straight with a metal detector or something since five o'clock," said Flynn whose small cottage was the only house on the Downs. "I can't think what they expected to find."

"Flatfooted idiots," said Gathorne-Hardy. "What's the traffic like?"

"They're really beginning to arrive now, sir," said the head groundsman.

"All right. I'm going to check the stables. I expect the first gallops will be starting shortly. See you at breakfast."

"Very well, sir," said Flynn and clipped back his phone. Breakfast with Gathorne-Hardy on Derby Day had become something of a tradition, which the little Irishman looked forward to. He climbed into his Land Rover and drove slowly down the famous hill. He looked up the straight to the enclosures, which were beginning to buzz with life. Already the old place was behaving like a child on its birthday, differently than on ordinary race days. Flynn loved his job. He had come over to England at fourteen with great ambitions to become a steeplechase jockey. Unfortunately, weight had sealed his intentions: after five years of bitter struggle with diet, pills, and the weighing scales, he had given up. Someone had got him a job as a gardener at Epsom. He had never gone home.

Flynn eased down Tattenham Hill. He passed the white double gates on the right that he would be opening in seven hours' time to admit the royal party. At Tattenham Corner people had already begun to arrive on foot from the station. Many carried heavy hampers and picnic baskets, while others pushed infants in prams. Cars were pouring onto the Downs over the track from the Old London Road.

At the bottom of the hill Flynn got out of the Land Rover to check the coconut mats, eighteen of them rolled up on each side of the road across the track. One of his ground staff was already there waiting to put the mats in position and to cover them with the grass cuttings; the first of the horses would shortly begin their morning canter. In the great race itself the runners would cross no less than four roads in all, covered with a total of seventy coconut mats. One of Flynn's many responsibilities was to see that they were laid properly in their place at the right time.

"See you later," he said to the groundsman and continued his drive up the straight toward the winning post. He took a personal interest in every blade of grass that made up the twenty-five acres of the racetrack. Under his direction the track was fertilized, cut, harrowed, and rolled. He had driven one of the tractors himself the previous Sunday when the track had been given its final cut before the Derby.

He made his way up the three and a half furlongs toward the winning post, the same route that later that day would be taken by the Queen. The right-to-left roll of the ground was quite pronounced; a horse had to come down the hill balanced to win this race. In the stands policemen were still probing with their sniffer dogs. To the right, near the parking lot and at the far side of the London road he could see the mobile police HQ that had been set up the day before. More uniformed policemen were gathered around in large groups and were being briefed.

Flynn's Land Rover was now level with the Members enclosure. The final touches were being put to bright displays of flowers inside the entrance and high up in front of the Royal Box. Flynn felt a touch of pride: all the flowers were cultivated under his supervision in the racetrack greenhouse behind the stables.

He pulled up level with the winning post and looked on down the hill toward the paddock. A horse and rider had come out onto the track from the stables: the morning gallops were about to begin.

SANDY MCKECHNIE SURVEYED the large-scale plan in front of him. "Can anyone think of any angle we may have missed?" he asked.

The men gathered around the head of C.13 shook their heads.

"As far as bombs go, sir, there's no worthwhile place left to put one," said Chief Inspector Dawson. "The place is as clean as a whistle."

The men were standing around a table in the large tent pitched beside the temporary parking lot. A steady stream of cars was arriving although it was only 6:00 A.M. Gypsy women with baskets were selling buttonholes of heather. Commander Lamont was going over the procedure to be used to shield the Queen on her arrival and later in the paddock. He spoke to twenty chosen sergeants who would each have up to thirty uniformed men in a squad. Dawson could hear Lamont's calm voice as he outlined in precise detail how the operation was going to work.

"Has everything been set up for body searches?" asked McKechnie.

"Yes, sir," replied Dawson. "The enclosures will remain closed to the public until nine o'clock. Anyone coming in then will be searched."

"All the passes issued?" asked McKechnie.

"All issued, sir," answered a burly little officer from the RPG. "Anyone who works here will have been issued with a yellow pass which they must display. Catering staff have got a blue pass and have been told they must remain at all times in the area they are working in. All consignments of drinks were searched yesterday. Fresh food arriving this morning is being searched about now."

"We will rendezvous back here at nine-thirty," said McKechnie. "Any questions?"

There were none. Dawson was impressed with McKechnie's grasp of the situation.

"If you don't mind, sir," he said, "I think I'll take a walk around."

"Good idea," said McKechnie. "By the way, we've had a look at the way the racecourse security people vet trainers, stable lads, and so on. It's pretty thorough, has to be. Just to be safe we have asked for a list of all visiting stable personnel to be given in to us as soon as possible. We'll have it run through the computer in the Yard just to be doubly sure there's nobody nasty about."

Dawson left the tent and turning right, walked down the public road that would take him past the back of the stands to the stables and paddock. Below him, a horse and rider cantered gracefully down to Tattenham Corner. Dawson paused to watch the fluid movement of animal and man; he had not been to the races for nearly ten years. Perhaps today would be enjoyable after all.

JEREMY CARVILL DUG the back of his heel sharply into the grass. There was a slight give, hinting at the hard bone of earth that lay four inches under the well-watered green turf. The going was perfect.

234

Jeremy was standing on the racetrack opposite the most famous winning post in the world. It was six-fifteen in the morning and he had a quite unbelievable hangover. He had woken up in the Ritz at five o'clock and crept out of the lavish, tentlike suite, leaving Yaw sprawled, snoring noisily. He had come to Epsom directly; halfway out he had asked the taxi to pull over while he had disembarked and spewed his guts out onto the hard shoulder of the M23.

Despite his condition Jeremy could already sense the excitement that was special to the day. He looked down the track up which would run in a little over nine hours' time, the twenty-four runners in the Derby Stakes, which for over two hundred years had been run on this very turf. To his right, sprawled over the undulating expanse of Epsom Downs, were hundreds of modern caravans and tents, the chief home of Europe's gypsies for this great week. From as far away as Hungary, Greece, and Turkey they had come in their gleaming mobile homes to join, as their ancestors before them had done, in the rite of Epsom Downs.

Sideshows were being erected outside some caravans while others were festooned with bright flags. Whole families sat at outdoor tables for breakfast: men stripped to the waist, olive-skinned matriarchs with formidable bosoms, dark-haired children with the jet-black eyes of the Balkans.

To Jeremy's left, the stands and enclosures rose in tiers, each section carefully segregated from the next. There was Tattersalls enclosure, which with the arrival of nearly one hundred bookmakers would determine the odds at which the Derby winner would be returned with all the precision of the London Stock Exchange. That calculation would be vital this day, not only for the thousands of people who wagered at Epsom, but for the millions of others betting on the race all over the British Isles and in places as far apart as Jamaica, Hong Kong, and New South Wales. Great sums of money would change hands in Tattersalls today, fortunes would be lost and won.

Above Tattersalls enclosure were long rows of private

boxes that would be later occupied by their top-hatted owners or by companies who had hired them for the day. Derby Day is not a day for serious business in the City of London. The race is run in mid-week, and all the City institutions are open as usual, but the recorded volume on the London Stock Exchange this day would be the lowest for over five months.

Jeremy's bloodshot eyes traveled left from Tattersalls into the holy of holies, the Members enclosure. He could see a team of men putting the finishing touches to a magnificent floral display that would please the Members on their walk from the lawn of their enclosure into the bar.

The steep Members lawn at Epsom, dotted with small, white garden seats, allows the Members to follow the Derby with an uninterrupted view over the Downs. As the horses sweep down Tattenham Hill and around the seemingly endless Tattenham Corner, Epsom's Members do not have to endure the shoulder-to-shoulder discomfort of those elsewhere on the course, crammed into stands, some for five hours before the race. As the horses make their dash up the final three and a half furlongs to the winning post, the Members need not worry unduly about following their choice if the race to the finish is a tight one: the last half-furlong and winning post at Epsom are exclusively opposite the Members enclosure.

Jeremy allowed his gaze to rise up from the Members lawn, up into the stand above and to the balcony of an extra-large box, like the terrace of a town house apartment. Even the Members at Epsom could not intrude into this box with its private rest rooms, kitchen, and dining room, without a very specific invitation. It is there that tradition is enacted every year when the trainer of the winning horse is presented to the reigning monarch. Jeremy's stomach did a somersault as he thought about it, and he held the running rail for support. The fresh air was gradually helping to make him feel a little less shattered.

He tested the ground again and walked on down the track toward Tattenham Corner. Other trainers were also out with much the same concerns as himself, some wishing for the ground to be a bit softer, others hoping that it might be a little more on top. He had seen Maxwell Rae coming out onto the track with a worried look on his face: Pavarotti liked more of a cut in the going. However, J. J. Reilly had smiled to everyone as he made his way across the Downs. Southern Cross was in splendid form.

Other horses were having a loosen up on the track, mainly coming down the hill to Tattenham Corner in a slow canter. Horses were not allowed to work on the straight half mile in front of the stands; too much traffic could damage the turf, which had been prepared with the meticulous attention of a lawn at Kew Gardens.

Two television crews had arrived, one in the Members enclosure, the other with hand-held equipment out on the course. They began setting up their gear, which would soon begin live, up-to-the-minute broadcasts for breakfast television. A bookmaker had arrived—for the benefit of TV—and was bawling out odds on the race to no one in particular.

Jeremy walked on down the track. He had left Stroker and Noble Lord walking from the stables across over the Downs toward the Derby start. He would meet them as they came down Tattenham Hill. The ground rose quite sharply in the furlong and a half before the winning post, posing an additional question to the stamina of a horse. To his left, Jeremy saw a convoy of Black Marias pull into an open enclosure next to Tattersalls. The doors opened and a small army of uniformed policemen got out. Security must be a nightmare on a day like this, he thought, with most of the royal family coming to see the race. Over half a million people would be in Epsom that afternoon as the horses entered the starting stalls at three-thirty.

STROKER FELT CHALKIE Charlesworth's hand press on the shin

side of his left boot. He eased himself upward and astride the colt in a motion so quiet that the horse barely knew he had been mounted. Then he helped his feet into the irons, suspended by very short leathers from their clips built into the bridge of the saddle. His knees were now level with his waist.

"All right."

He nodded at Zeid to let go of Noble Lord's head. Jesus, that's a weird one, he thought. Zeid reminded him of a man in a trance although he seemed to go about his tasks efficiently. The bugger has almost no blood in his face, he thought. Stroker nudged Noble Lord out over the Downs in the direction of the start. He saw Jeremy walk up the track to his left toward Tattenham Corner. God he looks rough. I bet he's shitting bricks, he thought.

The Downs were coming awake now, the life in the gypsy camps beginning to increase audibly. Stroker could see a line of double-decker buses with open tops make their way onto the Downs at Tattenham Corner. They would continue to arrive all morning and by lunchtime would be packed like sardines, facing the track, all the way from Tattenham Corner to the finish. Incredibly, even at this early hour some of the buses' occupants were high-spiritedly toasting each other's health with pint glasses of beer. Stroker grinned to himself. This was Derby Day all right.

Stroker Roche had already ridden the winners of two Derbys, one when he was an eighteen-year-old boy-wonder jockey, the other, ten years after that. But he had ridden the Epsom track more times than he cared to remember. He walked Noble Lord down a path through the Downs, past the gypsies' encampment, down into a hollow and up the far side.

Noble Lord arrived at the point from where in nine hours' time, the race would start. The automatic starting gates were already in place, their aluminum bars glinting in the early light. Stroker saw the two white boxes attached to the rail of the track: one was an old-fashioned telephone system connecting the start back to the steward's room; the other was an automatic timing device to record the minutes and seconds it took the race to be run.

Up ahead, going at a brisk pace over the first two furlongs, he saw Sapphire Prince, an English-trained, Arab-owned runner. We shouldn't have too much bother with him, thought Roche. Walking back down the track was the Irish challenger, Southern Cross, a beautiful colt, held by Noble Lord over shorter distances, but could he turn the tables over the one and a half miles of the Derby? Southern Cross's jockey was Gerry Walsh, a popular little Irishman riding full-time in England.

"You're looking a picture, Stroker!" Walsh called across.

"Thanks, mate," said Stroker.

He clicked his tongue ever so softly, and the half a ton of flesh and blood beneath him quickened instantly into a slow canter, up the rising ground of the racetrack that is the first furlong of the race. Police had closed the roads leading onto the track so that the horses could exercise.

Stroker was now at the far side of the Downs. The Derby start is at the base of a hill. The track itself is a series of up-and-down hills and bends, meandering through the Epsom Downs for one and a half miles. It is a supreme test of the thoroughbred horse: not only must he have stamina and speed, but also the balance to maneuver bends and gradients at full gallop, the nimbleness of foot to take advantage of openings that may present themselves for only two strides, and, most of all, the strength of character to concentrate on beating off his rivals over the last two furlongs, run in a virtual tunnel of deafening noise as half a million people on both sides of the track scream their choice home.

Stroker quickened Noble Lord's pace very slightly. They were at the first bend of the track, a right-hand one, bounded by woodland. Noble Lord had been drawn in position number twenty for the start. This meant that he would have the advantage up to this first bend. But the track at this point swung to the left and continued so uphill to the mile post. He would then be on the outside and at a disadvantage. From the mile post at the hilltop the track began to sweep, always to the left, downhill for half a mile until it eventually rounded into the straight at notorious Tattenham Corner. And that was make or break. As the field of horses surged down the hill, the weaker ones would not keep the pace and would begin to drop back sharply, like flotsam in a great racing tide. No matter how good you were, if you missed your position at this stage, the risks of being hampered by a horse going backward were enormous. By the time you arrived in the straight all that you would see was the tails of your rivals, racing beyond your reach.

The Epsom Derby was therefore a great test of a jockey as well as a horse; Stroker Roche did not intend to let any other horse or jockey screw up his chances this day.

They had now reached the top of the hill, and Stroker pulled up and walked Noble Lord in a small circle, talking all the while to the horse, his every jockey's instinct sharply honed, delighting in the colt's magnificent well-being. He had to admit Jeremy had done a great job of preparation—the horse was trained to the minute.

From where they walked, a magnificent view was enfolding in the summer morning. Below and to his right the village of Tadworth still slept, while straight in front, over the horse's ear was the sprawling mass of Greater London.

Stroker again nudged the horse gently, and they set off down toward Tattenham Corner in a slow, controlled canter. The gradient plunged sharply at this point. They reached the halfway stage of the descent, and the jockey allowed the horse's pace to quicken slightly. Noble Lord immediately lengthened his stride. The sweeping downhill track presented him with no problems, his balance perfectly preserved, leading with his inside leg. They were really motoring now, the colt taking a mighty hold of his bit, the jockey's iron wrists anchoring him from going flat out. Stroker could feel the powerhouse beneath him. If he was in the same position that afternoon, all he would have to do was to press the button.

The horse's ears were pricked as he strove to go even faster. He loved running. As they approached the bottom of the hill, Stroker could see Jeremy standing on the track. With difficulty he eased the colt up as they reached the trainer.

"O.K.?" asked Jeremy.

Stroker grinned broadly.

"It's not everyone gets to drive a fifty-million-dollar machine before breakfast," he said.

ZEID AND CHALKIE watched Stroker jog their horse across the Downs to the Derby start, then they turned to walk along the bottom of the track, back toward the stable yard, Zeid carrying Noble Lord's leading rein.

Their route took them past the presaddling enclosure with its rows of wide stalls to one side, past the paddock itself with the television tower beside it. Workmen were erecting a marquee at the back of the paddock, between the St. John Ambulance hut and a mobile bank. The grass in the paddock gleamed with health; soon the twenty-four most valuable colts in Europe would be prancing on it, watched by TV worldwide.

To the right and behind the paddock stood a building in the shape of an L, housing Tote facilities and a bar. Suddenly Zeid saw a large group of uniformed policemen with Labrador dogs emerge from behind it and walk down the track, heading straight in his direction. His heartbeat quickened. Instinctively he looked around him for a way of escape. The uniformed group had left the track and were approaching the paddock. They appeared to be looking directly at him. Zeid and Chalkie walked on. Zeid tried to keep the cork in his urge to run for it. He looked at them again. They had turned away into the Tote building.

Every muscle in his body had screamed with tension, but now he began to relax. The fact of being so near the place where his mission would be executed had brought the strain in him to a new pitch.

The police bastards were everywhere. The night before, when they had got in from Newmarket he had seen them, swarming all over the stands. They had even been out on the course itself with bomb detectors. The poor fools! he thought. Little did these English know of the master plan that was unfolding against them. Well they might send their armies to terrorize the poor people of a small, defenseless country, to plunder their little prosperity and abuse their women. Not defenseless any more. Soon they would pay the price of all cowards and thieves—and then perhaps they would leave Ireland to her own people.

Zeid's intense hate provoked in him a rage that surmounted any fear. Now it enabled him to breathe easily again as they approached the long, red-brick dormitory block beside the stables where he had slept the night before.

"The place is bloody crawling with coppers, isn't it?" said Chalkie.

Zeid looked at him sharply. He wondered if the head lad had noticed his reaction back there. Still it did not matter much whether he had or not. Only the wizened little man walking at his side now stood between him and the success of his crusade. It was time to remove that obstacle.

"I'm going down to check tack," Chalkie was saying. "You muck out, on the double, and then when Stroker gets back we'll have some breakfast."

Zeid grunted as he and Chalkie walked through the arch leading down to the stables, each showing their pass to the security man at the gate. As he returned his pass to his jeans pocket, Zeid's fingers checked the rounded shape of the small plastic object he had put there an hour before.

The yard was busy. Some horses had come in from their work and were being walked around while others were preparing to go out on the track. Buckets stood under gushing taps outside stables, barrow loads of manure were wheeled to the dung heap, bales of straw were carried on pitchforks to freshen the beds of horses now out on the Downs. The teams of men associated with each horse scurried about, all conscious of the special nature of the day that had begun.

"Morning, Chalkie!"

Chalkie turned to acknowledge the greeting from the head lad of another Newmarket stable.

"Morning, John!" he said. "See you at breakfast."

They walked toward their box, situated at the very back of the yard facing a line of beech trees. If the day got too hot the trees would provide invaluable cool for Noble Lord in the tense buildup before the race. Chalkie saw a group of Frenchmen gathered around Esprit du Calvados, the fancied French colt that had won two big races over there already. The crack French jockey was on board, and there was old Michel Lambret the great trainer, who had delayed his retirement for one year to train this colt.

Next to him was the American colt, Razzle Dazzle, who had been flown from New York where he was a popular star. Chalkie doubted if he stood much of a chance—there was an ocean of difference between racing on a circular dirt track in the States and the undulating grass switchback that was Epsom.

"How'r'ye, Chalkie?"

The voice came from over the door of a stable they were passing; it belonged to Sean Murphy, the traveling head lad of J. J. Reilly's stable.

"Morning, Sean," said Chalkie. "All well?"

"He's out with Gerry doing a small bit of work," said Murphy. "He'll run well, but you'll take all the beating."

"We're keeping our fingers crossed," said Chalkie. "See you later, Sean."

They reached Noble Lord's box at the back of the yard, a single line of stables facing the trees, built in red brick with plain asbestos roofs. The woodwork and half-doors of the boxes were painted in a dark green.

The sun had not yet penetrated to that part of the yard, which was still in shadow. Each stable had a feeding manger in its far left-hand corner and immediately to the right inside the door there was a wooden locker, built flush with the corner of the wall, where small items of tack and grooming brushes could be kept.

"I just want to get something from the locker," said Chalkie.

He walked into the empty stable ahead of Zeid and made his way to the right-hand corner. He bent to the locker and frowned. It had suddenly become quite dark. He turned his head. Why has the bloody fool pulled the top door shut? he thought. A vicelike hand suddenly clasped around his mouth, and he felt the stinging point of a needle as it plunged into his chest. In terror he tried wildly to burst free, but then his small body arched upward in the agonizing spasm of a massive cardiac attack.

Quietly Zeid let the limp body slide on to the straw. He left the stable, returning a moment later with a wheelbarrow. It took him only a few moments to fork some straw and manure on before wheeling it out, down the block to the steaming dung heap that was being busily replenished from the other boxes. Soon the cleanings from Noble Lord's stable would be far beneath the surface. The chances of the tiny, plastic hypodermic being discovered were remote.

JEREMY SAW THE flashing lights of the ambulance when he was halfway up the straight. Stroker had taken Noble Lord up Tattenham Hill and would come back to the stables via the start, making sure the colt was completely cool before returning him to the stable yard.

Now that the gallop was over, Jeremy would ring Penny and ask her to bring his morning suit and a clean shirt out to Epsom without delay. He would get a loan of Chalkie's razor. Christ, the prince had been demanding! Jeremy had only a faint recollection of the previous evening, and what he could remember he would have preferred to forget. The colt's gallop had made him feel slightly better. Stroker had reached a masterly understanding with the animal, only rarely achieved between horse and rider. The sight of them in an

244

extended gallop would make a cripple throw away his crutches and dance for joy.

Jeremy strolled past the winning post, down the hill to the stables. He was about to show his pass when he saw a familiar figure running out to him. It was Sean Murphy, J. J. Reilly's head lad.

"Oh thank God you've arrived, Mr. Carvill," the Irishman blurted. "I was going to run down the track to find you."

"What's the matter?" Jeremy asked, a great well of fear rising in his chest. His mind raced. Surely the horse was still out on the track?

"I'm very sorry, sir, but there's awful news," Murphy said.

"What fucking news?" Jeremy screamed.

"Chalkie Charlesworth, sir, we found him five minutes ago inside in the box. The ambulance has brought him off to Epsom. But he's dead, sir."

Jeremy staggered slightly backward to the red-brick wall, and the Irish head lad moved to steady him.

"Just take it easy, sir," said Murphy gently. "Don't upset yourself too much."

Jeremy felt lightheaded, unable to comprehend what he had been told. Incredibly his first feeling was not one of sorrow, but of relief: the horse was all right.

"Just let me take you down to the box, sir," Murphy was saying. "Chalkie was a great old friend of mine. Terrible thing it is to have happened to him on the day that you'll probably win the Derby."

"What happened to him?" Jeremy asked in a daze.

"He had a massive heart attack, sir. In the box. He was stone dead when we got to him. I was only talking to him a few minutes ago."

Jeremy, with Murphy at his elbow, made his way numbly into the yard and toward the block where Noble Lord was stabled. Word had obviously gone about the yard because everything was now subdued; a couple of trainers came up and murmured condolences to him.

"Frightful thing, awfully sorry," said Major Langdon.

245

"I liked old Charlesworth. Sorry, Jeremy," said someone else.

Jeremy turned the corner. A few lads who had been standing about walked away when they saw the trainer. Zeid sat in a wooden chair outside the box. He got up as Jeremy approached.

"What happened?" asked Jeremy. He was feeling a bit more clear-headed now.

"I was mucking out," said Zeid in his staccato voice. "I went to the dung heap. I came back. Chalkie was lying in the stable. He was dead."

Jeremy shook his head incredulously. "What did you do then?" he asked hoarsely.

"I think he must have come running up for me, sir," replied Sean Murphy. "That's how I knew. Isn't that right, young fellow?"

Zeid nodded. "That's right," he said.

"I called the ambulance," said Murphy. "There's a St. John Ambulance unit on duty, and they were here in a couple of minutes. They've taken him into the hospital in Epsom."

"Jesus Christ," said Jeremy and sat down heavily in the chair. "You're sure he's dead? I mean, who said he was dead?"

"The ambulance man," replied Zeid.

Jeremy sighed deeply. "O.K.," he said, "we still have a job of work to do. Murphy, thank you very much. I won't forget this."

"If there's any way we can help you," said the Irishman. "I'm sure Mr. Reilly will do everything he can."

"No. I think we'll just about manage, thank you. But I'll ask if I need help," said Jeremy. "Thank you so much again."

Murphy turned and left for his own stable.

"Now," said Jeremy, standing up. "I'll just see Stroker, tell him what has happened, and get the horse in. What a frightful thing. And this is the day that he had worked for all his life."

Zeid nodded.

"I shall have to go into the hospital straightaway," said

Jeremy. "We'll have to notify his wife. Oh my God, what shall I say?" He turned ashen-faced to the stable lad. "Zeid, you're in charge now, do you hear that? Do you understand?"

"Yes, sir," replied the swarthy youth.

"I'll come down here and groom the horse myself before he's saddled. But you're not to leave him out of your sight, is that clear?"

Zeid nodded. Jeremy turned to go back to the stable entrance. Stroker should be back by now, he thought.

"One other thing, Zeid," he said turning back, his face drawn with tension and fatigue, "you'll have to lead the horse around the presaddling enclosure and around the paddock before the race. That was to have been Chalkie's job . . ." and he fought to contain a sob. His voice trailed off.

The stable lad turned away from the trainer and began to busy himself in the stable: he did not want Jeremy to see the smile that had appeared on his face.

THE SUITCASE SKIDDED off the rubber conveyor and onto the metal baggage carousel of Terminal Three. The area was crowded with returned holidaymakers, eyes red-rimmed from the eight-hour overnight flight. It was 8:00 A.M.

Hope reached for his bag. Beside him, Debbie stretched out her brown arm with its chunky, white bracelet for a heavy suitcase. Hope caught the handle, and easily lifted the bag off.

"I've been looking for a baggage trolley," she said, "but I guess we're a little late."

"I'll carry it, no problem," said Hope. They walked toward Customs, and Debbie stopped and laughed, her very white teeth shining in her pretty face.

"Winston Hope," she smiled, "for a cop you are really something. Here you are falling for the oldest trick in the book—carrying a total stranger's baggage through Customs. I could have three kilos of the best Colombian in there."

Hope turned, his face perplexed, to look at the attractive girl with the lovely smile.

"Come on, Winston," she said, linking her arm through his. "I was really only kidding."

Together they walked through Customs and out into the concourse of the airport building. For the last two hours of the flight they had chatted like old friends of many years. It had seemed natural.

"We'll go back to my place and ring Scotland Yard," said Debbie. "I'm sure they'll want you to go in and explain everything."

They were outside the Customs area.

"I don't want to intrude," said Hope stopping. "Maybe I . . ."

"No discussion," said Debbie. She placed her suitcase beside his. "Now, sir, if you would be so good as to continue your good work . . " She inclined her head toward the two bags and then strode off toward a sign that indicated the Underground. Hope was left with little option; he picked up the luggage and hurried in pursuit.

It was ten-thirty when they emerged into London's busy traffic. Debbie led them past shops and through squares of terraced houses to a newly painted, white front door at the end of a quiet cul-de-sac. The house had been converted into flats. She was carrying a bag of groceries, which they had stopped for. Hope brought up the rear.

"Well here we are," she said cheerfully. "I'm on the top."

They entered a small hall that led to two further entrances. Debbie's accumulated mail lay neatly stacked on a white, marble-top table with a newspaper. She put them into the grocery bag, opened the right-hand door, and climbed the narrow flight of stairs.

"Can you manage?" she called back.

"O.K.," said Hope. "I can manage fine."

He transferred both suitcases to his right hand and made his ascent of the stairs in reverse pulling the bags behind him.

The little flat was bright and cheerful. There was a main living area, with a small kitchen with pine fittings tucked into the corner. Double windows opened onto a tiny roof garden. At the back there was a sofa of the type that comes in sections and a coffee table with a smoked-glass top. Deep-red hessian hung on the walls. A bathroom led off a small passage inside the front door and another door, presumably to the bedroom, faced it.

"Home sweet home," Debbie smiled. "Whew! It's a long trip."

She put her bag on a shelf in the kitchen.

"Now what's it to be? Coffee? Eggs and bacon?"

"Sure," said Hope, "that would be real good."

"O.K., Sergeant Hope," she said. "You sit over there," she pointed to the sofa, "and I'll do the work for a change."

Hope sat down and began to flick through the daily newspaper on the table. He was trying to work out in his mind the best course of action. He was sure that today was the day ringed in the calendar, but it could have signified a thousand other things—and the more he thought about it the more it seemed likely to him that any explanation was more probable than the one that he was now pursuing. He would call Scotland Yard after breakfast. He knew the way police forces worked: if he made an appointment first, outlining his story, then he would be treated all the more seriously when he got in. Anyway, they would by now be familiar with the case.

"How do you like your eggs, Sergeant Hope?" asked Debbie. She looked over to where he sat, and her face dropped. Hope was sitting absolutely frozen, staring at the newspaper. He half rose from the sofa pointing incredulously.

"What is it?" she asked, coming out from behind the worktop to him.

"It's, it's him," stammered Hope.

"It's who?" asked Debbie. Hope was staring down at a large photograph in the centerfold that showed a group of men standing around a horse.

"It's him," repeated Hope, pointing his finger at a dark-haired youth at the horse's head, turning slightly away from the camera. "It's the man whose photograph I saw in New York. I swear it."

"Let me have a look," said Debbie. She turned the paper to her. Emblazoned across the top of the page was "EVERY-ONE'S FAVORITE!" The story was about the horse that was on everyone's lips, the fifteen-million-dollar wonder-colt who would that day start as the shortest-priced favorite of the century for the Epsom Derby.

"Oh Jesus," said Debbie, closing her eyes and resting her forehead on the heels of her hands.

"It's him," said Hope again.

"I'm sure it is," she said wearily. "Do you know what day it is today?"

"It's June third," he replied.

"Yes. It's Wednesday June third," she said. "It's Derby Day over here. Today is the day of their most famous, richest horse race. Most of London will be there—including guess who?"

Slowly Hope began to understand what she was saying. She had flicked to another page that contained a full description of the dazzling pageant of royalty that would unfold at Epsom that afternoon.

"She'll be at the races?"

"That's right. And so will he," said Debbie pointing to the photograph. "He's working in the stable that trains the favorite for the race."

Hope leapt to his feet.

"Where's the phone?" he shouted. "We must stop her."

Debbie stood up.

"Just a minute," she cried. "Who are you going to call? The Palace? They'll think you're some kind of a nut! Anyway she'll have probably left by now. It's nearly eleven."

"Than we must phone the police and tell them," said Hope. "Give them a description so they can arrest him."

"Arrest who?" she asked. "A stable boy? What reason would they have to do that? Who are you? And how long would it take you to convince them of your story?"

250

"Where is this Derby?" Hope asked.

"It's at Epsom, twenty miles from London," said Debbie.

"Then that's where we're going!" shouted Hope. "How do we get there?"

"By train," she said and grabbed a phone book. "Oh Jesus!" she said as she misdialed and started again.

"Here, let me do it," Hope said. "Where's the number?"

Debbie pointed, then ran into the bathroom and began brushing her hair. She could hear Hope speaking. She came out still brushing vigorously. "You got it?" she asked.

"Every twenty minutes from Victoria," he replied. He was at the door. "Brush it later," he called and ran down the stairs, three at a time, in front of her.

IN HIS OFFICE on the twelfth floor of New Scotland Yard, the Commissioner of the Metropolitan Police picked up his buzzing telephone. His back stiffened involuntarily as he heard the voice on the other end.

"Yes, sir," he said, "of course, sir. I have a direct line of communication set up. No, nothing at all, sir."

"I wanted to talk to you personally," said the Home Secretary. "The rumors that have started flying around are horrendous. One would think we were about to be invaded."

"I think the situation is under control, sir," said the commissioner. "We have set up a quite unprecedented security operation out there."

"Have you see the morning papers?"

"I have, sir."

"The PM has been on to me," said the Home Secretary. "Wanted to know if Special Branch had picked up anyone worthwhile."

"Nobody, sir," said the commissioner. "If there is something going on they've kept it very quiet."

"Too bloody quiet," said the Home Secretary. "Still, let's hope it's just a scare. We're probably jumping to conclusions."

"We're treating it extremely seriously, sir," said the commissioner.

"What about this damn fellow who came in through Scotland?" asked the Home Secretary.

"We're still trying to trace him, sir, but as you can imagine he could be anywhere," said the commissioner. "I shall let you know the moment we have anything."

"I've complete confidence in you," said the Home Secretary and hung up.

The commissioner replaced his receiver and stared at it for a moment. He had been briefed that morning by Jim Abbott. He was sure nothing had been overlooked. He snatched up the telephone again.

"Ask Jim Abbott to come up here right away," he said to his secretary. Then he swiveled around in his chair and looked morosely out the window.

MAJOR GATHORNE-HARDY left his office to walk the short distance to the stable yard. A balding, fit-looking man was standing just outside the door.

"Excuse me," he said. "I'm looking for the clerk of the course."

"I'm the clerk of the course," said Gathorne-Hardy. "What can I do for you?"

"Ah, good morning, sir. Chief Inspector Dawson, Special Branch," said Dawson producing his ID. Another bloody policeman, thought Gathorne-Hardy.

"Roger Gathorne-Hardy," he said. "Anything the matter, Chief Inspector?"

"No, sir," said Dawson. "If you had a moment, I was wondering if we could walk around the stables, just to familiarize myself with the place."

"Just on my way there," said Gathorne-Hardy.

They walked briskly to the stables, Dawson showing his pass to the security officer at the gate.

"Quite a production for you today," said Dawson to the clerk of the course.

"It used to be easier," said Gathorne-Hardy darkly.

"Yes," replied Dawson. "I'm sure the extra security hasn't helped."

"Hasn't helped?" said Gathorne-Hardy. "It's only quarter past eleven, and I'm told the traffic is already backed up three miles the other side of Epsom. We're going to get a lot of stick, you know, closing our main car park on the busiest day of the year."

"We had very little option," said Dawson.

The bustle of the early morning was over, and the yard was sunny and peaceful. They were standing at the center of the yard.

"Where do you want to go?" asked the Major.

"Just a quick tour," said Dawson. "Anything unusual your end this morning, sir?"

"Apart from the fact that our racecourse is more like a military encampment, everything is as usual," said Gathorne-Hardy. They rounded a corner and nearly bumped into the tall figure of Jeremy Carvill carrying a small suitcase.

"Good morning, Jeremy," said Gathorne-Hardy.

"Oh excuse me. Good morning, Major," said Jeremy. "I'm just rushing to get changed. My owner will be here shortly, and we're due to have lunch."

"Frightful business this morning," said the clerk of the course. "Very upsetting for you before the big race. I'm very sorry."

"I know," said Jeremy shaking his head. "It hasn't quite registered yet. He was my right arm, been with me from day one. He was as fit as a fiddle at six o'clock this morning."

"Frightful business," said Gathorne-Hardy. "I won't keep you, you're in a hurry. Best of luck this afternoon."

"Thanks very much," said Jeremy and with a nod to Dawson ran toward the dormitory building.

"What was all that about?" asked Dawson.

"That was Jeremy Carvill," replied Gathorne-Hardy. "He's training the favorite for the Derby. His head lad, Charlesworth, dropped dead in the stable just before breakfast."

"I saw an ambulance earlier on," said Dawson. "That must have been him."

"Most likely," said Gathorne-Hardy. "They took him to Epsom Hospital. I understand there will be a routine post-mortem later on."

They were at the back of the yard where a line of boxes faced the trees.

"Do you want to see the favorite?" asked the clerk of the course.

"Why not?" said Dawson.

They walked up to the box and looked in over the half-door. In the comparative gloom they could see a gleaming black coat being brought to an even brighter shine by a dark-haired stable lad.

"Morning," said Gathorne-Hardy.

The stable lad jumped, causing the horse to jink away from the wall.

"Sorry if I startled you," said Gathorne-Hardy. "Clerk of the course. Just checking if everything is in order."

Dawson saw a pale face with wild eyes, a slightly off stare, and a drooping mustache.

"All right," came the reply. "Just grooming."

Gathorne-Hardy nodded.

"Mustn't upset these horses," he said to Dawson. "That one there is worth nearly fifty million if he wins this afternoon as he's expected to."

Dawson whistled softly.

"That's put my fiver in its place," he said with a laugh, glancing back as they walked away from the box at Noble Lord to whom the stable boy was now talking in a soothing voice.

"All these employees have been checked out and cleared in advance I believe?" he said to Gathorne-Hardy.

"Absolutely. No one can come in here without a special pass and number. To get that pass they have had to apply to the Jockey Club in advance. There's far too much money in here today for us to be anything less than one hundred percent sure of who's who. Far too much."

They were back at the exit area. The lively figure of Jimmy Flynn was coming toward them. He had spent his Derby breakfast with Gathorne-Hardy listening to the old clerk of the course rattling on about the police.

"Jimmy, this is Inspector . . . sorry, I've forgotten your name," he said.

"Dawson," said the Special Branch man, shaking the head groundsman's hand.

"Anything to report, Jimmy?" asked Gathorne-Hardy.

"The Downs traffic is moving all right," said Flynn, "but I hear that Epsom is twice as bad as usual and that's terrible. It's the car parking."

Gathorne-Hardy nodded his head curtly.

"I know," he said.

"There's also a huge crowd of people building up at the entrance to the enclosures," said Flynn. "The police are searching everyone coming in, and that's leading to big delays."

"I think I'll go over and lend a hand," said Dawson. "Thank you for your time, Major, Mr. Flynn."

He walked up onto the track and turned left in the direction of the enclosures, two furlongs away. Major Gathorne-Hardy and Jimmy Flynn watched his bald, receding head.

"These policemen are going to make an absolute bollocks of the day," said Major Gathorne-Hardy.

IT WAS THE first time since he had been a POW in 1944 that Colonel Freddy Newell had been body-searched. The brawny police officer did not waste any niceties on the senior steward either: having expertly patted the colonel's outstretched arms, chest, and back, he ran his fingers down the outside of the striped-suited, bony legs and then briefly but firmly up into the crotch of the Jockey Club's foremost arbiter. At a closed booth nearby, his wife, Lady Honor, was receiving the same treatment from the hands of a police-woman.

Following their searching, the Newells made their way to the special entrance lobby to take the elevator that would bring them up to the Jockey Club rooms.

"What a nuisance for everyone," said Lady Newell.

"I'm very glad to see it," said Colonel Newell pressing the elevator button. "I heard this morning," he lowered his voice, "that there has been another bomb scare, and the police are taking it very seriously."

"How awful," said Lady Newell. "There's something about it in the paper." They stepped into the lift.

"These terrorists are taking over our lives, I'm afraid," said her husband. They stepped out into the paneled rooms of the Jockey Club. A small, beaming man with a huge mustache came toward them.

"Honor, Freddy, come and have a drink," he said, standing on his toes to kiss Lady Newell on the cheek.

"How nice to see you, Binkie," said Lady Newell.

Binkie Goldman was a Russian Jew who had made his fortune in electronics twenty years earlier. Now his time was divided between his two great interests: sailing and horse racing. Goldman had stud farms in Australia and Canada as well as in England. His tireless patronage of racing and his great wealth had assured Goldman's election to the Jockey Club. Today, the supreme authority at Epsom in all matters relating to horses was vested in Colonel Newell, Binkie Goldman, and Lord Hugh Llewellyn, a crusty septuagenarian who had yet to arrive.

"Glass of champagne?" asked Goldman.

"Well, I suppose since it is Derby Day, just one," said Newell. Lady Honor had gone to the powder room.

"Have you heard about the scare?"

"Yes," said Goldman, "but even if I hadn't it wouldn't take much working out, would it? I've never seen so many police-men. There must be a thousand of them here."

"Life must go on," said Newell. "We cannot allow our society to be compromised by threats from the Irish, or the PLO or anyone else."

"I know what I would do," said Goldman. "I'd do a Begin on them. Send in a couple of B52s over Ireland and bomb the shit out of them. These terrorists are walking around the streets over there, you know, free as the breeze."

"Well, I'm not sure if it's quite as simple as that," said Newell. His wife had returned and Goldman handed her a drink.

"Oh how kind, Binkie," she said. "Have we got our nice table at the window again?"

Goldman made a face.

"Afraid not," he said. "The famous Prince-what's-his-name, the chap who owns Noble Lord, is coming up for lunch with young Carvill. They asked specifically for the window. I thought it better not to make a fuss."

"Absolutely," said Newell. The amount of money that this Arab was spending on racing was mind-boggling. He had single-handedly raised the average at last year's yearling sales by twenty-five percent.

"Looks like his horse is a good thing," said Goldman. "As far as the bookies are concerned, he's gone by."

"Oh, what price is he?" asked Newell.

"Two to one on."

"Oh dear," said Lady Newell. "That means I shan't get very much back for my pound."

"Back something else, darling," said the colonel. "Back a complete outsider to beat him."

"That's right," said Goldman looking at his race card. "Why not try Southern Cross, the Irish colt? Ran a blinder in the Guineas."

"Oh I couldn't desert Stroker, not at Epsom," said Lady Newell.

There was a buzz of excitement around the small bar and dining room. A number of people were looking out of the window, down the track. The Newells and Goldman took their glasses and walked to the front of the room until they had a panoramic view of Epsom Downs.

Way to their left, up near the six-furlong start, bright sunlight glinted off the highly polished roofs of half a dozen maroon Rolls-Royces as they began to make their slow, stately way down Tattenham Hill, toward the most famous corner in thoroughbred racing, their passage cheered by hundreds of thousands of happy, holidaying people.

The royal party was about to arrive.

COMMANDER MCKECHNIE REPLACED the telephone receiver. Jim Abbott had been uncharacteristically edgy, he thought. Must be getting a lot of pressure from higher up. The operation had gone smoothly so far. Of course the security arrangements had meant delays and inconvenience, but that was the price one had to pay.

He had just got the word that the Queen and her party were safely up in the Royal Box. The procession and arrival had gone without incident, the police forming a two-deep barrier around the sovereign and her guests. McKechnie's anti-terrorist squad were all over the roofs and hidden at strategic points around the paddock and out on the Downs. None of them had reported anything.

Chief Inspector Dawson, who had been on the telephone at the back of the tent, came out.

"Everything seems to be going smoothly, sir," he said to McKechnie.

"Yes, thank goodness," said the head of C.13. "Anything from Special Branch? That's what I'm really interested in. As soon as we can catch up with a couple of these bastards then this sort of operation won't be necessary."

"Nothing that I've heard, sir," said Dawson.

"I'm advocating a complete review of our immigration laws with Eire," said McKechnie. "We cannot allow these people this sort of access any more than we can the Libyans, for example."

"It certainly does not make life any easier," said Dawson. "However this O'Neill man is reported to have come in from Northern Ireland. There's very little we can do about that—no more than if he was a Welsh nationalist."

"The Queen is safely in and upstairs," said McKechnie changing the subject. "We have only this paddock business left as our main worry. Christ, what would life be like if this was par for the course each time she stepped outside the Palace?"

"Pretty awful," said Dawson. "Nothing more on the Caribbean aspect of this thing, sir?"

"Nothing," said McKechnie. "However that's something I want to get to the bottom of. Someone knows a lot more than we do. I want to meet that someone."

THE CREAM SILVER Shadow with the dark windows drew up at the side entrance to the Ritz at twelve-twenty. Two dark-skinned men ran down the few steps and stood on either side of the back door. They surveyed the area immediately around the car, then one of them nodded to a third man situated back inside the hotel. A moment later the figure of Prince Abdullah bin Yasir al-Fahd, owner of the favorite for the Derby, swept out. He wore robes of dazzling white, the only color provided by the hand-stitched keeper on his headdress, which was worked in reds and greens and golds. Enormous dark glasses concealed his eyes. He entered the air-conditioned comfort of the car and sank back with relief in the luxury of the wide rear seat.

His head had been lifting from his shoulders all morning from the effects of the cocaine and alcohol the night before. He felt like a wet rag. If it had not been for the oxygen tent in which he had breathed for twenty minutes earlier on, he could not have mustered the strength to get up at all. It had cost a small fortune to have the unit fitted up at such short notice. But he knew from experience it was worth it. The inhalation of pure oxygen put you back on top like nothing else. But where was Jeremy?

He vaguely remembered the young trainer leaving. The drug had blurred the fine edge of his appreciation, leaving him with only the vague outline of what had happened. He had been trying to contact Jeremy all morning but with no success. They had got through to Epsom racetrack, but the trainer had left—someone said for a hospital. Yaw shuddered. Perhaps the fool had overdone it last night and was now being sedated somewhere.

"All ready, Your Highness?" asked the driver.

Yaw nodded, and the great car slipped out into the Piccadilly traffic heading for Battersea Heliport. The prince's eyes were now beginning to adjust to the interior darkness. He pressed a button, and a large opaque glass screen slid noiselessly up to isolate the back from the driver.

"Good morning, Your Highness."

Yaw started. He looked to his right. A staggering-looking girl sat perched on the small jump-seat. She wore a black leather mini-skirt and a simple white blouse. She sat with her elbows on her bared, brown knees, her luxurious mane of auburn hair cascading forward, her teeth sparkling in a wide smile. There was something vital and animallike about her that caused the Prince to swallow hard. He had seen her before but he had no idea of her name.

"Good morning," he said.

"Do you remember phoning me last night?" she asked.

"I think so," said Yaw.

"You naughty boy, Prince," she said with a giggle. "Here, let me take off poor Prince's dark glasses." She leaned over and removed the large shades. Yaw's eyes blinked.

"I hope your horse wins today," she said softly.

"So do I," said Yaw.

"I would like to be able to afford to have something on it," said the girl.

The prince put his hand into a fold of his robe and brought out a fat wad of notes, which he put on the seat beside him.

"Oh, you're so kind," purred the girl.

She slid from her perch until she was kneeling between the prince's knees. Her fantastic hair smelled of subtle fragrances. The vibrations from her glorious young body were electric. Yaw began to feel immeasurably better.

"Your Highness is so very kind to little me," she murmured and began softly to peel up the skirt of his robe from the ankles. He leaned forward and unbuttoned the top of her blouse. It slipped down from her round, golden shoulders. She wore nothing beneath.

As they swept down toward the river, Yaw was oblivious to the envious stares of the people they passed, hurrying to their lunch. It was nearly half past one.

"COME ON!" CRIED Debbie as they reached the tube station.

Hope had paused for a moment to admire the magnificent cream car with the black windows that had just gone past. He hurried after Debbie's scurrying figure, down two flights of steps to where the tickets were sold, both on automatic machines and by a man behind a small, barred window.

"Do you have any change?" asked Debbie.

Hope shook his head.

"Shit," said Debbie under her breath and joined a queue at the ticket window. A group of about ten children with their teacher was in front. The teacher reached the window and produced a document for the ticket clerk.

"Just a minute," Debbie heard the clerk say as he disappeared. She looked around. None of the other ticket offices was open. There was a shop in one corner selling sweets and cigarettes.

"Get some change, quickly," she said to Hope. "I'll stay in the line."

Hope fumbled for a five pound note and went over to the shop. A fat youth chewing gum slouched behind the raised counter.

"Could you please change this?" Hope asked.

"Naw, sorry, short for change."

Hope looked back to the ticket office: the line had not moved. He picked up a bar of chocolate, and the youth took the five pound note. He handed Hope back a handful of coins and Hope rushed back to Debbie.

"Got it," he said.

She took the coins and went to a ticket machine. "Christ, these don't give change," she groaned and went back to the kiosk.

"Please sir, can you give me tens?" she asked as winningly as she could.

"Sorry," said the youth, "short of tens."

"Fuck you, Mister," hissed Debbie.

Hope turned to the barrier where a blue-uniformed ticket collector stood. With a jerk of his head he signaled Debbie to follow him. The collector's attention was momentarily elsewhere, and Hope and Debbie ran through the barrier, toward the escalator that would take them down to the bowels of the station.

"This way," said Debbie and turned left at the bottom of the escalator. A train stood by the platform. With all of a second to spare she and Hope jumped in.

"What time is it?" she asked him.

"It's one thirty-five," he said. "We have almost two hours to the Derby. You say this place is only twenty miles away. We should do it easily."

"Let's hope so," said Debbie.

Two minutes later, a sign saying "Victoria" flashed by. Debbie and Hope hit the platform as the doors opened.

"Follow the British Rail signs," she yelled.

The Underground was busy and the slow-moving up escalator was blocked solid when they got to it. Debbie began to elbow her way upward.

"Go easy, love," said a man in overalls, "it's completely jammed up there."

"I'm sorry, but this is an emergency," said Debbie.

They made little progress; eventually the top was reached.

Grabbing Hope by the hand she tore for the exit. Their way was blocked by a chubby, black ticket collector.

"Excess ticket desk is over there," he said to her protesting figure, indicating another window with a long line.

"We haven't time to queue," cried Debbie. "This is life or death!"

"Sorry," said the collector. "That's the rules."

Hope produced a wallet and flicked it open, showing his badge.

"Antiguan Police Force, man," he said. "Now stand aside."

The ticket collector's mouth opened; and he stood back as Hope and Debbie raced through. Then his face split in a wide grin, and he raised his right fist.

Victoria station was, at the very height of the tourist season, like a set for the Tower of Babel. People of every origin and color swarmed all over it, producing a great swell of noise over which an incomprehensible loudspeaker dispensed information with a high-pitched whine. Large notice boards clicked and whirred, showing arrivals and departures at the different platforms. People pushed luggage trolleys around in a seemingly aimless fashion; a large group of Japanese waited to be led to a train; special British Rail wheelchairs transported the disabled to and fro; crowds of people gathered around machines that dispensed Pepsi, Nestlés chocolate, your photograph in color or in black and white, change, chewing gum, and, above the whole demented scene, gray pigeons flitted in the domed arches of the station, periodically dispensing their droppings on the teeming hubbub below.

"This way," shouted Hope and ran to a ticket window, one of a long line.

"Two to Epsom," he said breathlessly.

"Return?"

"Yes, return."

Hope flung some coins into the small metal carousel, set in the window.

"Which platform?" he shouted.

"Consult the notice board and listen for announcements."

Hope and Debbie raced toward a notice board, scanning it feverishly. There was no mention of Epsom. They rushed on. A black porter leaned on a railing. Hope ran up to him.

"Epsom, which platform?" he asked.

"Fourteen, my friend, straight down," said the porter. "Nice day, lady," he remarked with an approving grin as Debbie hurried by.

Fourteen was located farther along the station; it took them awhile to weave through the dense crowds. The ticket collector who sat in his box checked his watch and looked at the platform behind him.

"I think you've missed it," he said.

"Which train?" asked Hope, catching Debbie by the arm.

"On the left, the left!"

The rear carriage jerked as it reacted to the starting pull of the diesel locomotive up front. Hope sprinted for it, pulling Debbie so that her feet barely grazed the surface of the platform. His legs pumped. He was almost level with the accelerating door of the carriage. He could see a group of men standing inside drinking from bottles. A platform inspector was looming up, his hands waving. A whistle shrilled. Suddenly one of the men inside, a 250-pound six-footer, saw the frantic face through the glass. He flicked open the heavy train door.

"Come on, mate!" he cried with assurance, grabbing Hope's outstretched hand and applying a mighty tug. Hope sailed through the air into the doorway, the minute, flying figure of Debbie still in his airborne grasp behind him. The large man shut the door with a bang and looked out. There was a great cheer from the other men. Hope and Debbie lay on the floor, struggling for their breath as the train gathered speed.

"Going to the races?" asked the big man.

There was another great cheer and someone handed Hope a frothing bottle of beer.

"Thank you," he gasped. "Good luck."

"Good luck to you, mate," said the man. "Hope you back the winner."

Debbie leaned across from where she sat and with her hand wiped Hope's gleaming wet forehead. Then she kissed him gently on the cheek.

"Well done," she whispered. He smiled, and they both climbed to their feet.

The train was clipping on over the river, past gas tanks, a large power station. It flashed through silent Battersea Park station: Hope could see a clock suspended from the platform roof. It was ten minutes to two o'clock.

MAJOR GATHORNE-HARDY stood in the center of the parade ring as the horses made their way out to the start of the first race. Colonel Freddy Newell, the chief steward, stood at his side. The sun blazed down on the huge carnival scene, causing the men in their striped morning suits to perspire freely.

"The going should be absolutely perfect, Roger," said Colonel Newell.

"I was just saying that to Flynn," remarked Gathorne-Hardy. "I can never remember it better. It's a great credit to him and his staff."

"You're very lucky," said the chief steward.

"Should suit the favorite for the big race," said Gathorne-Hardy. "I think a lot of people have come here today just to see him. He's a real talking horse."

"Yes," said Newell. "The papers certainly don't oppose him."

"He's a lovely sort of horse," said the clerk of the course. "Beautiful action, unique specimen. I saw him out this morning. He's very ready."

Newell looked about him briefly.

"His owner arrived for lunch about twenty minutes ago," said the senior steward, "complete with a lady friend. Caused quite a stir."

"Really?" said Gathorne-Hardy.

"Well, she wasn't what you might say dressed Derby Day. However, I think she had other—uh—compensating attributes which caused one to overlook her informal attire."

"Such as?"

"Such as the most bloody marvelous pair of legs I've seen in a long time. God, if only I was twenty again!"

The two men laughed and began to walk back up the track from the paddock in the direction of the enclosures. In the thinning crowd around the parade ring, half a dozen Special Branch men, some in formal morning suits, mingled with the crowd, scanning each face with their eyes, searching for a familiar mug shot, casually brushing anyone who looked suspicious to verify if that bulge was in fact a smuggled firearm or not.

And high up in the stands, sharpshooters from C.13 scanned the milling crowds with their binoculars, tireless in their vigil to protect the middle-aged woman who was just finishing her strawberries in the box immediately below them.

THERE WAS A great roar of approval from the crowd as Stroker drove the filly up the inside rail through a gap little bigger than a dental cavity.

The jockey on the leading horse had turned around in his saddle to grab a quick look to his right. They were inside the last furlong, and he was sure he had it sewn up. It was a costly mistake. His mount lost precious balance for an instant and rolled out toward the center of the track. At once the jockey knew he had looked the wrong way. He desperately tried to regain his forfeited momentum, now aware out of the corner of his left eye of the flailing, driving powerhouse that had come to rob him.

"Come on, my son!" screamed fifty thousand delirious post-lunch punters as their first dividend of the day punched his way to the line. "Come on Stroker!"

Stroker passed the winning post and stood up in his stirrups on the still galloping horse. That's a good omen, he thought. Always nice to start off with a winner on a day like this. He eventually pulled up, past the stands, on the hill that led down to the paddock. He turned around and jogged back up the track to the Winner's circle in the Members enclosure.

"Well done, Stroker!" shouted the crowd, as he vaulted out of the saddle. Stroker grinned. If I'm back here after the Derby, that'll do, he thought. The next race was for apprentice jockeys who would not be riding in the big one. He unbuckled the girths and scooped the saddle from the heaving back of the first winner. The animal's trainer patted Stroker on the shoulder, and the little man scurried off under the stands to the weighing room where he sat on the seat of the large Avery scales. The clerk of the scales noted the weight.

"One down and one to go, Stroker?" he asked cheerfully.

Behind the official scales a man in a small office announced some minor changes for the second race. Stroker climbed from the seat and walked into the jockeys' changing room, a spartan place with gray and yellow tiles on the floor, wooden benches along the walls, and plain wooden tables running down the middle.

Stroker's valet was waiting with his colors for the Derby, the green stars shining back and front on the gleaming white silks. The room was very busy, filled by several dozen of these diminutive men, some of them millionaires many times over. They changed in rooms like this most days of the week all over England, but the tension today was special.

There was only one Derby Day. So much depended on their skills in the next two hours—and for the younger ones, or those on unfancied horses, there was always the chance that today might be the day on which they got the unexpected break. It had happened many times before: the favorite could fall or fail to stay the distance or be just plain sick. The horse under you might have decided that he liked what he was doing and begin to run for the first time in his life. If you streaked past that famous post with the rest of them behind you today, your career went up a notch.

Even Stroker, a veteran of many years, did not escape the strain. Noble Lord was widely assumed to be a sure winner, and this fact increased rather than helped the weight of stress that he began to feel. Poor old Chalkie Charlesworth's dropping dead had not helped either. What a pity, thought Stroker again. What a piss-awful hand poor old Chalkie had been dealt.

"Feel like a sauna, Stroker?" asked his valet.

"No, John, thanks," he replied. "I'll think I'll grab a cuppa."

After he'd dressed, he walked into a small refreshment room furnished with a sink, a fridge, and a few tables. He made himself a very weak cup of black tea and sat down in a chair. Another Newmarket jockey, Wally Tigget, a contemporary of Stroker's and an old friend, came and sat down. He was riding Pentle Bay in the Derby and wore dark-blue silks with white collar and cuffs.

"Butterfly time?" he asked. Tigget had difficulty keeping his weight below the one hundred and twenty to one hundred and twenty-one pounds necessary in order to weigh out with a saddle at one hundred and twenty-six, the standard weight for the Derby. There would be no prerace cup of tea for him.

"Yeah, a bit I suppose," said Stroker. "There's a lot riding on this one, isn't there?"

"Always is, young man," said Tigget, "always is. Listen, I forgot to say it but, Jesus, Stroker, I was very upset to hear about Chalkie Charlesworth. He and I went back a long way. How's your guvnor taking it?"

"How d'you think, bloody awful," said Stroker. "I saw him before the first and he was the color of skimmed milk. I'd say he hit it a bit of a lash last night as well. Christ knows what he'll do with Chalkie gone. He bloody ran the yard."

"What a shame," said Tigget, "on the day you'll probably win the Derby too. Nearly malicious, isn't it?"

"As far as poor May Charlesworth is concerned, I'd say

bloody malicious," said Stroker. "This was to have been their meal ticket. Lot of good it is to her now."

"Come on," said Tigget standing up. "I'm sure you'll persuade Carvill to honor his promise. Let's go out and have a look at the second."

Stroker finished his tea and put on a checked jacket over his silks. Then the two little men walked into the sunlight.

ZEID WAS COMPLETELY calm.

Jeremy had just checked the horse for the last time before the parade; he had left for the weighing room where he would pick up the jockey's saddle.

Zeid had followed him down to the end of the stable block and watched the tall figure of the trainer make his way from the yard, under the arch, past the security guard. The bastard had a few drinks on board as well by the smell of him. Jeremy was really rattled by Chalkie's death. It was nothing to the shock in store for him, thought Zeid, as he groomed the colt's long back with a rough cloth. The animal snorted with pleasure. There were five minutes to go before he would lead the horse to the presaddling ring.

Walking quietly to the door of the stable, Zeid glanced outside, then leaned out and quietly brought the top half inward to shut. There had been no one outside. He turned his attention to the flush white locker in the front right corner of the stable. Inserting his finger in a hole at the center of its door, he pulled it open.

He removed grooming tack, a blanket, and some rags that he had placed there an hour before. His fingers brushed cold steel and then grasped and withdrew the bulbous Type 64 from its hiding place. His head spun with pleasure. Only a little more time, and he could give up this act of being someone else. All he had to do was keep his cool; keep steady, concentrate and kill, the American instructor in the desert had taught him.

Concentrate and kill.

It would not be any different to the thousand other times when he had scored ten out of ten in the snapshot, often in conditions a lot tougher than they would shortly be. He had done it running, with the sun in his eyes, in the brief twilight, as well as at walking speed. And this little beauty would ensure his getaway.

He fondled the Chinese gun with affection, sensitive to every curve and indentation of its muzzle and breech. They would never know from where the shot had come, there would be no noise, no gas escaping in the wake of the subsonic bullet. The race would be canceled and the horses returned to their stables. That night he would travel north to a planned rendezvous with Seamus O'Neill. They would be back in Belfast in thirty-six hours, returning home as heroes.

The thought of the hateful woman lying dead on the green turf caused him to lick his lips. He felt himself begin to harden involuntarily.

He shook his head and untied a small rag.

Concentrate.

Three rimless cartridges lay in it, and Zeid selected one, which he loaded into the breech of the gun. He then pushed a bar in the upper part of the breech to the left: when the pistol was fired the breech would remain open, achieving utmost silence since the slide of the gun would not blow back in the usual way.

He had one shot, but it was enough. He laid the gun down and untied the horse's leading rein from its ring on the wall. Then he picked up a folded, blue string cooler from the straw floor; it was intended for the horse's sweating flanks, for after the race that would never be. He arranged the blue sheet on his left forearm and with his right hand placed the gun in his now-concealed left.

Then he opened the door of the stable and, leading with his right hand, he walked toward the exit of the stable yard with the Derby favorite.

A number of horses were ahead of him. He could see Esprit du Calvados, on his toes, just going out onto the track, Razzle Dazzle, the American colt, behind the Frenchman, and the Irish runner, Southern Cross, looking resplendent, his jetblack coat glistening in the afternoon sunlight.

Noble Lord sensed the uniqueness of the occasion and began to prance sideways as they emerged onto the end of the track, which curved around to the paddock entrance. Zeid chucked sharply at the silver harness chains that connected the lead to the horse's bridle, and as he did so the colt reared straight up, flailing the air with his forelegs. The sudden movement almost dislodged the Type 64 from Zeid's left-hand grasp, and he stumbled. A number of people had stopped to look at the magnificent horse, erect on his hind legs, snorting indignantly through flared nostrils. Then the colt came down, and Zeid patted him soothingly having quietly readjusted the cooler, which had nearly slid off.

Concentrate. Concentrate and kill he thought, his ears humming.

They had arrived at a small wooden hut at the entrance to the presaddling enclosure. A man in a black bowler hat was handing out white, numbered armbands to the lads as they led in the runners. Zeid's heart missed a beat. The lads in front were putting theirs on the left arm. It would be an impossibility for him to do so without putting down the gun and cooler, with the huge risk of the Type 64 being seen. His mind raced.

Concentrate.

They hadn't thought of this.

Concentrate.

He was now at the hut, and the man looked at him questioningly.

"Number please?" he asked Zeid.

"Twelve."

The man fished around and produced the armband. In a smooth movement Zeid transferred the gun and cooler to his right hand and forearm. It was an enormous gamble. If the colt played up at all, gun and cooler would be jerked to the ground. Zeid stuck out a straight left arm to the man.

"Please," he said.

The man frowned and then smiled.

"Oh, a bit fractious is he? Never mind."

The man slipped the armband up the proffered arm. The youth transferred the cooler back and walked on.

The bowler-hatted official turned to the next entrant. There was something odd about that last lad, he thought, something weird, as if he didn't really fit in. Then he looked at his race card. Number twelve was Noble Lord, the horse they were all talking about. Must be the tension of having the favorite for the race, he thought and handed out the next number.

AT EACH STATION the train stopped, and more racegoers climbed on. Hope and Debbie were wedged face-to-face in the center of the carriage. Empty beer bottles skittled around the floor, and somewhere at the back of their compartment a child had been sick.

Hope looked out the window at the settled afternoon. They passed green parks where normal people were walking dogs, playgrounds with children on swings and slides, white-shirted couples playing tennis, people walking slowly through the cemetery of a church.

He counted stations, Balham, Mitcham Junction, Hackbridge, Carshalton. Following the great effort of catching the train, his confidence in their mission had greatly ebbed to be replaced by a sense of anticlimax. What was he, an insignificant policeman from a tiny, unknown country trying to do in London? What a fool he would look when he got back to Antigua. He began to sweat at the very thought of it.

"We're nearly there," said Debbie as the train pulled out of Ewell East. "Let's hope there's a taxi." She had inquired from one of the other racegoers in the train how to get out to the track.

All at once signs saying "Epsom" flashed past, and the train stopped. With difficulty they squeezed out of the carriage and found themselves at the end of a pushing, good-humored crowd all waiting to go down the short, steep flight of stairs that led out of the station. Two collectors gamely tried to check the arriving passengers' tickets. After a minute or two they abandoned the idea, and the crowd surged out toward Epsom's High Street.

Hope held Debbie's wrist tightly. To the right of the station entrance a long line of taxis were methodically picking up fares. Hope ran down the line and jumped in the back of the first free cab.

"You got to wait in line," said the driver.

"Please," Debbie implored him. "We have to make the Derby. It's a matter of life and death!"

"Oh all right," said the driver, punching his meter and wheeling out of the line. He drove down the road, around a little roundabout, and into the center of Epsom.

"What are you going to do?" asked Debbie.

Hope drew in a deep breath.

"I'll go straight up to the first policeman I see, I'll show my credentials and ask to be taken to the officer in charge. I'll explain that wherever the Queen is, she is in extreme immediate danger and appropriate action must be taken. Then I'll show them this," Hope took out the newspaper with the photograph from his jacket, "and ask to go with them to help identify and arrest whoever this is."

He looked out of the window. "This traffic is not moving, you know," he said.

"I'd noticed," said Debbie. "It's two-thirty. The Derby start is three-thirty."

"If he plans to make his move sometime before the race, then we may have a problem," Hope said.

"As an employee of a racing stable could he get nearer the Queen than if he wasn't?" asked Debbie.

"I haven't any idea," replied Hope. "But why else would he be in a racing-stable if it didn't give him an advantage?"

"Assume he is a terrorist, then that's his cover," Debbie said.

273

"Work on the assumption that at some point, being with the horse gives him an entrée which the normal everyday terrorist does not have." She could see the driver looking at them.

"He's with the horse that's favorite for the race," she said. "Maybe the Queen presents a cup or trophy to the winner and that's when he plans to get her."

"Possible, but unlikely," said Hope. "Too much left to chance. What happens if the horse doesn't win? No, it's more general than that."

He looked out of the cab window. A woman with a pram whom they had passed over five minutes ago was level with them again.

"This is hopeless," he said. He slid back the glass partition. "How much longer before it frees up?" he asked the driver.

"It doesn't," he replied. "Been like this all bleeding morning. They've closed the regular car park up there with this massive security operation and . . ."

Hope wasn't listening as the driver went on; he looked at his watch.

"How far is it?" he interrupted.

"How far? About a mile and a half I should think," the driver said.

Hope opened the door and jumped out, flinging some money over the seat.

"Let's go," he said and began to run up the footpath following the endless line of barely moving cars. Debbie ran beside him; they were in a residential area lined by houses and apartment buildings, shrubberies and trees. Hope looked down: Debbie was panting already. His feet were hitting the pavement one stride for every two or three of hers. The road inclined slightly upward. His open jacket flapped annoyingly at his sides, and he removed it as he ran.

"Here," he said, shoving it into Debbie's hands, "I'm going to go on."

"Go ahead," she panted. "I'll see you up there."

Hope nodded briefly at her and accelerated away.

"Good luck," she yelled after his fast-receding figure.

Hope settled down to run seriously, pacing himself with the knowledge of an athlete. The road darkened and began to climb in a series of curves through an area with dense woodland to the right. He was running very fast now, about the equivalent of a four-minute mile, his long legs stretching out to meet the rising ground, devouring the road in front of him. The traffic was inching forward periodically, many people sitting with their engines turned off until the next move. To his left he saw a large cemetery. There was a funeral in progress; a small group of mourners stood around an open grave. He ran faster. The hill turned to the left and became steeper. He pressed himself more. His feet pounded the road. A group in a stationary car gave him a loud cheer. His lungs were hurting now, but he kept on. A patch of green appeared at the top of the hill. He increased his pace, throwing himself up the road. He emerged from the shadows of the trees into the bright sunlight, running flat out. There was a large area cordoned off with police tape. Beyond this he saw the backs of the stands, people milling around, groups of uniformed policemen. He was almost there. He gave the last two hundred yards all he had, sprinting with his head forward, his legs pumping agonizingly.

Three young RPG officers turned to see the spectacle of the man careering toward them. He got to them and stopped, completely out of breath, bending forward, his hands on his knees.

"You all right, mate?" asked one of the officers.

"The Queen," gasped Hope. "Where's the Queen?"

The policemen looked at each other.

"You want to see the Queen?" one asked.

"Where is she?" asked Hope as he gulped air. The policeman looked at his watch.

"I would say at this moment she is going down to the paddock to see the horses," he said.

Hope jerked upright.

"Horses?" he shouted. "She sees the horses? Stop her, quickly, stop her!"

"We've got a right one here," said the policeman, out of the side of his mouth to his colleague.

"Are you in trouble, sir?" he asked Hope.

"I'm a policeman too," blurted Hope and realized with horror that his ID credentials and the vital photograph were in his discarded jacket. "Antigua and Barbuda. Stop the Queen going near the horses!"

He could see one of the officers raising his eyebrows. They weren't going to believe him. He would have to get in there himself. Abruptly he turned and ran toward an entrance.

"Come on, lads," cried an RPG officer as he set off in hot pursuit. Half a dozen other policemen had observed the incident from a distance and took up the chase. Without difficulty they cornered Hope by the high iron railings.

"Let me in!" he shouted. "You don't understand!"

"Take him up to the tent and cool him off," said an officer with three stripes. A group of amused onlookers observed Sergeant Hope being frogmarched by four uniformed men up the road toward Tattenham Corner.

SEAMUS O'NEILL HAD not bargained for the body search. The policeman had been cheerfully apologetic but thorough. His hands had probed the silk back of the waistcoat, the gray frock coat, even the band of the topper. He thanked God that he had had the foresight to keep the SIG-Sauer in its compartment in the long, leather binoculars case. They had removed the field glasses and had a quick look inside. A moment later he was in. Delaney was already there; she had no problem, always traveled clean.

They had been hanging around London Bridge for an hour and a half waiting for a train. Security, they had said. A lot of good their security would do them, the bastards, he thought. It was half an hour now to the Derby parade. The place was alive with police. He had tried to get a glimpse of the quarry during the national anthem, but there had not been a hope. He had not seen Kelly yet, but there would be time enough.

He entered the gents cloakroom and locked himself in a cubicle. Placing the leather case on the water cistern, his fingers ran down the stitching until they found the catch they sought. A moment later the reassuring pistol was in his hand. He checked the magazine. Its full capacity of eight bullets was in place. He shoved the SIG, barrel first, into his trouser belt in the small of his back. Then readjusting his frock coat, he flushed the toilet and walked outside. Setting his hat at a jaunty angle, he offered his arm to the attractive red-haired woman with the wide-brimmed hat who had been waiting. Then they both set off in the direction of the parade ring.

Up ahead of him, what looked like a thousand blue-uniformed cops were milling about on the track. The royal party was leaving for the paddock.

JEREMY CARVILL ADJUSTED Noble Lord's girths and cast his eye lovingly over the horse, like a painter giving his masterpiece one last, fatherly appraisal. The enclosed saddling box was dimly lit, but even still the colt positively glowed.

"Right, Zeid, off you go," said Jeremy. "It's in the hands of the Almighty now."

Zeid turned his head abruptly at the remark.

"Come on man, off you go," said the trainer, opening the door and allowing the sunlight to blaze in. Several hundred people were gathered by the rail of the presaddling paddock. The swell of noise behind them in the main paddock flooded into the box. Zeid bent down to pick up the blue rug.

"What do you want that for?" asked Jeremy testily. Zeid looked up at the trainer, his eyes ablaze. The white flourish of a robe caught Jeremy's attention: Yaw was outside with his friend of the afternoon and Penny Carvill.

"Oh never mind, come on," said Jeremy. "Once around this ring and then into the paddock."

Zeid walked the horse out smartly as he was told and set off

in a clockwise direction around the oval-shaped ring. Spectators leaned over the rails eager for a sight of the favorite.

"Here he is. Here's Noble Lord," Zeid heard them say. The
sight of the Arab in his flowing robes strengthened his confidence. They were not alone today in their work. They had
powerful friends—friends even more powerful than the great
imperial bitch within.

He concentrated hard on her image.

Kill.

It made him feel good. The tension slipped from his
shoulders. He began to walk with a more relaxed swing,
somewhat like the horse he was leading. He was beginning to
enjoy himself.

Turning left, he led Noble Lord into the paddock.

WALKING THROUGH THE Members enclosure to the paddock,
Chief Inspector Dawson heard the shrieks of the bookies. He
paused to watch the frantic activity.

"Take five to two," they shouted from their raised positions
on timber boxes.

The bookies beside the Members enclosure had draped
rugs inscribed with their names over the rails that separated
the Members from the cheaper Tattersalls enclosure. Serious
men in top hats walked up to the rails and whispered instructions in the bookie's ear. There was a nod, the bookie leaned
down to his penciler to record the transaction, and the client
walked away. No money changed hands. Dawson saw a
small, thickset man with a large cigar in his mouth approach
the rails. There was the usual whisper. The bookie asked the
small man a question, then nodding vigorously he turned, not
to the penciler but to another man standing behind. Whatever
he said had an electric effect. The other man ran at full speed
along the rails and stopped by the rug of another bookie.
There was more whispering. Then an explosion of activity.
Men ran up and down shouting at each other. Bookmakers out
in Tattersalls could be seen hurriedly wiping the chalk quotes
from their boards.

"Take three to one," Dawson heard and then a new cry. "I'll lay seven to two, Southern Cross."

Dawson smiled and walked on through the Members out onto the track that led to the paddock. He showed his badge to one of the constables on the gate. The royal party had just been driven down: Dawson could see the maroon Rolls parked at the ring and the great wall of black that was nearly a thousand policemen gathered in the same place. Everything is going pretty well, he thought; this is the last test of the security.

A sharp crackle from the walkie-talkie in his pocket caused the nearby policemen to turn around. He put it to his mouth.

"Chief Inspector Dawson?"

"This is Tent HQ, sir. We have a call here from Epsom District Hospital for you. A Dr. McCausland. Says it's most urgent."

"Does he say what it is?" asked Dawson.

"No, sir. He insists on speaking to you personally. He's holding on."

"I'm on the way," said Dawson and began to run back up the deserted lawn, the Members having all left for the paddock. His call earlier that morning to the hospital had been simply by the book. Follow up any loose ends, anything that is out of the ordinary, that does not fit in. Now he had a heavy feeling in his stomach as he sprinted out the back of the stand and up the road to the tent. Commander McKechnie had left for the paddock.

A police constable was holding the mobile phone at the back. Dawson hurried to it, past a number of officers who were leading a protesting black man into the tent.

"Chief Inspector Dawson here," he said, out of breath.

He listened intently to the doctor on the other end.

"You're quite sure?" he asked several times.

He put a finger in his left ear to hear better; the West Indian's voice was booming.

"You're quite sure?" he asked once more.

"Ninety-nine point nine percent," said the doctor on the other end. "We'll have to wait for the full postmortem, but if he wasn't injected with some sodium cardio-toxic substance then I'm a Dutchman."

Dawson thanked him and replaced the phone.

". . . Antigua and Barbuda," he heard the voice at the front of the tent. Dawson's mind raced. The dead man worked in the favorite's stable. There had to be a connection. He turned to the radio operator.

"Get me Commander McKechnie," he said.

". . . Caribbean police force," Hope boomed. Dawson froze. He walked to where the large black man was being held.

"Who is this man?" he asked the inspector-in-charge.

"Says he's a police sergeant from Antigua, sir. Wants to stop the Queen going into the paddock."

Dawson's ears screamed. The initial briefing came flooding back, the FO, the Caribbean tip-off that had started it all. He shoved aside the men holding Hope.

"Let him go," he shouted. The black man's shining face showed great agitation. "I'm Dawson, Special Branch. What's going on? Quick!"

"Sergeant Hope, Antigua and Barbuda police, sir. There's a man here with the horses who is going to try and assassinate the Queen."

"Commander McKechnie on the line, sir," said the radio man.

"Hold him a second," said Dawson. "What does this man look like, Sergeant Hope?" he asked.

"I had his photograph, sir, but it's . . . I will know him if I see him."

"Then follow me," cried Dawson. He turned to the radio operator. "Tell the Commander I'm on the way! Full-scale alert on everyone *inside* the paddock! Get the Queen out, *now!*"

He ran at full tilt back down the road to the stands.

"Keep with me," he shouted back to Hope. The two men sprinted shoulder to shoulder to the back of the stands scattering groups of heather-selling gypsy women as they ran. Dawson had his chief inspector's pass out.

"Emergency," he yelled to the inquiring police officers on the gate. Hope kept right behind Dawson's hurrying figure. They were out on the Members lawn and running down to the gate leading onto the track. Dawson rushed through, but a number of officers blocked Hope's way.

"Let him through, for Christ's sake!" Dawson bawled.

Now they were on the green turf of the racetrack itself, scorching down it. They were oblivious to the cheers that greeted their dash, the Englishman compact and fit, a competent runner, the West Indian a natural athlete, his long strides matching the other man's with an easy rhythm. Now they were going downhill, flat out. A couple of plainclothesmen had recognized Dawson and were following behind. They could see the entrance to the paddock less than a hundred yards away, blocked solid with policemen. Clutching his pass high Dawson began to shout.

HE ADJUSTED THE butt of the gun under the cooler so that the end of the nozzle was right at the edge of the blanket; another millimeter, and it would be seen. It took a bit of getting used to walking so close to the wall of police; he had gradually led the horse in nearer the center of the ring. That way he was farther from their searching eyes—and nearer to her.

She had come in just a minute ago when he was at the far end of the paddock. Now he approached where she stood, chatting to several men who held their hands behind their backs. He was surprised that she was so small in real life, small and quite pale, with a big, blue hat. As he drew level she turned suddenly in his direction to admire Noble Lord. She was so near he could see the pupils of her eyes.

Concentrate.

He readied the gun.

Now he was at a less favorable angle. The horse jinked slightly, and he chucked it with the leading rope. He walked on, his view obscured. His heart pounded. He rounded the top of the ring and headed down again. This time he came level but the shot was not on: Jeremy and the Arab were between him and the target; she was standing more to the other side of the ring.

When I come up the far side next time, he thought.

He steered the horse even more to the right so that when he came around the bottom and up again he would be no more than five or six yards away—an easy shot.

He felt a broad smile spreading on his face. This was happiness—the assurance of success, the achievement of all ambitions, the execution of someone who stood for everything he hated, the inflicting of maximum pain on the enemy. And it was all so easy, so simple, just a squeeze and that was it. He wanted to laugh. Look at all those fools, standing like dummies. If only they knew!

A man walked over to the royal party. Zeid frowned. The man was talking to the target. She had inclined her head to listen. The horse danced to the right, and Zeid increased his step. They were at the end of the paddock. He could see her talking to a man in a tall hat and turning as if to go. He swung up the side of the paddock much farther in than the other horses.

Concentrate.

The gun was rock steady in his hand. He could see her pause and then walk slowly in the same direction. But he was gaining. In ten more strides he would be level.

There was commotion at the mouth of the paddock. The rows of policemen had parted, and two men burst in. Forget them. Concentrate and kill. Five more strides. Concentrate. She had stopped at the noisy intrusion. Even better. One of the men, a black, was looking around urgently. Concentrate. Now he was almost level. She was side-on to him. He wanted to get her in the face. He eased the cooler back to insure an uninterrupted flight for the bullet. Concentrate. The snout of the Type 64 came peeping out. He began to squeeze.

All at once there was a great cry. He was aware of a hurtling black mass to his left. She turned to look, her face in a frown. He had her. Kill. He pulled.

Sergeant Hope left the ground in a great leap. He had seen the man almost immediately. Why was he walking the horse almost up the center of the paddock? In mid-air he saw the barrel of the gun. He was coming right down on top of it. A knifelike pain shot into his upper chest. The men rolled together onto the ground. The horse had reared straight up and, now free, galloped down the paddock. The frenzied gunman got up again, his eyes deranged. There were loud screams and a fusillade of gunfire. His body jerked backward as a dozen bullets hit it and then slumped to the ground.

Hope rolled away. There was intense confusion. The royal party and most of the owners and trainers were lying flat on the grass. Horses reared and fought to get free from the encircling wall of policemen who had all tried to converge on the center of the paddock.

The pain was enormous. Hope tried to stand up, but the effort was too much. He was losing blood rapidly. The paddock began to revolve crazily.

He passed out.

TWENTY-TWO

IT TOOK EVERY ounce of strength in Stroker's body to restrain Noble Lord.

From the moment that the starting gates had flown open, the colt had taken a massive hold. He knew this was a race. They covered half a furlong and had just crossed the first matted road, the entrance to a local trainer's yard. The Irish horse had a pacemaker in, and he was taking them along at one hell of a clip. Stroker tried to settle his horse, tried to drop him off the pace. Even though this was the Derby, he still could not get the earlier events of the afternoon out of his head.

Pandemonium was far too mild a word for it. The Queen bundled into her car; the parade ring alive with gun-toting policemen; loose horses everywhere; Jeremy and the prince taken away for questioning. The race had been put back an hour and a half—some said it would be canceled completely, but the Queen herself had insisted it be run. Why else had she come to Epsom? she said.

And to think that that little bastard, whoever he was, had knocked off Chalkie Charlesworth and then nearly succeeded with the Queen of England. The whole thing was incredible.

He wondered how the poor black bloke was. Poor bugger. If it had not been for him there certainly would have been no Derby.

They were working their way over from the right to the left-hand rail, bobbing along, two furlongs behind them. The horse was more settled now, about mid-division, one off the rails. The pacemaker was still flat out. Stroker could see Pavarotti two from the front, his jockey with a double handful. Pentle Bay was up there in the first four or five, going nicely for Wally Tigget. Noble Lord was about tenth. Stroker glanced right. Southern Cross was matching strides with him, little Gerry Walsh sitting quietly, perfectly balancing his mount.

"How're you going?" he yelled to Stroker.

"So far so good," shouted Stroker.

"If I were you, I'd head for Liverpool,' shouted Walsh. "I think they'll put the lot of you in jail when this race is over."

Stroker smiled grimly. He could just be right.

He felt the jarring as they crossed the mats on Walton Road. All along the left-hand side of the course thousands of people stood cheering. They were still climbing. The wind whipped at his face as they neared the top of the Downs. To his right Stroker saw movement. The Frenchman, Esprit du Calvados, was making his move. He wanted to be up front for the descent. Let him off, thought Stroker, as the French champion jockey urged his colt on.

They flashed past the mile start. Now they were at the very top of the hill. Tadworth to the right, and away below to the left, the winning post, enclosures, and paddock where just two hours ago half the world had almost witnessed the first televised assassination of a crowned head of state.

Suddenly, the long, left-hand descent had begun and the pace moved up a notch. They were plunging downhill, past the six-furlong chute. This was where class would tell. If a horse crossed its legs on the hill, the lights would go out in a big way for horse, jockey, and anyone close behind.

Noble Lord was perfectly balanced. Stroker let out a reef. The colt moved up two places. Stroker still kept him one off the rails. They were really motoring now. Some horses ahead were going backward. It was like dodging along a crowded sidewalk. Stroker passed the Irish pacemaker, now almost stopped. He passed Razzle Dazzle, the American, dead as a dodo. He weaved to avoid the dying Frenchman. Pentle Bay was still hard at it, plugging along now in the lead. They were halfway down, five furlongs from home.

To his right Stroker could see Southern Cross, tracking him like a shadow. He stole a look left. Pavarotti was trying to get through on the rails. Here we go, thought Stroker and kicked his colt up a gear.

The response was immediate. Noble Lord lengthened his action. They were reaching the bottom of Tattenham Corner, matching strides with Pentle Bay. Already the intense roaring of the crowd nearly half a mile away could be heard, like thunder or the crashing of a great sea. Pentle Bay was tiring but would not give in yet. Noble Lord took it up.

Stroker felt, rather than saw, Pavarotti coming through on his inside. They had reached the base and crossed the Old London Road. Three and a half furlongs from home. The grass shone in the sun, undulating away like a green ribbon. The cheering was deafening. Southern Cross came up to his right boot. Stroker prepared to set sail. He balanced his mount and then crouched low over his withers, his kicking legs urging the colt to go for home.

They sprinted up the straight, opening a large gap between them and their pursuers. One and a half to go. The crowd was delirious. There would be no close ones this time. Stroker chanced a quick backward look.

It was a miracle that he did not hit the ground headfirst: his left arm grabbed a fistful of mane to stop him falling; his nose cracked hard against Noble Lord's shoulder; his whip was gone. The right stirrup leather had sheared clean away.

There was a great gasp from the crowd. Noble Lord had

completely lost his momentum and had lurched toward the center of the track. Instinctively Stroker kicked his left stirrup free and straightened up. Now his legs hung straight down in the manner of jockeys in the old prints. He tried to regain his balance. Southern Cross was nearly level again. Instinct took over. Stroker began to flail his arms and legs in unison like a demented jack-in-the-box. Noble Lord slowly tried to pick up his stride. Southern Cross had gone a length up on the inside. Noble Lord had veered away from the running rail and was racing at an angle up the center of the track. Stroker could see Gerry Walsh, his opportunity not missed, drive for the post two hundred yards away. There were just the two of them.

With a supreme effort Stroker brought his unsupported knees as far as he could and pummeled them into the base of his horse's neck. There was a wall of noise. But Stroker was oblivious to everything except the need to peg back the couple of yards between them and Southern Cross. His hands and arms threshing in a circular, urging frenzy, his entire small body ramming for home with every stride, he rode the race of his lifetime, exhorting the colt beneath him to do what he had been born for.

Inch by agonizing inch the gap began to close. They were running out of time. Noble Lord had never been ridden in this manner, but there was no mistaking the urgency being transmitted by the madman on his back.

His head was at Walsh's stirrup. Gerry Walsh gave his colt everything. Stroker felt the power beneath him. He had only a vague idea of where the line was. He threw his balled-up body between the horse's ears. They were dead level. He could do no more. The post flashed by. Half a million people were on their feet. The air was full of top hats. He set about trying to pull up. It was all over.

Whatever the result, he had done his best.

POLICE CONSTABLE GEOFF Little stood outside Tattenham Corner station. From his position, he had seen the horses sweep around Tattenham Corner and up the straight. A fruit vendor had his transistor on. The near apoplectic radio commentator was reporting on what had taken place inside the last two furlongs.

"And as if we haven't had enough drama today we have just witnessed the incredible spectacle of Stroker Roche getting the favorite home in the Derby, for my money by a short head, without, and I repeat in case you've just joined us, without stirrups. What a fantastic performance. We don't know yet exactly what happened . . ."

Constable Little smiled. He had put a fiver on Noble Lord; his only bet of the year was in the Derby, but it was one that he always looked forward to. Epsom was his local beat. He strolled away from the door of the station. Crowds were already leaving the course for the early trains back to London. What a day, thought Little. All these extra men drafted in at God knows how much expense, and still some nut comes within a whisker of pulling it off. He shook his head. There was word of a witch-hunt in the Metropolitan Police for allowing such a near thing. Constable Little had not seen any of the action in the paddock, but he had received a blow-by-blow from the mobile HQ.

He surveyed the growing crowd. Family groups on their way home, punters in high spirits, people on a truly historic day out. A man in a morning suit hurried along, holding his topper in his hand. He had a bushy mustache. His face was dark and agitated, and he was perspiring. I bet he lost his shirt, thought Little. As the man went by, something fell from his pocket. It was a race card, its glossy cover a souvenir of Derby Day. The man walked on, not noticing.

"Excuse me, sir."

The man turned slightly but kept going. Constable Little bent down and retrieved the card.

"Sir, excuse me just a moment," said the policeman, raising his voice.

To Little's amazement the man then did an extraordinary

thing. Throwing his top hat to the ground, he put his right hand under the tails of his coat to the small of his back. Training rather than logic took over. Constable Little covered the few yards between them in less than a second. He saw a blur of black as the SIG-Sauer appeared. He leaped, catching the man's readying right arm. The pistol went off with a loud crack. The two of them fell backward on the road, the man snarling like a wounded animal. People began to scream. Two other policemen appeared.

Seamus O'Neill's day at the races was over.

DEBBIE SAT WITH a cup of coffee in the waiting room of Epsom District Hospital. Chief Inspector Dawson sat beside her. He had been in and out, keeping up with the continuing security operation. He was elated by the news that O'Neill, the INLA man whom the whole of England was looking for, had been caught outside Tattenham Corner railway station. His woman companion had been missed, however; the police were still looking for her. The media were beside themselves over the whole affair. The London *Evening Standard* had rushed out a special edition:

"THANK GOD!" screamed its full-page headline.

Dawson looked at the pretty girl as she lit up another cigarette. It had been nearly two hours since Hope was brought in. The operation had got underway immediately the ambulance had arrived. The efficiency of the hospital was impressive, but the surgeon in charge declined to put any percentages on his chances of success. Hope had caught the slug full on in the chest; the fact that it had not killed him outright was some indication that luck was on his side.

An estimated fifty million people had seen the attempt in the paddock and Sergeant Hope's dive. The outline of Hope's dash from the Caribbean was filtering out. Now there were four TV crews and over fifty reporters outside the hospital, and more were on the way. The day was turning into the media event of the decade. Questions were being asked about the security operation. The Commissioner of the Metropolitan Police had arrived an hour ago. Debbie got up and paced the room that had been allocated to them.

"I wish they would tell us something," she said.

"Try not to worry," said Dawson. "These things take time—no news is good news."

"I know, I know," she said, sitting down again. "God, he's so brave. Imagine yourself or anyone for that matter doing what he did. It's incredible."

"The whole thing is incredible," said Dawson. "I mean what sort of people are they out in Antigua to try and sit on something like this?"

"They tried to completely isolate him, you know. They were transferring him to some rock out in the ocean."

Dawson shook his head.

"Thank God they didn't," he said. "That whole New York business—that took great courage too from what you tell me."

"Yes," replied Debbie, "he was sent up there to follow up on the murder of his brother-in-law, Ernest Wilson, who was a small-time crook. The Antiguan Police Commissioner wanted to show the U.S. government they were doing something to try and stop drugs being run through Antigua—so he gets this crazy idea to send Sergeant Hope to New York."

"Our assistant commissioner has been back on to the Foreign Office," Dawson said. There are chaps in there who need to be roasted, spend their time playing God. This is off the record, but I think they're more interested in protecting their sources than the lives of the royal family."

"What was their source in this case?" Debbie asked.

"We're still only guessing, but we think someone in the Antiguan police commissioner's office, perhaps his secretary. He may have overheard Sergeant Hope's story or read his report."

"The commissioner sounds like a nut case," said Debbie.

"That's putting it mildly," said Dawson. He scratched his head. "But what was the connection in New York?" he asked. "How did Sergeant Hope link in with this INLA plot?"

"In Ernest Wilson's apartment he found a book of giveaway

291

matches, from a fashionable French restaurant on First Avenue. Unless his brother-in-law had been working there, the matches did not fit—there was no way it would have been in character for him to eat there. So Sergeant Hope goes along and sees this guy Sir Tristram Hoare who's been in Antigua three weeks before. Far too coincidental."

"Yes, but hold on," said Dawson. "Explain how the matches get into the brother-in-law's apartment in the first place?"

"They were in the briefcase," said Debbie. "All Ernest Wilson ever got from Sir Tristram Hoare's briefcase was a packet of matches." She sighed. "One presumes there were papers to do with the gunrunning, maybe even information about today, but Wilson was practically illiterate anyway. The mob in New York didn't know that: they murdered him for what he might have known."

The door opened, and the surgeon came in dressed in a green smock and trousers, white cut-off rubber boots, and a tight green skullcap. He carried a small metal dish.

"Relax," he said with a big grin. "He's doing fine, he's going to be all right."

"Oh thank goodness," said Debbie and sat down heavily.

"His breastbone deflected the bullet into the right lung," said the surgeon. "We had a bit of a dig to get at it, and he lost a hell of a lot of blood, but the worst is over. He's a very strong man. He'll be as fit as a fiddle again in two weeks."

Dawson looked at the dish.

"This is the little bugger that nearly did it all," said the surgeon rattling the dish. Dawson looked in at the snub-nosed rimless bullet. "Never seen one of these before," said the surgeon.

"I know, we had a look at the gun," said Dawson. "Chinese by all accounts. God knows how they got it in there."

Debbie stood up.

"Can I see him, please?" she asked in a small voice.

"I can't see why not," said the surgeon. "He was beginning to come around a bit on his way back from theater."

They walked down a corridor with tall windows through which the late afternoon sun was shining. Two policemen stood on either side of a door. They went quietly in. The figure in the bed was very gray; a blood transfusion unit stood beside him. The sheets were drawn up to his neck concealing the surgery that had taken place in the body below. Hope was breathing steadily. He opened his eyes.

"Debbie," he said. "Debbie."

She made her way to the bed, fighting to keep back the tears, to hold the hand of the man she had first met less than twenty-four hours ago.

"It's going to be fine," she whispered warmly. "It's been a big success."

He smiled.

Dawson put his head over Debbie's shoulder.

"We're going to be thanking you for a long time to come, Sergeant Hope," he said.

Hope closed his eyes.

Suddenly the door of the room flew open. A white-coated doctor rushed in and over to the surgeon. He whispered urgently. The surgeon frowned. The door opened again, and a police constable stepped in. He motioned to Dawson and spoke quickly in the Chief Inspector's ear. There was the sound of many feet walking along the corridor and the noise made by a group of people speaking in hushed voices.

The policeman caught the door handle and holding it open, stood at rigid attention. Hope, the effects of the anesthetic wearing off with every second, became aware of something going on. He opened his eyes and managed to raise his head an inch from the pillow. Even the sunlight flooding into the room could not match the dazzling brilliance of his smile.

Although the last time she had done it had been years ago in a school play, Debbie rose from the side of the bed and executed a perfect curtsy.